PENGUIN BOOKS

leaving tangier

TAHAR BEN JELLOUN was born in 1944 in Fez, Morocco, and emigrated to France in 1961. A novelist, essayist, critic, and poet, he is a regular contributor to *Le Monde, La Repubblica, El País,* and *Panorama.* His novels include *The Sacred Night* (winner of the 1987 Prix Goncourt), *Corruption,* and *The Last Friend.* Ben Jelloun won the 1994 Prix Maghreb, and in 2004 he won the International IMPAC Dublin Literary Award for *This Blinding Absence of Light.*

LINDA COVERDALE has translated more than fifty books, including Tahar Ben Jelloun's award-winning novel *This Blinding Absence of Light.* A Chevalier de l'Ordre des Arts et des Lettres, she won the 2006 Scott Moncrieff Prize and the 1997 and 2008 French-American Foundation Translation Prize. She lives in Brooklyn, New York.

leaving tangier

· *a novel* ·

TAHAR BEN JELLOUN

Translated from the French by
LINDA COVERDALE

PENGUIN BOOKS

PENGUIN BOOKS
Published by the Penguin Group
Penguin Group (USA) Inc., 375 Hudson Street, New York, New York 10014, U.S.A. • Penguin
Group (Canada), 90 Eglinton Avenue East, Suite 700, Toronto, Ontario, Canada M4P 2Y3 (a divi-
sion of Pearson Penguin Canada Inc.) • Penguin Books Ltd, 80 Strand, London WC2R 0RL,
England • Penguin Ireland, 25 St Stephen's Green, Dublin 2, Ireland (a division of Penguin Books
Ltd) • Penguin Group (Australia), 250 Camberwell Road, Camberwell, Victoria 3124, Australia
(a division of Pearson Australia Group Pty Ltd) • Penguin Books India Pvt Ltd, 11 Community
Centre, Panchsheel Park, New Delhi – 110 017, India • Penguin Group (NZ), 67 Apollo Drive,
Rosedale, North Shore 0632, New Zealand (a division of Pearson New Zealand Ltd) • Penguin
Books (South Africa) (Pty) Ltd, 24 Sturdee Avenue, Rosebank, Johannesburg 2196, South Africa

Penguin Books Ltd, Registered Offices:
80 Strand, London WC2R 0RL, England

First published in Penguin Books 2009

5 7 9 10 8 6 4

Copyright © Editions Gallimard, Paris, 2006
Translation copyright © Linda Coverdale, 2009
All rights reserved

Originally published in French under the title *Partir* by Editions Gallimard, Paris.
This work is published with the support of the French Minister of Culture—National Center of
Books. Ouvrage publié avec el concours du Ministère français chargé de la culture—
Centre national du livre.

LIBRARY OF CONGRESS CATALOGING IN PUBLICATION DATA
Ben Jelloun, Tahar, 1944–
[Partir. English]
Leaving Tangier : a novel / Tahar Ben Jelloun ; translated by Linda Coverdale.
p. cm.
ISBN 978-0-14-311465-9
I. Coverdale, Linda. II. Title.
PQ3989.2.J4P3713 2009
823—dc22   2008021598

Printed in the United States of America
Set in Requiem • Designed by Elke Sigal

Contents

Translator's Note

Leaving Tangier is about leaving home: emigrating, going into exile, taking leave of one's country, one's friends and family, even one's senses. The many ties that bind the characters in *Leaving Tangier* to what they have left behind tug on their heartstrings in different ways, some of which evoke geographical, historical, or cultural references to a world that may well be unfamiliar to an American reader. I have provided endnotes to illuminate the meaning of such allusions, and an asterisk by a word in the text means that the term is explained in these notes at the end of the book.

leaving tangier

My Cameroonian friend Flaubert says "Here I am!" when he's leaving and "We're together!" to say good-bye. A way to ward off bad luck. In this novel, those who leave aren't planning to return, and when they leave someone, it's for good. Flaubert, who studied a few pages of *Madame Bovary* in school, has promised to read this entire book as soon as summer vacation begins, when he goes home.

I

Toutia

In Tangier, in the winter, the Café Hafa* becomes an observatory for dreams and their aftermath. Cats from the cemetery, the terraces, and the chief communal bread oven of the Marshan district gather round the café as if to watch the play unfolding there in silence, and fooling nobody. Long pipes of kif pass from table to table while glasses of mint tea grow cold, enticing bees that eventually tumble in, a matter of indifference to customers long since lost to the limbo of hashish and tinseled reverie. In the back of one room, two men meticulously prepare the key that opens the gates of departure, selecting leaves, then chopping them swiftly and efficiently. Neither man looks up. Leaning back against the wall, customers sit on mats and stare at the horizon as if seeking to read their fate. They look at the sea, at the clouds that blend into the mountains, and they wait for the twinkling lights of Spain to appear. They watch them without seeing them, and sometimes, even when the lights are lost in fog and bad weather, they see them anyway.

Everyone is quiet. Everyone listens. Perhaps *she* will show up this evening. She'll talk to them, sing them the song of the drowned man who became a sea star suspended over the straits. They have agreed never to speak her name: that would destroy her, and provoke a whole series of further misfortunes. So the men watch one another and say nothing. Each one enters his dream and clenches his fists. Only the waiters and the tea master, who owns the café, remain outside the circle, preparing and serving their fare with discretion, coming and going from terrace to terrace without disturbing anyone's dream. The customers know one another but do not converse. Most of them come from the same neighborhood and have just enough to pay for the tea and a few pipes of kif. Some have a slate on which they keep track of their debt. As if by agreement, they keep still. Especially at this hour and at this delicate moment, when their whole being is caught up in the distance, studying the slightest ripple of the waves or the sound of an old boat coming home to the harbor. Sometimes, hearing the echo of a cry for help, they look at one another without turning a hair.

Yes, she might appear, and reveal a few of her secrets. Conditions are favorable: a clear, almost white sky, reflected in a limpid sea transformed into a pool of light. Silence in the café; silence on all faces. Perhaps the precious moment has arrived . . . at last she will speak!

Occasionally the men do allude to her, especially when the sea has tossed up the bodies of a few drowned souls. She has acquired more riches, they say, and surely owes us a favor! They have nicknamed her Toutia, a word that means nothing, but to them she is a spider that can feast on human flesh yet will sometimes warn them, in the guise of a beneficent voice, that tonight is not the night, that they must put off their voyage for a while.

Like children, they believe in this story that comforts them and lulls them to sleep as they lean back against the rough wall. In the tall glasses of cold tea, the green mint has been tarnished black. The bees have all drowned at the bottom. The men no longer sip this tea now steeped into bitterness. With a spoon they fish the bees out one by one, placing them on the table and exclaiming, "Poor little drowned things, victims of their own greediness!"

As if in an absurd and persistent dream, Azel sees his naked body among other naked bodies swollen by seawater, his face distorted by salt and longing, his skin burnt by the sun, split open across the chest as if there had been fighting before the boat went down. Azel sees his body more and more clearly, in a blue and white fishing boat heading ever so slowly to the center of the sea, for Azel has decided that this sea has a center and that this center is a green circle, a cemetery where the current catches hold of corpses, taking them to the bottom to lay them out on a bank of seaweed. He knows that there, in this specific circle, a fluid boundary exists, a kind of separation between the sea and the ocean, the calm, smooth waters of the Mediterranean and the fierce surge of the Atlantic. He holds his nose, because staring so hard at these images has filled his nostrils with the odor of death, a suffocating, clinging, nauseating stench. When he closes his eyes, death begins to dance around the table where he sits almost every day to watch the sunset and count the first lights scintillating across the way, on the coast of Spain. His friends join him, to play cards in silence. Even if some of them share his obsession with leaving the country someday, they know, having heard this one night in Toutia's voice, that they must not give in to the siren call of sadness.

Azel says not a word about either his plan or his dream. People sense that he is unhappy, on edge, and they say he is bewitched by love for a married woman. They believe he has flings with foreign women and suspect that he wants their help to leave Morocco. He denies this, of course, preferring to laugh about it. But the idea of sailing away, of mounting a green-painted horse and crossing the sea of the straits, that idea of becoming a transparent shadow visible only by day, an image scudding at top speed across the waves—that idea never leaves him now. He keeps it to himself, doesn't mention it to his sister, Kenza, still less to his mother, who's upset because he's losing weight and smoking too much.

Even Azel has come to believe in the story of she who will appear and help them to cross, one by one, that distance separating them from life, the good life, or death.

2

Al Afia

Whenever Azel leaves that sea-green circle of silent and lonely reverie, he feels cold and shivers slightly, no matter what the season. Instinctively, he turns away from the night, refusing to enter it. He walks in the city, speaking to no one, imagining that he is a tailor, a special kind of couturier, sewing the narrow lanes to the wide avenues with white thread, as in that story his mother used to tell him when he had trouble falling asleep. He wants to find out if Tangier is a man's jellaba* or a bride's caftan, but the city has grown so much that his quest becomes hopeless.

One February night in 1995, Azel decided to abandon his sewing, convinced that Tangier was no longer a garment but one of those synthetic wool blankets brought back from Belgium by émigrés. The city was hidden beneath a fabric that trapped warmth without dispelling humidity. Tangier no longer had any shape, any center; instead, it had lopsided public squares from which cars had dislodged the peasant women who once came from Fahs to sell their fruits and vegetables.

The city was changing, and its walls were cracking.

Azel stopped at the Whiskey à Gogo, a bar run by a couple of Germans on the rue du Prince-Héritier. He hesitated an instant before pushing open the door. He was one of those men who believe everything that happens to them is written in the order of things, perhaps not in the great celestial Book, but written somewhere. What must happen, happens. He had very little freedom. He'd learned this at his mother's knee, yet he occasionally struggled against determinism through action, finding pleasure in changing his routines simply to defy the tyranny of fate. That night, pausing for a moment at the door, he had a presentiment, a sort of crazy desire to rush toward his destiny.

The place was strangely calm. A bleached blonde was serving the men drinking at the bar. One of the two German guys was at the cash register. He never smiled.

In the dark room, men were alone with their whiskey bottles. Everything was sinister and murky. Azel stopped short when he saw a stocky man drinking a lemonade at the bar. His back was turned, a back as wide as a flagstone, with a thick neck. Azel recognized him and thought, *Mala pata!* Bad luck: it was the caïd, the local gang leader, fearsome and powerful, a man of few words and no heart. People called him Al Afia, "the fire." A well-known *passeur,* he smuggled boatloads of illegal emigrants so determined to sneak across the straits—to "burn up" the ocean—that they would set fire to their identification papers, hoping to avoid being sent home again if they were arrested.

Al Afia didn't burden himself with feelings. That man from the Rif Mountains* had always been a smuggler. As a child, he'd accompanied his uncle on nights when boats arrived in Al-Hoceima to pick up merchandise. His job had been to keep watch, proudly handling the binoculars with expertise, like an army commander scanning the horizon. He'd hardly known his father, who had died in a truck accident. The uncle had taken the boy under his wing and made him a trusted lieutenant, so when this protector had disappeared in turn, Al Afia had naturally taken his place. He was the only one who understood how everything worked, knew the right people to see about a problem, had contacts in Europe whose phone numbers he'd memorized, remembered families who needed help because the father, uncle, or brother was in prison. Al Afia was not afraid of anyone and cared only about his business. People said he knew so many secrets that he was a walking strongbox. This was the man at whom Azel, primed by a few beers, now began shouting, calling onlookers to witness.

"Look at that fat belly, a crook's belly, and that neck, it really shows how bad this man is—he buys everyone, of course, this country is one huge marketplace, wheeling and dealing day and night, everybody's for sale, all you need is a little power, something to cash in on, and it doesn't take much, just the price of a few bottles of whiskey, an evening with a whore, but for the big jobs, that can cost you, money changes hands, so if you want me to look the other way, let me know the time and place, no sweat, my brother, you want a signature, a little scribble at the bottom of the page, no problem, come see me, or if you're too busy, send your driver, the one-eyed guy, he won't notice a thing, and that's it, my friends, that's Morocco, where some folks slave like maniacs, working because they've decided to be honest, those fellows, they labor in the shadows, no one sees them, no one talks about them when in fact they should get medals, because the country functions thanks to their integrity, and then there are the others, swarming everywhere, in all the ministries, because in our beloved country, corruption is the very air we breathe, yes, we stink of corruption, it's on our faces, in our heads, buried in our hearts—in your hearts, anyway—and if you don't believe me, ask old Crook's Belly over there, old baldy, the armored safe, the strongbox of secrets, the one sipping a lemonade because monsieur is a good Muslim, he doesn't drink alcohol, he goes often to Mecca, oh yes, he's a hajji*—and I'm an astronaut! I'm in a rocket, I'm escaping into space, don't want to live anymore on this earth, in this country, it's all fake, everyone's cutting some deal, well, I refuse to do that, I studied law in a nation that knows nothing of the Law even while it's pretending to demand respect for our laws, what a joke, here you have to respect the powerful, that's all, but for the rest, you're on your fucking own. . . . As for you, Mohammed Oughali, you're nothing but a thief, a faggot—a zamel . . . an attaye . . ."

Azel was shouting louder and louder. One of the cops at the bar, outstandingly drunk, went over to whisper in Al Afia's ear: "Leave him to me, we'll charge him with threatening our national security . . . securi-titty. . . ."

Al Afia's thugs would obey his slightest signal, and he had to shut this little loudmouth up. He glanced at him. Two bruisers grabbed Azel and tossed him outside, punching him savagely.

"You're crazy, busting your ass to piss off the boss—anyone would think you wanted to wind up like your pal!"

Azel's first cousin, Noureddine, had been more than a friend—
he'd been like a brother to him. Azel had hoped that one day his
sister Kenza might marry Noureddine, but their cousin had
drowned during a night crossing when Al Afia's men had over-
loaded a leaky tub. Twenty-four perished on an October night
the Guardia Civil of Almería claimed was too stormy for any attempt at rescue.

Al Afia had flatly denied receiving any money—even though
Azel had been right there when Noureddine had paid the smuggler twenty thousand dirhams. That man had more than one
death on his conscience—but did he even have a conscience? His
varied business interests were flourishing. He lived in a huge
house in Ksar es-Seghir, on the Mediterranean coast, a kind of
bunker where he piled up burlap bags stuffed with money. People
said he had two wives, one Spanish, one Moroccan, who lived in
the same house and whom no one had ever seen. Since kif trafficking wasn't enough for him, every two weeks he filled some old
boats with poor bastards who gave him everything they had to
get to Spain. Al Afia was never around on the nights the boats
left; one of his men—a chauffeur, bodyguard, burglar, never the
same guy—would supervise the operation. Al Afia had his
snitches, his informers, and his cops as well. He called them "my
men." Every so often, taking great care not to alert the police in
Tangier, the authorities in Rabat would send soldiers to stop the
boats and arrest the *passeurs,* and that's how a few of Al Afia's
henchmen landed in jail. As long as they were imprisoned in

Tangier, Al Afia looked after them as though they were his own children, making sure they had a daily meal, supporting their families. He had his connections in the local prison, where he knew the warden and above all the guards, whom he tipped even when none of his pals were in residence there.

He was a past master at corruption, expertly assessing every man's character, needs, weaknesses, neglecting no aspect of anyone's personality, and he had a finger in every pie. You'd have thought he had a doctorate in some outlandish science. Al Afia could read only numbers. For everything else, he had loyal and competent secretaries with whom he spoke a Riffian dialect of Berber and a few words of Spanish. Everyone considered him a generous man: "wears his heart on his sleeve"; "his house is yours"; "the dwelling of Goodness"; and so on. To one man he would offer a trip to Mecca; to another, a plot of land, or a foreign car (stolen, obviously); to yet another, a gold watch, telling him, "It's a little something nice for your wife." He paid the medical expenses of his men and their families and night after night he offered drinks to everyone at the bar that had gradually become his headquarters.

3

Azel and Al Afia

War had been declared between Azel and Al Afia a long time ago. Well before Noureddine's death, Azel had decided to leave one night, and had already paid the *passeur*. At the last minute, however, the voyage had been canceled, and Azel had never been reimbursed. He knew that by himself he could do nothing against that monster, a man so feared, so loved—or rather, protected—by those who lived off his generosity. Now and then, especially after a few beers, Azel would let off steam by insulting him, calling him every name in the book. Al Afia had pretended not to hear him until that night, when Azel addressed him by his real name and called him a *zamel*, a passive homosexual. The ultimate shame! A man so powerful, so good, lying on his belly to be sodomized! That was too much, the little jerk had gone too far. A serious lesson was in order: "You pathetic intellectual, hey, get this, you're lucky no one here likes guys, otherwise you'd have gotten your ass plowed a long time ago! You spit on your country, you badmouth it, but don't worry—the police will see to it you wind up dissolving in acid. . . ."

Azel had studied law. After passing his baccalaureate exam with distinction, he'd received a state scholarship, but his parents couldn't pay the rest of his tuition. He'd been counting on his uncle, who practiced law in the nearby town of Larache, to give him a job, but the uncle had had to close his office after some complicated business cost him most of his clientele. In fact, those clients had left him because he refused to do things the way everyone else did, which had earned him a bad reputation: "Don't go to Maître El Ouali—he's an honest man, you can't make a deal with him, so he loses every case!" Azel had realized that his future was compromised, and that without some kind of pull he'd never find work. Many others were in the same boat, so he'd joined a sit-in of unemployed university graduates outside the Parliament in Rabat.

A month later, when nothing had changed, he decided to leave the country, and headed back to Tangier on a bus. Riding along, he even imagined an accident that would put an end to his life and his impossible predicament. He saw himself dead, mourned by his mother and sister, missed by his friends: a victim of unemployment, of a carelessly negligent system—such a bright boy, well educated, sensitive, warmhearted, what a pity that he got on that damned bus with those bald tires, driven by a diabetic who lost consciousness going around a curve. . . . Poor Azel, he never had a chance to live, did everything he could to break free—just think, if he'd managed to set out for Spain, by now he'd be a brilliant lawyer or a university professor!

Azel rubbed his eyes. He went up to the bus driver and asked him if he had diabetes.

"Heaven forbid! Thank God, I'm as strong as a horse, and I place my life in God's hands. Why do you ask?"

"Just to know. The newspaper says that one in seven Moroccans has diabetes."

"Forget it—you shouldn't believe what you read in the papers. . . ."

Leaving the country. It was an obsession, a kind of madness that ate at him day and night: how could he get out, how could he escape this humiliation? Leaving, abandoning this land that wants nothing more to do with its children, turning your back on such a beautiful country to return one day, proudly, perhaps as a rich man: leaving to save your life, even as you risk losing it. . . . He thought it all over and couldn't understand how he'd reached such a point. The obsession quickly became a curse: he felt persecuted, damned, possessed by the will to survive, emerging from a tunnel only to run into a wall. Day by day, his energy, physical strength, and healthy body were deteriorating. Some of his friends found relief from despair by taking up religion and soon became regulars at the mosque. That had never tempted Azel, however; he was too fond of girls and drinking. Someone had contacted him, even offered him work and the chance to travel— a beardless man, who'd spoken in polished French about the future of Morocco, specifically "a Morocco returned to Islam, to righteousness, to integrity and justice."

The man had a tic, blinking nervously while he chewed on his lower lip. Pretending to listen to him, Azel repressed a smile and imagined him running stark naked through the desert. That did it: the man seemed ridiculous. Azel paid no further attention to what he said. Azel had no use for that morality: most of his pleasures were forbidden by religion! He firmly refused the man's offer and realized that the fellow was actually a recruiter for some very shady causes. Azel could have given in and made himself a bit of money, but he felt afraid, he had a presentiment, remembering a neighbor who'd joined a militant religious group only to vanish without a trace at a time when men were going off to Libya and on to Afghanistan to combat the atheism of the Russian Communists.

Six months later, the recruiter had tried again, inviting Azel to dinner "just to talk." Azel couldn't manage to take seriously this man who, in spite of his nervous twitches, was managing to attract some lost souls to religion. Azel was interested in his methods and the logic of his arguments, however, and he tried to learn who was behind this movement, but the recruiter was on to him. He anticipated Azel's questions, which he answered with a knowing air, confiding in him as though he'd been an old friend.

"I studied literature, I even defended a thesis at the Sorbonne. After my return to Morocco, I taught French literature, and then I worked as an inspector of schools. I traveled around the country, seeing what people like you don't get to see, and I heard the voice of traditional, rural Morocco. No one brainwashed me, and no, I'm not some lunatic: I know what I'm doing and what I want. Our political parties have failed miserably because they haven't learned to listen to what the people are telling them. They've missed the boat. I'm particularly angry at the Socialists, who believed in taking turns at the political trough, who played the power game without doing anything to bring about change. The king used them, and they went along with it."

He paused and looked into Azel's eyes. Placing a hand on his shoulder, he bit his lower lip—without blinking, this time—before continuing.

"No one in power respects the message of Islam. They use it, but do not apply it. And our plan is precisely to do something different. We know what the people want: to live in dignity."

When he stopped to blow his nose vigorously, as if to disguise his nervous tics, Azel began to stare at him and once more saw him naked, in a warehouse this time, being chased by a huge black man and yelling for help. Catching up with him, the colossus slapped him, laughing uproariously.

While the recruiter continued presenting his tedious arguments pieced together from every which where, Azel escaped into a daydream: he was now sitting on the terrace of one of the big cafés on the Plaza Mayor in Madrid. The weather was lovely, people were smiling; a German girl, a tourist, asked him for directions, and he was inviting her to have a drink. . . . Suddenly, the recruiter's voice grew louder, hustling him back to Tangier.

"It's intolerable that a sick man who goes to a state hospital should be turned away because the hospital cannot take care of him. That is why we actively intervene wherever the state is ineffectual. Our solidarity is not selective. This country must be saved: there are too many compromises, injustices, too much corruption and inequality. I'm not claiming to fix every problem, but we don't stand around with our arms crossed waiting for the government to serve its citizens. I've been enriched by French culture, the culture of law, of rights, the culture of justice and respect for others. I found things in Islam that share this enlightenment, in sacred Muslim texts as well as in those of the golden age of Arab culture. I would like you to open your eyes and give meaning to your life."

Suspecting that Azel had little interest in his speech, he repeated that last sentence several times.

"I know, you're like many of your comrades, obsessed by the idea of leaving, of fleeing this country. That's not just the easy way out, it's also the most dangerous. Europe doesn't want us. Islam frightens them. Racism is everywhere. You think you'll solve your problem by emigrating, but once you get out—if indeed you do reach a safe harbor—you'll miss your culture, your religion, your country. We are against emigration, legal or clandestine, because our problems are things we have to solve here and now, without counting on others to fix them for us. Once more, I do not claim that religion is the answer to everything. No: religion, it gives you confidence, self-confidence, and that's what opens doors for you."

The man had his nervous tics under control, and Azel was listening more attentively to him, yet he still couldn't stop wondering about the life he might have somewhere far away. Then he remembered his missing friend, Mohammed-Larbi.... There was no point in talking to the recruiter about the fate of a man who had probably joined an Islamist organization. Azel felt like having a glass of wine, but the restaurant did not serve any to Moroccans. Besides, the recruiter would have taken it the wrong way. Azel wanted to provoke him, to tell him that religion should stay out of politics, that one should improve people's living conditions without forcing them to hang around mosques. Then the recruiter offered him the chance to teach some law courses in a private school where he was the principal. Despite the meager salary, Azel was actually tempted to accept, but when the other man led him to understand that from time to time he would be sent on missions to the kind of countries where Moroccans didn't need visas, Azel lost interest. It was Europe that had captured his heart, and his longing to emigrate there was simply overwhelming.

When the two men said good-bye, they promised to keep in touch.

"If you ever manage to slip into Spain," the recruiter added, "let me know: I'll put you in contact with some reliable friends over there."

Again, Azel had a vision of him naked: in a hammam, a Turkish bath, getting a massage.

4

Noureddine

The following night, Azel couldn't sleep. Why was he so obsessed with leaving Morocco? Where had the idea come from, and why was it so tenacious, so violent? Afraid of his own thoughts, he wavered between that uncontrollable desire to leave and the recruiter's proposals, which he couldn't completely dismiss. Insomnia gave frightening intensity to these tortured ruminations. Careful not to disturb his sleeping family, he went out on the balcony, which overlooked the Marshan cemetery. A lovely silvery light shone so brightly that the sea seemed like a white mirror. Azel counted the tombs, looking for Noureddine's grave. He couldn't manage to picture what that superb body disfigured by salt water must look like now. Azel had been the one to go identify the corpse of his cousin and friend. The other victims had been disfigured, perhaps even mangled by sharks, but Noureddine's body, although bloated, had been untouched. All around them were weeping families; some of them hadn't even known about the attempted crossing. Among the dead Azel had noticed two women and a child, covered with a white sheet, and it was then that the governor had swept into the morgue, furious in his distress.

"This is the last time! Hey you, cameraman, come over here and film these bodies! All Morocco must see this tragedy! It has to be in the evening papers—too bad if it spoils people's appetites! We've had enough! *Basta!* We're sick of it! This must stop. Morocco is losing its strength, its young people! Where's the police chief? Get him here right away. We're going to seal off the coasts!"

Azel had never forgotten even one detail of that scene, or the suffocating smells from those bodies nourished, only a few days before, by the dream of a better life. Nor would he ever forget Noureddine's milk-white eyes, or his right hand clutching a key. As a child, Azel had been horribly afraid of death and everything about it. He could spot a corpse-washer at any distance, so anxious was he to avoid any handshaking or eating out of the same plate with them. He hated that cloying incense burned around dead bodies. He had always refused even to look at the face of someone who'd died. It was stronger than he was, an irrational fear, a phobia that haunted him. When he was ten years old, Azel had run to hide at a neighbor's house on the day his own grandfather was buried, convinced that death was contagious and that its shadow would come carry him off at night under its cloak. The first time he ever forgot his fear was when he'd had to go claim Noureddine's body. He'd handled all the administrative procedures to bring his friend home. Paralyzed by their son's death, Noureddine's parents had wept and refused to accept what had happened. Kenza, clothed all in white, was not allowed to attend the funeral: the women had to stay home, it was the custom. She screamed out her grief, weeping both for her cousin and for her fiancé, suffering over her own fate as well. Noureddine had been buried that same day, because of the advanced decomposition of the body. Azel's efficiency had astonished everyone. The *tolba*, men learned in the Koran, had gathered in the front room, where they read silently from the Book and chanted a few prayers together. Before going on to the cemetery, the cortege stopped at the neighborhood mosque, where a man with a strong, loud voice recited the *Janâzatou Rajoul*, "the burial service for a man." The prayer was spoken in front of the body, well wrapped in its white shroud and adorned with a piece of green and black embroidery. A few minutes later, Noureddine was carried by Azel and three other friends to his grave. The *tolba* began the prayers of farewell; the body was placed in a narrow hole and quickly covered with earth, flat stones, and cement. It was all over very quickly. The family distributed bread and dried figs to some beggars and the *tolba*. Azel stood among the relatives to receive condolences. He was sobbing. When people urged him to set aside his anger, to follow the path of wisdom and patience, Azel took that as nothing more than a conventional formula, the kind trotted out on such occasions. He would never forget his friend! And he would never give up trying to avenge him in some way.

Azel smoked a cigarette out on the balcony, then tiptoed back to bed, where he began wondering once again about the abrupt disappearance of Mohammed-Larbi, the friend who had probably been lured into some Islamist group, although the young man's father kept saying that was impossible. His son, he insisted, was a nonbeliever who did not observe Ramadan and often got drunk, in fact his drinking was a dreadful burden for the family and their neighbors.

"Exactly," a policeman had explained. "That's just the type of guy who interests the Islamists. They've got ways of winning them over. And once he's in, they give him a passport and some visas—counterfeit, obviously, but the recruit doesn't know this, and they send him off to a Muslim country like Pakistan or Afghanistan for training, where another team takes over, a tougher bunch, and the goal becomes clearer: taking revolutionary action to cleanse Muslim countries of native and foreign infidels. The whole procedure takes from three to six months, because the brainwashing doesn't start right away, they take their time and above all apply the most sophisticated techniques, they're experts, well organized, cleverly set up, they don't waste their efforts, we know that from men who've become disillusioned and escaped from them, guys who suddenly realized what was going on, but what can you do about all this? We're vigilant, but these people play on religious faith, irrationality, weakness of character, whereas our sole advantage is spotting the fake documents. Their recruits don't travel by airplane, however: they choose busy times in the ports, at night, and sometimes they slip a bill or two into the policeman's or custom official's hand and that's that. I know, I shouldn't be telling you this, but it's the truth: the Islamists' main ally is the corruption they claim to be fighting, because it's thanks to baksheesh that they manage to slip past the border police. Your son will turn up one day, old man, and you won't recognize him, he'll have changed, so let us know, and you'll be doing your country a great service. . . ."

Mohammed-Larbi had been a restless youth, rebellious and, above all, desperate. During the riots in Beni Makada, a slum neighborhood in Tangier targeted by the authorities during an antidrugs campaign, he'd been arrested and had spent a few days in police custody. He was a quiet high-school student, but sometimes, enraged at the country's predicament, he would insult the authorities and opposition figures alike, calling them all incompetents. Azel was convinced that he'd joined an Islamist group and was now in some sort of "liberation army." Although Azel had often called him a hothead, he'd liked Mohammed-Larbi, and was sorry he hadn't spent more time with him in the days before he disappeared.

Azel depended for support on his sister, who worked as a nurse in a clinic and for private patients as well, since the clinic didn't pay very much. The boss was a surgeon—a short guy, very fussy, with that way skinflints have of always talking about money, whether it's the price of tomatoes or a scanner—and he paid Kenza the minimum wage, telling her, "You're learning the business." In one day he earned what his employees took home in a year, which didn't prevent him from praying five times a day, visiting the holy places each spring, and making a pilgrimage every two years. Before each operation, he demanded payment in advance, in cash. He was as famous for his greed as for his surgical skills. People even said that for love of money he had betrayed his best friend. And yet he slept soundly, beaming with satisfaction. Kenza had no choice. She preferred her exhausting job to the unstable existence of her friend Samira, a colleague who had become a "hostess" in what was essentially a prostitution ring. Samira went on trips with men she didn't know, to parties where she took dangerous risks. Everything had been marvelous at first, glamorous and easy. People asked to dance with her, never to sleep with her. That suited her fine. But all that gradually fell apart. How many times had she come running to Kenza, terrified, badly beaten, raped!

Azel had given up looking for work, at least in the ordinary way—a letter enclosing a résumé. He'd gotten nowhere like that. He'd looked all over the place, in the civil service as well as the business community, but he'd lacked the backbone to venture into that predatory world. All in all, Azel was a nice guy, not a tough guy. Poor boy! He had no idea he was on the wrong track. No one had warned him: after creating hell, bastards go to heaven! His obsession pursued him everywhere: the thought of leaving! He cherished it, clung to it. Meanwhile, he barely managed to keep going, trying to sell used cars, acting as an agent for a realtor, and he'd even waited patiently at the French consulate on behalf of a man who could afford to pay him two hundred dirhams for the five hours on line. Azel managed to earn a little money, enough to buy some contraband cigarettes, purchase name-brand clothing on credit. . . . As for girls, his friend El Haj, a distant cousin of Noureddine's, was the one who took care of slipping a hundred-dollar bill between their breasts.

5

El Haj

El Haj and Azel made a strange pair. They weren't the same age, didn't share the same interests. Fascinated by this young man's story, El Haj wanted to help him. El Haj was as physically repulsive as Azel was attractive. Azel's relationships with girls were episodic but straightforward: sex was the object, nothing else. To him, falling in love was a luxury, especially since there was nowhere to take a girl in Tangier, even just for a drink. You needed a car, money, a job. Everything that foreigners had and he did not, in this city that enticed and infuriated him. El Haj welcomed Azel warmly at his beautiful house on the Mountain. El Haj loved to party. Like certain men of the Rif, he had enjoyed a period of easy money and foolproof business schemes, but unlike his friends, he had abandoned that life to concentrate on enjoying himself. He was married, but had been unable to father children, and his wife spent part of each year in her native village in the Rif while he stayed on in his big house. Every two years, he took her on a pilgrimage to Mecca. She was satisfied with that and in re-turn, she left him alone. In Tangier, he liked to organize dinners with friends, and would put Azel in charge of inviting girls. The real estate agent for whom Azel did small services had introduced him to a good network of girls who liked to have fun: drinking, dancing, and eventually, sex, as well as getting a few presents or—to put it bluntly—cash. This wasn't wicked or sordid. Many girls were students of some kind, others said they were secretaries or had lost their jobs, while some were young divorcées who craved excitement but hadn't much money, and there were girls brought along to the parties by their older sisters so they could join this life, young and naïve girls, pretty and pleasing, often from modest backgrounds but sometimes from well-off families, too. The network, which contained several categories of girls, was run by Khaddouj, the *qawada*, a procuress of about forty who found recruits in the hammam and through her friend Warda, a hairdresser. Thanks to the success of the cell phone (and especially to the fact that you could continue receiving calls for six months after your credit ran out), the girls were available at any hour of the day or night. Azel did not consider them prostitutes, but simply "social cases." That was El Haj's favorite expression, and he had a whole theory on this subject.

"In our beloved country, there are only two reasons to go out with a woman: either you intend to marry her and are therefore a goner, or you want to make her your mistress, which means, can you afford her? Because they're demanding, they want a furnished apartment, a monthly salary, gifts from time to time—which is normal, of course, but has nothing to do with what we ourselves want, because really, what are we looking for? We're looking to enjoy ourselves with pretty little sweeties to whom you slip a few bills at the end of the evening: you're not tied down, you're not committed, you'll never be two-timed, you're having fun, they're having fun, and what's great is, you won't ever see the same ones twice, it's ideal for the libido, change—it's the key to permanent desire, my friend! They're cute, and besides, they're all social cases. And us? We're helping them! Plus above all, they're really liberated, no taboos, no won't-go-theres, they do everything and are more expert than European women, believe me, I wonder where they learn all that, you start thinking there must be a sex school where they show porno films! No, Moroccan women are superb, they're beautiful, desirable, clean, and that's important, they're always at the hammam, they wax their legs and mounds, they drive me crazy, when I'm with them I forget my diabetes and everything else. . . . They're truly nice, they never mention money, they arrive like guests to enjoy a pleasant evening, they relax and let you know that not only are they available but they've come there only for you! And then, their skin, it's the softest, the most voluptuous—can you imagine, when skin has the fragrance of cinnamon, amber, musk, every perfume you ever dreamed of, in no time you're in heaven and you close your eyes so you'll never fall back to earth, that's why I like Moroccan women, they start with almost nothing and presto, they're fabulous. Yes, my friend, we're lucky, and I know, you don't agree, you're going to lecture me about poverty, exploitation, vice, morality, the status of women, justice, equality, privilege, even religion, I know what you're going to tell me, but: let yourself live, and enjoy your youth. . . ."

Many of those girls were in love with Azel, but he discouraged them, telling them the truth about his situation: "I'm twenty-four, I have a diploma but no money, job, or car. Yes, I'm a social case, too—just drifting, ready to do anything to get the hell out of here, leave this whole country behind except for some memories and a few postcards, so I'm not made for love, and you deserve better, you should have luxury, beauty, poetry. . . . I already tried to burn up those eight or nine miles between us and Europe, but I got cheated—so I was luckier than my cousin Noureddine, who drowned only a few yards from Almería, can you imagine?"

The girls listened to him; some of them cried. They all came from families where loved ones had tried to leave the same way. Siham, the oldest, admitted that she'd made the crossing only to find the Guardia Civil waiting for them on the beach at dawn in camouflage, as if they'd been at war. She'd been arrested, interrogated, then sent back to Tangier—and a beating by the Moroccan police. Since then she'd come up with other ideas but still hoped to leave and get as far away as possible. She'd been disgusted by what she'd heard said about girls who tried to get a life by emigrating.

"When a man burns up the straits, they say he'll find work; when it's a woman, particularly if she's pretty, right away she's going to be a whore! There are well-known networks in the Gulf states, and if you can just get to Libya, where you don't need a visa, things are all set up to move you on to Dubai or Abu Dhabi. You have to put up with being pawed by those fat slobs; some girls like that, or let's say, they like what they can get for it. Me, if I ever get to emigrate, it'll be to take care of my parents. My sister works for two families, in Milan, where old people are abandoned by their own children and grandchildren, so they turn to young

women from the Maghreb—Moroccans, Tunisians, Algerians—
who prepare their meals, accompany them to the hospital, take
them out for walks, read to them, in short, give them what they
need. It's good work. It's what I dream of doing. My sister is
looking into how I could get a visa."

When El Haj put on some music, Siham and the other girls
got up to dance. Watching them, Azel felt moved, and wished he
could take them one by one in his arms to hug them close. He was
happy, but sensed the fragility of such emotions. That evening he
made love with Siham.

"Will you take me with you if you manage to leave the country?" she asked him afterward, and then admitted that she was
hoping to marry a Frenchman or a Spaniard.

"Me too," replied Azel.

Giggling, she corrected him: a Frenchwoman or a Spanish
lady! Azel thought for a moment.

"What does it matter," he said solemnly, "as long as I fulfill my
dream. . . ."

Siham sat on the edge of the bed and cried. He put his arms
around her, wiped away her tears with the back of his hand, and
hugged her tightly.

"In this country, you don't confess to a woman that you love
her; it has something to do with sexual modesty, apparently. I,
however, am telling you!"

"You love me? Then say it again."

"It's not easy."

"And what does it mean, to love me?"

"That I love to be with you, I love to make love to you. . . ."

"But you can't be thinking of spending your life with a girl who slept with you the first time you met, a girl who's not a virgin anymore!"

"You know, I don't want to be like all the others here. Virginity, for me, it's more of a problem than anything else. I don't like to deflower a girl, it puts me in a panic, all that blood. . . ."

"Then tell me 'I love you.'"

"Some other time, when you won't be expecting it."

Siham lay down on her stomach and began to fondle Azel's sex with her right hand.

"Since you love me and aren't telling me so, *I'm* going to tell you everything I think!"

And she rattled off all the words for "penis" she knew from reading *The Perfumed Garden,* by Sheik Nefzaoui,* followed by all the words for "vagina," emphasizing the vowels and taking pleasure in this linguistic inventory. Then, when she felt Azel finally grow hard, she told him to penetrate her anally.

In Arabic, her command had something pornographic about it, something exciting and at the same time unbearable. Azel lost his hard-on.

"You're teasing me! I won't take you from either the front or behind."

"Too bad—at least give me a summery, see-through dress I'll put on in the hot weather when it's windy; I won't wear panties and that way people will see my belly, my crotch, my buttocks, and all the men will keel over in front of me!"

Laughing, they got dressed again. Before they left the room, Azel summoned the courage to ask, "Why did you want me to take you from behind?"

"Girls who want to hang on to their virginity let themselves be taken that way, so there's no risk. That's what I did for a while and I didn't like it at first, it hurt, and then strangely enough I began to enjoy it. Ever since, I've liked to change pleasures now and then, but you, you didn't seem crazy about it. . . ."

"No. When I was a kid, in my teens, I did it a few times with boys, never with girls. I don't like it much. I'm sorry about what happened just now."

El Haj had collapsed in the living room with a girl in each arm. He was snoring, and the half-naked girls were smiling broadly. Unwilling to wake him, Azel offered the girls, who had each received a hundred-dollar bill, a ride home in El Haj's car.

Afterward, Azel drove across the city in silence with Siham holding on to his arm. She felt like doing something madcap and impulsive, but Azel was in a gloomy mood, so in the end she went home. At around five in the morning, Azel found himself alone on the esplanade of the boulevard Pasteur, which offered a fairly clear view of the lights of Tarifa, directly across the straits. He took the harbor road, driving past the ruins of the Gran Teatro Cervantes, and decided that as soon as he became a Spanish citizen, he would come back to restore it. At the harbor entrance he was accosted by a policeman in a foul temper.

"Hey, you! Where're you going?"

"To watch the boats leave!"

"Get out, we've got enough problems with the Spanish and those Africans always skulking around. . . ."

"Don't worry, I'm not going to burn up the straits, only watch the trucks get loaded on. I've got the right to envy those crates of merchandise! I'd like to be one of them—not be inside one, I'd suffocate—but *be* one, delivered to a warehouse in Europe, in a land of prosperity and freedom, yes, a simple, cheap pine box, an anonymous crate on which I'd like to have written in red letters: 'Fragile,' and 'This side up.'"

"You're nuts!"

"Completely! Here, take some cigarettes."

The policeman helped himself and asked Azel to just leave him alone.

"Tell me frankly, come on, between ourselves, wouldn't *you* like to take the place of one of those crates?"

"Fuck off!"

"Calm down, I'm joking."

"Go wherever you want, and if you find a good deal, come and get me. I'm fed up, too. But cut out that business about the crates. You know what my wife calls me? *Sandok el khaoui:* empty crate! All because I don't earn enough to offer her everything she wants. Know what I get a month? Two thousand dirhams. I pay eight hundred in rent, and we live—we survive—on the rest. So beat it, stop bothering me!"

Azel walked along slowly, taking particular pleasure in the rumbling engines of the big trucks. He went over to them, breathing in the odors of diesel fuel as if he were sniffing a bouquet of roses.

He ran his hand over a wheel, studying it and wondering how far away it could take him. He asked the two workmen loading the truck what merchandise they were carrying. Clothing, only designer goods: Boss, Klein, Zara, garments from Italy, Spain, everywhere but Morocco!

He saw himself as a mannequin dressed in some of the clothes and packed in one of those crates, sent off to a store window in Paris or Madrid. He imagined having himself modeled in wax, crossing the border disguised as a display dummy, a lifeless object instead of a breathing human being. The idea made him laugh. It scared him, too. He continued looking around, peeked under the truck, and remembered the story of that teenager who'd hidden in a place like that. Once across the Spanish border, he'd run off only to be caught by some hunters who'd handed him over to the police. European radio and television stations had broadcast his story as an example of the madness that came over certain young Moroccans. The Moroccan consulate had picked up the unfortunate adventurer and sent him home, but as soon as he'd arrived in Tangier he had sworn to do it again.

Other trucks were loading heavier cargo. Azel went over to the boats that would soon be leaving. Everything was quiet. The cops were having their breakfast; one of them was reading a paper. The article was explaining that Spain had recently installed an electronic surveillance system along its beaches, with infrared and ultrasound equipment, ultra everything, along with automatic weapons. . . . The illegal aliens could be detected even before they'd decided to leave their country! With that paraphernalia, the Spanish cops were now able to foresee everything as soon as a Moroccan showed the slightest inclination to cross the Straits of Gibraltar: the mere *thought* would provide the Spanish with detailed information on the guy in question: age, name, past, everything, they'd learn everything. That's progress for you. Now the Moroccans would just have to behave themselves! No more dreaming about Spain, thanks to a new law and all those technical innovations. At the slightest suspicion, the lights of the Guardia Civil pop on and the electronic gear detects the would-be emigrant, who will be turned back before he even leaves his house. No need to search through loaded trucks anymore.

Like a child who discovers the sea for the first time, Azel was impressed by the size of the ships. He loved the noise of the engines and the shouts of the sailors. Standing on the dock, he imagined himself as a captain or commander in a white uniform, and closing his eyes to savor these moments, he gave orders with brisk precision. It must have been around seven in the morning. A huge steamship was about to come alongside, and Azel was fascinated by that mass gliding along the placid water. When he waved to a woman passenger leaning over the rail, she did not react, but he didn't care, so what. What he wanted, at that very instant, was to be in a cabin on board, where he would hole up, waiting for the ship to leave again so he could go smoke a cigarette out on deck. There he would chat with a German tourist taking a cruise with his wife to celebrate their golden anniversary. Feeling seasick, Azel would take some medicine and go lie down on clean sheets to listen to the sound of the waves carrying him away, far away from Tangier and Africa.

Visions crowded into Azel's mind like a dream sequence in a

movie. He saw himself dressed all in white, accompanied by Olga, an Austrian opera singer visiting her brother, who was spending the summer on the Mountain. Her brother's friends were all homosexual, yet Olga had met Azel at his house, spotting Azel from a distance, sniffing out the man who loved women. And she had not been mistaken. Just what was he doing at Monsieur Dhall's house? Shorthanded, the head chef had asked him to come help out, although in fact Azel wasn't waiting on the guests, but welcoming them, showing them where to go. Olga had taken him by the arm to lead him to the far end of the garden. In silence, they had kissed for a long time. She was quite forward, which bothered Azel, but he'd gone along with it. Then someone had summoned him, so he'd detached himself from the clutches of the Austrian beauty to rejoin the chef.

Azel looked up to find the steamship drawing slowly alongside the quay. He helped the dock workers install the gangplank. As they left the ship, the passengers were laughing. Azel wanted to go aboard, slip off somewhere, and stay on the ship. It was too risky. He noticed a gray cat trying to sneak past the guards onto the ship; chased away with a kick, he still didn't stop trying. The policemen and customs officials knew the cat well, and used to comment sarcastically about his stubborn desire to get out of Morocco. Even the cat was fed up: he, too, wanted something else from life, and needed tenderness, caresses, a kind family who would spoil him. The cat wanted to go away because he knew instinctively that it was better "over there," and he had his obsessions like everyone else, coming stubbornly every day to try his best to jump onto that vessel bound for Europe. Perhaps he was a

Christian cat who might have belonged to some Spaniards or English people, since there was no one to rival them for protecting and loving animals so much, whereas here a cat or dog is treated like an intruder, we chase them, hit them, so it was perfectly normal that this gray cat wanted to leave, too! Once, he had jumped, missed the gangplank, and been saved by a fisherman who took pity on him.

Azel broke off his reverie and walked away with his hands in his pockets. When he encountered the cat, he greeted him as if he'd been human.

"So you want to leave as well, you've caught the virus of departure too, haven't you—you don't feel at home here, where you're mistreated, kicked, you dream of a better, more comfortable life in a big bourgeois house. . . . Hey, don't give up, you'll get there some day."

The cat listened attentively, meowed, and vanished.

Leaving the harbor, Azel stopped a moment in front of the cop, to whom he gave his almost full pack of cigarettes.

"Here, they're American, real ones, black market. Smoke—and take a big hit of the tar that will make its home in your lungs. Well, so long, pal!"

To get back to town, Azel drove to the rue Siaghine* and the Grand Socco. The streets were eerily calm. As usual, the ground was strewn with filth. He wondered for the hundredth time why Moroccans were clean at home and dirty in public, and remembered what his history teacher at the Lycée Al Khatib had taught him, that Morocco's tragedy was the exodus from the countryside. Rural people flooding into the city continued to live like peasants, throwing their garbage out their front doors—in short, not changing their behavior one jot. And it's all the fault of the heavens, it's the drought that forces thousands of families to leave their land to come beg in the city.

That morning, there were many more stray cats than usual. They weren't even fighting, they were feasting. Azel saw a beggar rummaging through a garbage can and felt ashamed. The man fled.

At the Grand Socco, Azel sat down on a wobbly stool and ordered a bowl of fava bean puree. "I love this dish," he thought; "I'll have some here because I'm not sure I can get any *over there.*" He was as happy as the cats, although the image of those little creatures head-down in the garbage cans made him sick.

6

Miguel

Wounded, thrown to the sidewalk, Azel was still conscious. The two men standing over him were about to finish him off. His stomach and ribs hurt, but deep down he was proud: he'd had the courage to attack a monster, perhaps the most powerful man in the city. Until now, no one had dared defy him and tell him to his face what everyone thought. Azel felt a kind of euphoria that gave him strength in spite of his injuries. Convinced that this night belonged to him, he knew at that moment that his life was going to change.

Just when Azel, trying to get up, was stomped back to the ground, Miguel López's car pulled over. The two attackers fled. Miguel and his driver got out to carry Azel back to the car. Then they drove off to the Old Mountain, where Miguel had a handsome house with a view of the medina and a stretch of the sea.

He was quite an elegant man who dressed with exquisite taste. He loved flowers so much that he spent an hour every morning arranging the various bouquets in the house, expressing his mood and inclinations through that day's choice of blossoms and color combinations. He spent the summer in Tangier and the rest of the year in Barcelona or traveling around the world to organize the exhibitions at his art gallery. A generous man, he had a passion for Morocco because of the quality of life there, its infinite variety. It was only natural for him to come to the aid of a man who'd been knocked down, and he didn't understand why the customers in the bar were just sitting there, letting those thugs do their dirty work.

Miguel was close to one of the king's cousins, a man who had his entrée at the palace and had placed Miguel on the list of those whom protocol would welcome there without question. Miguel was thrilled to appear at the court of Hassan II two or three times a year and to be considered a friend of Morocco, an artist expected to speak well of the country and—most important—defend it against criticism.

Miguel was a worldly man at heart. He adored parties where he could rub shoulders with celebrities, which amused him and made him feel proud, in a way. He had known many sorrows, and had decided to put his trust in lighthearted merriment. Posh society affairs provided all the frivolity he needed to forget his mistakes, failures, and heartaches.

Why, then, did Miguel want to tear Azel from his own world to take him home to Spain? At first, he wanted to help Azel. Only after seeing him a few times did he realize that a fling or even a serious affair was possible. Whenever Miguel forced a man to become involved with him, he regretted it, but he found a kind of perverse pleasure in feeling lonely and sorry for himself. He loved the "awkwardness" of Moroccan men, by which he meant their sexual ambiguity. He loved the olive sheen of their skin. And he loved their availability, which marked the inequality in which the relationship was formed, for the lover by night was thus the servant by day, casually dressed to do the daily shopping, wearing fine clothing in the evening to stimulate sexual desire. The old concierge in an apartment building where an American writer and his wife lived had said it best.

"That type, they want everything, men and women from the common people, young ones, healthy, preferably from the countryside, who can't read or write, serving them all day, then servicing them at night. A package deal, and between two pokes, tokes on a nicely packed pipe of kif to help the American write! Tell me your story, he says to them, I'll make a novel out of it, you'll even have your name on the cover: you won't be able to read it but no matter, you're a writer like me, except that you're an illiterate writer, that's exotic—what I mean is, unusual, my friend! That's what he tells them, without ever mentioning money, because you don't talk about that, not when you're working for a writer, after all! They aren't obliged to accept, but I know that poverty—our friend poverty—can lead us to some very sad places. People have to make do with life, that's how it is, and me, I see everything, but I don't say everything! We're all hung up by our feet, it's like at the butcher shop: you ever seen a sheep hanging from its neighbor's hoof? No? Well, Moroccans who go with Christians, it's the same thing!"

The next morning, Miguel knocked on the door of the room where Azel had been put to bed. He wanted to know his guest's name, what he did, how he was, and why he'd been in that bar.

When there was no reply, Miguel knocked again before quietly opening the door. Azel was sleeping on his back, half-covered by the blanket. Miguel was stunned by the candid expression on his face, and the beauty of his bruised body. Deciding to let him sleep, Miguel tiptoed out. He felt agitated, and poured himself more coffee, which he rarely did because of his heart condition. He went from one room to another, then out onto the terrace to try to compose himself. He had the strong impression that this young man was going to turn his life upside down—he was convinced of this in a kind of blazing and inexplicable intuition. Although he would have liked to talk to someone about what had happened, about his feelings, Miguel forced himself to calm down and wait until lunchtime.

The situation brought back memories he had long struggled to repress, of the time when he used to flee his parents' house to haunt the bars of Barcelona, longing for a love affair that would relieve his melancholy and loneliness. His parents—a Catholic mother and a Communist father—could not imagine why their son was slumming around with depraved men. They made life hard for him, barely even spoke to him. One day he was beaten up when he tried to stop a fight between two drunks. He couldn't possibly have gone home with his right eye all swollen, his parents would have questioned him too much and might even have asked the police to investigate the men he was meeting. As Miguel was getting to his feet, wiping away the blood trickling from his forehead, a hand had offered him a white handkerchief, and for a few seconds he'd seen nothing but that scrap of white fabric, delicately perfumed. Slender, with long fingers and dark freckles on the back, the hand belonged to a tall, middle-aged man wearing a gray felt hat and smoking a cigar. The man had walked away with a firm step, but noticing a slight affectedness in his movements, Miguel had followed him without a word. For Miguel, that was the beginning of a complicated and painful story of love and sex. He had left his parents' house only to become a slave in debt to his rich and powerful rescuer.

Brushing this already ancient history away with his hand, Miguel told himself that the young man still sleeping in his room had nothing like that to fear. Around noon, Azel appeared, timid, embarrassed at finding himself there, apologizing for having slept too long.

"Sit down, you must be hungry."

"No, I'd just like an aspirin and a large glass of water."

"What's your name?"

"Azz El Arab, but my friends call me Azel, it's simpler."

"What does your name mean?"

"The pride, the glory of the Arabs! It means I'm the best, someone precious, beloved and good. . . ."

"Hard to live up to, no?"

"My father supported Nasser and was a nationalist with a passionate interest in the Arab world. Unfortunately, the Arab world of today is a shambles. So am I, by the way. Speaking of which, I would like to thank you for what you did last night."

"Please, don't bother. Here, eat something."

Azel felt more at ease, and asked Miguel about his work, his travels, what he was doing in Tangier. Actually, he was trying to find out if his rescuer could help him obtain a visa for Spain, but he did not mention that, and at one point took advantage of his host's brief absence to slip away.

Miguel was annoyed. He asked his driver if he knew the boy, but Khaled shook his head.

"You will find him and bring him back, nicely, don't use any force."

"Understood, monsieur."

Khaled was hurt, but didn't dare show it in front of his employer, who was pretending to have forgotten that the two of them had once had an intimate relationship. Miguel sometimes displayed a remarkable ability to forget. Obliged to swallow his disappointment and make the best of things, Khaled had gotten married, determined to put an end to that episode and all the gossip and mockery of his friends at the café.

Anyway, it wasn't the first time Miguel had asked him to bring him home some tipsy kid he was planning on helping, and Khaled didn't even feel like warning Azel, whom he knew by sight from having seen him a few times hanging around bars with other guys like him.

Fetched by Khaled, Azel showed up again at the villa the next day, accompanied by his friend Siham. Without comment, Miguel received them with attentive courtesy. Azel introduced Siham as his fiancée, and she played along. Azel quickly turned the conversation to the topic that obsessed him: leaving. Being reborn elsewhere. Leaving by any means possible. Spreading your wings. Running along the sand shouting out your freedom. Working, creating, producing, imagining, doing something with your life.

Azel had no need to convince Miguel, who listened while he

thought things over and wondered about all the questions tumbling pell-mell through his mind: Did he want to help Azel or keep him for himself? How could he do both? Miguel had lost much of his youthful vigor, but one thing was certain: he would make that man his lover. Although his seductive powers had waned, Miguel hoped to create a bond of friendship in place of love. Cheered by the prospect of a sexual liaison with Azel, Miguel watched him talk, move, walk, even show off his fiancée, and was delighted. It was Siham who had the courage to ask the question.

"Could you help us get a visa?"

Irritated by the bluntness of her request, Azel apologized to Miguel, adding, "You know, more and more young people today dream only of leaving, just leaving this country behind."

"I do know, and it's distressing," replied Miguel. "You're not the first to ask me for help. When a country gets to the point that the 'best' of its children want to leave, it's a terrible thing. I'm not passing judgment on all this, but I admit that while I do understand you, my hands are tied. I had the same dream when I was your age, although my circumstances were different. Spain was unlivable. Franco just wouldn't die, and his religious and military regime infested everything. Well, I had the amazing luck to win a prize at the École des Beaux-Arts, and I left Barcelona for New York. That saved me. I felt as if I were passing from darkness into energy and light. I'd been stifling in that cramped, hypocritical existence, where everything smelled stale, as if dust were clinging invisibly to objects, clothes, hair, and especially the soul. All Spain smelled moldy. People were choking. The country came alive only for soccer and the corrida."

Without answering, Azel stood up and walked nervously around the living room.

"Come on," he told Siham. "We've taken up enough of this gentleman's time."

"Call me Miguel."

"Yes, Miguel. Well, see you soon!"

That evening Azel joined his pals from the neighborhood at the Café Hafa, where they were playing cards. The lights of Tarifa were twinkling; unable to bear the sight of them, Azel asked Abdelmalek to change places with him, and sat with his back to the sea.

"Don't want to gaze at the forbidden land anymore?" asked Abdelmalek.

"What's the point of staring at that horizon? So near and yet so far . . ."

"Remember Toutia?"

"Why?"

"Simply because she haunted us and we were putty in her hands."

"No, we were so kiffed-up that we invented visions. Toutia never existed!"

"Someone saw you at the Spaniard's house. Watch out—he adores Moroccan boys," said Saïd.

"It's incredible, everyone knows everything in this city! I feel like emigrating just because of that."

"You think you'll have a nice quiet life over there?" asked Ahmed.

"At least I won't have to see your lazy faces anymore!"

"If you manage to bamboozle the Spaniard," asked Abdelmalek, "you'll help us?"

"I have no intention of bamboozling anyone."

"Come on, you sleep with him—and you're all set!"

"I can't stand being touched by a man."

"You'll see when you get to it, you'll be thinking only of your visa."

"So you, you could go to bed with a man, caress him, kiss him as if he were a woman, get hard and come and everything?"

"Men, they're not my thing, but when you got to, you got to: close your eyes and think of your girlfriend, it's a question of imagination, and then remember what it's going to get for you, it's just being practical."

"But that's prostitution!"

"Call it whatever you want, I know a lot of guys who do that in the summer, even some who end up leaving in the *zamel*'s baggage. Once abroad, they run off with a woman, get married, and become citizens, you know, that pretty burgundy passport. Afterward they come back here all arrogant and triumphant. There're others who flutter around old ladies, Europeans or Americans, wrinkled bags wearing too much makeup, alone, but so wealthy. . . . I knew one guy, that was even his specialty, he'd stake out the Café de Paris to await his prey. You know he wound up marrying a Canadian who gave him her nationality, with all her inheritance as a bonus? When he got back to Tangier he was so rich he was unrecognizable. He'd dyed his hair, he wore designer clothes and talked to us in a kind of beginner English. He thought he was impressing us. Well, we felt sorry for him. One day a truck to-taled his cute little brand-new Mercedes."

"And?"

"He died!"

"You mean God called him to His bosom because he went wrong?"

"Don't mix God up in this. He died because in this country the roads kill day and night, that's all."

Azel put down his cards, lit a pipe of kif, and after taking a few drags, handed it to Abdelmalek. His friend hadn't really told him anything he didn't already know. It was late, and Azel didn't want to go home yet. He stopped by the Whiskey à Gogo. Neither Al Afia nor his henchmen were there. A few cops were sitting at the bar. One of the waiters, Rubio, leaned over to Azel.

"Things are happening. Seems the minister of the interior has been ordered to clean up the country. They've arrested some guys. People say Al Afia is already in Spain or Gibraltar."

Azel looked the other customers over one by one and had the feeling something serious was about to go down. There was an oppressive silence, an uneasiness. The place felt strange, com-pletely different. The bar had to be under surveillance. Azel wanted to leave but found he couldn't move. He was caught.

He called Rubio over.

"What's going on?"

"I told you, it's the disaffection: on the radio they were talk-ing about a cleansing."

"You mean a 'disinfection'?"

"Yes, something like that. They arrest everyone first, they sort them out later. You know, it's like in the story of the guy running down the street who tells all the other men to run, and when one of them wants to know why, the guy says because we're in danger, there's a nutcase with a huge pair of scissors cutting the balls off everyone with more than two, so the other man says but I'm fine, I'm normal, I've got just the two, and then the first guy says yes but he cuts first and counts later!"

"Even when it's serious, you're telling jokes!"

"You've got to laugh, at least once a day. Okay, let's get serious again. Seems Hallouf is on the run, Hmara and Dib are locked up and along with them, a whole lot of kids who haven't done anything, although you never know. I'm giving you friendly advice: get out of here, go home, and stay there for the time being, because something doesn't smell right. It's like that often here in Morocco: they leave you alone for years and one day decide to pounce, to make an example, so you'd better make sure that example isn't you! You remember that business with the middle-class kids the king had arrested for using drugs? No, you were too young; he went after the children of the bourgeoisie simply to show that he could, that no one was safe, and at the same time to send a signal to the drug dealers."

Just as Azel was getting ready to go, undercover cops poured into the bar.

"Identity cards, get out your ID cards, and fast!"

Azel didn't have his on him. He felt guilty immediately.

"Those who don't have one, get in the van, come on, speed it up, we've got a full night's work ahead, Rabat's orders."

Azel obeyed and waited in the police van with a few other unlucky souls: two street bums, a whore, and five young men, a couple of them with bloody noses. Azel remembered that Abdelmalek had given him a bit of kif, but right then one of the cops came over and screamed at him, "Don't move, you sonofabitch!"

The cop frisked him and found the kif—not much, but enough to justify his arrest and a lengthy interrogation that allowed the police to expand their investigation, moving from the hunt for drug traffickers to antiestablishment kids with diplomas but no work. Everything was getting mixed in together. It was a long, cruel, painful night. Azel was worn out from telling his life story and insisting that he wasn't a dealer in anything, that he had no connection to Al Afia, that he'd even gotten beaten up because he'd insulted him. Nothing doing: the police had orders to find drug dealers, and Azel was the ideal patsy. The interrogation resumed the next day, this time with other cops as well, sent specially from Rabat. The atmosphere had changed.

"Whom do you work for? Who hired you? Who's your boss?"

Azel did not reply. He was slapped so hard his head rang, then strong hands shoved him back onto his chair and punched him in the stomach.

"I'm going to make it easy for you, you bastard," said the cop. "Your boss is Al Afia, Hallouf, or Dib? Who's the guy you get the drugs for, the stuff that goes out at night to Europe? Confess! Which of the three is your boss?"

Again, blows, increasingly savage ones.

"You'd better get this, you smarty-pants graduate: our-beloved-king-may-God-keep-him-and-grant-him-long-life has decided to disint . . . disaff . . . anyway, to clean all the sons of bitches who bring shame on our fatherland out of northern Morocco. His Majesty is fed up with seeing our nation's good name slandered in the international press because some fat pigs are filling their pockets selling drugs. It's over, all that careless laissez-faire. So you're going to assist the police and His Majesty our-beloved-king-may-God-keep-him-and-grant-him-long-life by telling everything you know about that scum, where they're hiding and which one you work for!"

The cops were imitating actors in American movies. They were chewing gum while they slugged him, thinking that was macho.

Bent double with pain, Azel had a sudden idea.

"I work for Monsieur Miguel."

"That's not a Moroccan name!"

"No, he's from Spain, his name is Miguel Romero López."

"What we want is any Moroccans involved in the drug trade, not the others. What's he do, your Miguel?"

"He doesn't have anything to do with drugs. He's an art dealer, he has a gallery in Spain. He lives on the Old Mountain and I work there as an assistant, a secretary."

A few more punches to the ribs knocked Azel from the chair. One of the cops made a phone call using some kind of coded language, and when Azel heard Miguel's name a few times, he understood that the police were checking up on him. Then the two cops from Rabat tackled him again, cursing him, furious because they'd just found out that Azel wasn't a trafficker after all, so they still had to find at least one before dawn. Leaving Azel lying on the floor, they went out to smoke a cigarette. That's when the two local guys decided to take action.

"You're some cutie, hey, tell us, *zamel*, does he fuck you or is it you fucks him? I've always wanted to know who's the top and who's the bottom in those pervert couples. Anyway, we don't hand over our asses, we do the screwing and you'll find out what we do with guys like you!"

They locked the door and took turns hitting Azel. After that one of them held him down on the ground while the other pulled off his trousers. Then he tore off Azel's underpants, spread his legs, spat between his buttocks, and tried to penetrate him. To make it easier for him, the other policeman knocked Azel out. They spat on him some more, then shoved a kind of broomstick up his anus, which was so painful it brought him around. The men kept hitting him, spitting on him, and taking turns entering him.

"Take this, *zamel*, pansy, little scumbag, you've got a cute ass— an intellectual's ass is like a big open book, but us, we don't read, we ride, hey, here's some more, bitch, slut, yes, this is what you do with the Christian, he gets on his belly and you stuff him, well, we're stuffing you and you're going to love it, you'll beg for more until your butt becomes a sieve, a real train station, here's more, goddamn intellectual, you're crying, crying just like a girl, tell me, tell us that you're sobbing with pleasure, ah, *dinemok*, fucking whore, you've got a girl's ass, not even any hair, you're just made for pulling a train. . . ."

The floor was splattered with blood, vomit, and urine. Half fainting, Azel could not stand up. Opening his eyes a few hours later, he vaguely recognized Miguel, who had come to get him. The cops explained that they'd saved Azel just when some crooks were about to rape him in a hotel room on the rue Murillo.

"It was a fight over some kif; we intervened because the hotel concierge called us. Luckily, we got there in time. We found him on the floor, pants down. . . . Have to watch out who you hang with, in this city!"

Azel's face was grossly swollen and he walked with difficulty, supported by Miguel's driver.

"I can guess what happened," said Miguel when they'd gotten back to his house. "I'll call a doctor."

"No, definitely not, I'm ashamed, ashamed!"

"Listen: we absolutely must get a medical certificate and prosecute them. I have a few excellent contacts in Rabat. What they did was intolerable—the king did not give them carte blanche!"

"But a policeman's word is worth more than mine! The king doesn't give a damn—what he wants is for nothing to change, he doesn't bother with the details."

"All this is bad for Morocco's image! If the press finds out, there'll be hell to pay!"

"The press? If the papers ever tell the truth one day, they'll be shut down."

Azel remained at Miguel's house for several days to recuperate. He phoned his mother to reassure her, explaining that he was in Casablanca looking into a job offer. When Kenza came to see him, he told his sister the truth and begged her not to tell anyone.

Feeling as humiliated as Azel did, she promised she'd do everything she could to help him get out of Tangier and the country.

The disinfection campaign was grinding up its victims. Some
drug traffickers were arrested; others managed to get away. Bank
employees involved in money laundering were sent to prison
along with customs officers who'd closed their eyes to what was
going on. In the collateral damage, a few innocents were con-
victed of threatening the security of the state. The minister of
the interior took advantage of the situation to arrest a few of
those troublesome jobless intellectuals on various charges and
send them to prison. The press played along, reporting on the
progress of the campaign. Trials flew by at top speed as the whole
country held its breath. Businessmen predicted a grave economic
crisis, explaining privately that the nation functioned in part
thanks to all that dirty money, and that now the traffickers would
stash their wealth in foreign banks, and no one would be safe. A
politician argued that the indictment of innocent people was
useful because it spread doubt and fear, thereby dealing an indi-
rect blow to the opposition. Questioned by deputies after his
speech, the minister of the interior justified his action.

"The country is ravaged by the plague of corruption and the
drug trade, so what could be more reasonable than hunting down
those gangsters? We've been ordered to disinfect the country,
and that's what we're doing, it's only natural. Justice is on the job,
of course; some judges have had the courage to attack those who
thought they were above the law because they personally knew
this or that figure in government. Nothing doing: there will be no
compromises. If heads must fall, they will fall, and I cannot imag-

ine that anyone among these honorable representatives of the people will protest. Our judiciary is independent, our police force is sound, and we should rejoice in this advance along the path of progress laid out by His Majesty our-beloved-king-may-God-keep-him-and-grant-him-long-life."

An elderly deputy, much respected, rose to address the minister.

"We agree, *monsieur le ministre*, that disinfection is necessary. But why not start with those close to you, with your own family? Everyone knows that your son has made some particularly sweet business deals thanks to the doors you opened for him. You must set a good example if you wish to be credible. As it happens, *monsieur le ministre*, you lecture everyone yet act as if *you* were above reproach. Since His Majesty has decided to clean up this country, let the cleansing be thorough: tidy up your own corner and do not take advantage of these times to imprison those who oppose your politics of repression."

"You are the senior member of this venerable assembly, and I will refrain from answering your unfounded accusations."

The president of the assembly decided to bring this incident to a close by calling a one-hour recess.

It took Azel two weeks to get back on his feet. His nights were restless; he was taking sleeping pills, but his dreams churned with scenes of violence. And although Miguel urged him repeatedly to file a complaint against the two policemen, he refused to do so.

7

Lalla Zohra

Azel's mother, Lalla Zohra, was worried. Ever since her son had started coming home late at night, she'd been waiting up for him. She would park herself in front of the television in the living room and stay awake until he returned. Although her daughter Kenza kept telling her that was ridiculous, Lalla Zohra did just as she pleased and refused above all to believe that her son was slumming in the city's bars and cafés. Like all mothers, she suspected something; she sensed that Kenza was hiding the truth, and feared that Azel might try again to burn up the straits.

"I know my son, he cannot stay in one place, he cannot accept being supported in this life by any woman, even his sister. He has his pride, and I know he's busy doing everything to go over there, to Spain. May God protect him, may God grant him the power to withstand the demon, to outwit the sons of sin! But why does he not call, why this silence? Perhaps he is ill? In hospital? Let it not be that. . . . Our hospitals are in such a state that we must pray that no good Muslim will ever be forced to set foot inside."

She was a woman from Chaouen, a little village where traditions were still respected, where modern life had not turned everything topsy-turvy. She could neither read nor write, but watched the news every night on television. She had learned numbers so she could use the phone.

Azel vaguely remembered his father, who had died in a traffic accident when Azel was young. He'd worked in a cement factory, and the insurance had brought a bit of money to the family, which for a time received some state assistance every year in the form of a few sugar loaves, cans of oil, and one bag of flour. The sugar came in a blue wrapper Azel had loved so much he'd used it to wallpaper his room. His mother had found a job. Like many women of her region and generation, she'd been involved in smuggling: she'd been a *bragdia* the way others were seamstresses. The people in the south said *contrabondo;* those in the north, *bragued.* She would take a night bus to Ceuta, wait for the border to open at five in the morning, and dash with hundreds of other women into the covered wholesale market. There she bought things she could easily resell: Dutch cheese, Spanish jam, pasta, American rice, shampoo, toothbrushes—in short, whatever she could hide under her clothing. This slender woman fattened herself up in minutes and crossed back over the border with a basket of goodies for her children. At least that's what she told the customs officer to whom she slipped fifty dirhams for his silence. She earned the difference in the exchange between the peseta and the dirham: in other words, almost nothing.

To enter Ceuta, a Moroccan city occupied by the Spanish for five hundred years, the locals needed neither passport nor visa, only their identity cards. Lalla Zohra had had hers laminated to protect it, and she kept it with her at all times. "With this, we can eat!" she liked to tell her daughter.

At first she'd enjoyed smuggling, hurrying through the market to get back before everyone else, sell faster, and go home. She was young, the mother of two children whom she left in the care of a neighbor, an honest woman who'd never managed to have children of her own. With time and fatigue, the market work had taken its toll: Lalla Zohra had gradually lost her enthusiasm, going less and less often to Ceuta, sometimes content now to resell what others had purchased.

Lalla Zohra had dreams for Azel, envisioning him as a doctor or an important official, and she hoped to marry him off to a girl from a good family. As for Kenza, who'd had less education than her brother, she was working and waiting for better days. Kenza's favorite pastime was dancing, especially to Middle Eastern singing, which she loved. She was truly talented, and was asked to perform at every family party. She would let herself go, playing up her charm and shapely figure. Sometimes she agreed to dance for neighbors, who would give her a token payment afterward. Her mother would accompany her there, keeping an eye on her. Kenza could have become a professional, but in that society, a girl who dances for a living is inevitably considered a person of easy virtue. That's how it is. Lalla Zohra pretended to be worried about her daughter, who had not found herself a husband, but she was obsessively concerned about the future of her son, whom she spoiled shamelessly. Azel was feeling more and more stifled by her possessive love.

When she saw him come home so pale and thin after his stay with Miguel, Lalla Zohra began wailing.

"Who did that to you? What happened? Why did no one tell me anything? Oh, my God, I knew it, I had a bad dream and refused to believe that dreams could be true—I'd lost a tooth, they were sticking it back in with a bitter paste, and so *that's* what it was: my son almost died! You didn't burn up the sea? You didn't cross the straits, did you? Speak to me, tell me what happened. . . ."

Khaled had entered the house after Azel, bearing huge baskets of provisions sent by Miguel, all the fruits and vegetables of the season plus half a sheep and several large sea bream. Khaled now withdrew and his master appeared, dressed in a handsomely tailored white gandoura* and matching babouches. Miguel presented Lalla Zohra with a magnificent bouquet of flowers.

Thinking for a moment that her visitor had come to ask for Kenza in marriage, Lalla Zohra called her daughter, who arrived, blushing and lovely, to shake Miguel's outstretched hand and express her gratitude.

"Azel has told me about you. Thank you for all you have done for him!"

"But it was only natural. Tell your mother that I'm delighted to meet her. Azel is a friend, and I would like to help him."

Lalla Zohra was perplexed. Who was this man, as elegant as a woman, and perfumed like one? And so good-looking, too! What did he want?

Azel asked his mother to prepare a good lunch for them, but Lalla Zohra begged off, explaining that there was not time enough to do the meal justice and insisting that Miguel come eat with them the next day.

A light scent lingered in the family's little house after Miguel was gone. Lalla Zohra had understood, yet struggled to convince herself that he had come there for Kenza.

"Don't you think, daughter, that he's a touch old for you?"

"Yes, but what does it matter—he's a kind and sophisticated gentleman. There are not many Muslim men as generous and refined as that Christian."

"What you're saying is stupid," said Azel bluntly. "It's not a question of being Muslim or Christian. Anyway, we're experts at disparaging others and criticizing our own community. The Arabs have agreed never to agree about anything, everyone knows that, so we must throw out all those clichés."

"I only meant that I like the man," protested Kenza, "but as you know, I'm not the one who interests him!"

Pretending not to have heard that last remark, Lalla Zohra asked Kenza to go buy a white tablecloth at Fondok Chajra, the bazaar where she sold all her smuggled merchandise.

"Tomorrow, my children, this luncheon must be perfect. And now, Azz El Arab, you will tell me everything."

Laughing, Azel gave his mother a hug. She had tears in her eyes, and so did he.

The next day, Lalla Zohra's modest home was filled with joy. She had repainted the entrance with blue-tinted whitewash and now awaited impatiently the arrival of the man she considered a stroke of good fortune. Although she said nothing, she so hoped that Azel would find work anywhere at all, with anyone! To her, Miguel was at least an ambassador or a consul—someone influential somewhere, in any case.

Lalla Zohra did not leave the kitchen during the entire meal. She ate nothing, and waited until teatime to make a brief appearance. Miguel was happy, brimming with constant praise for the delicacy of her cooking. He kept calling her Hajja; each time she corrected him, saying, "No, no, not yet: next year, *Insha'Allah!*"

Miguel invited Azel and his sister to the party he was giving to mark his coming departure, and asked Azel to arrive a little early to help out. Everything had to be impeccable. No false notes.

"Elegance and flamboyance," said Miguel. "Flowers, ah, flowers: the whole house must have flowers! Table service entirely of silver, of course! The champagne, chilled, but not too much, just enough. The servants must be on their very best behavior. Jaouad and Khaled, you must be clean-shaven. Above all, do not wear perfume, and do not serve almonds or tidbits that satisfy hunger. The aperitif should stimulate the appetite, not cut it!"

Everyone who was anyone in Tangier was there, the luminaries of the city as well as Miguel's closest friends. The dinner had been prepared with extraordinary attention to detail; everything had to be in the most exquisite taste, and Miguel would not have allowed the slightest imperfection. By nightfall, the villa was thronged with a beau monde that seemed to have stepped from another era. An elderly princess from a distant land might rub shoulders with a former government minister or a few film stars long faded from memory. People discreetly pointed out an old lady dressed all in blue, said to have been for many years the king's mistress, but that was a secret, of course. It was even said that she'd had a child by him, but that was only a rumor, naturally. She was a lovely lady who had made a few movies for a while, until the king, apparently, had asked her to stop: a wise decision, moreover, because her acting . . . Wearing one of Miguel's fine white gandouras, Azel was welcoming guests and showing them around, and he looked like an Oriental prince or a character in the black-and-white films of the fifties. Suave and reserved, he circulated among the crowd as if he lived there. Noticing his good manners, Miguel was pleased to have lured him into his circle, and yet he was uneasy, feeling a pang in his heart he could not explain. Watching this handsome young man, he suddenly felt like crying, but let nothing show and busied himself taking the most attentive care of his guests. That evening, his life was taking a new turn: Miguel was not so much celebrating his departure as he was presenting his new friend. His guests whispered, laughing as they watched the servant in the white gandoura: Not bad, that young man, even rather classy! Miguel has lucked out for once! Think it will last? Who knows? But you don't know what you're talking about—the fellow's just a servant, not Miguel's new lover, don't be silly! Listen, me, I'd try him out. Maybe he likes women, too. . . . Hush, quiet, here comes Miguel!

Cocktails were served on the terrace, which overlooked the straits. Miguel had indeed put flowers all through the house. Wearing a pistachio green caftan of his own creation and a superb coral necklace, Miguel was resplendent. He talked about his recent trip to India and his desire to return there as soon as possible, even hinting that he hoped to take Azel along with him. Since things were now clear to his friends, they wanted to know who this new boy was, to approach him, chat with him, find out what he was like. Azel, however, hid in the kitchen. As for Kenza, she was bored. She had come because it would have been difficult for her to refuse Miguel's invitation. But just what did he intend to do with her brother? She hadn't been fooled, and abruptly she, too, felt like crying, but she forced herself to smile. In this worldly company whose existence she had never suspected, the men were inaccessible. "One day, yes," she told herself—"one day I'll meet the man of my dreams. He'll be tall, and kind, and good, and sexy, and it won't matter whether he's a Muslim or a Christian. In this country, though, it's all so difficult. If I don't go along with what's expected, I'll end up an old maid and be looked down on as a *hboura*, worn out and useless."

Miguel came over to Kenza, took her arm, and introduced her to Ismaël, the only straight single man at the party. She noticed that he had clammy hands. That was a sign: this man was not for her. She went through some polite conversation anyway: Tangier-the-east-wind-the-houses-on-the-Old-Mountain-the-Europeans-who-snap-them-up-the-rise-of-Islamism-Spain-seen-from-afar-in-clear-weather . . .

She was irritated with herself for babbling so tritely to a man with sweaty palms and empty eyes to boot. Kenza changed her approach, becoming provocative.

"Tell me frankly, Ismaël: what are you doing here tonight?"

"I'm a guest, like you!"

"Yes, but what do you have to do with this crowd? I mean, are you here to blend in, to join their tribe?"

"I'm here because I like to treat myself occasionally to a nice piece of Christian ass! So there!"

Kenza was pleased to have ticked him off, and with a smile, she disappeared. On the way home, she kept seeing all those faces from a Tangier frozen forever in the 1950s.

Before his flight out, Miguel obtained a visa application form from the Spanish consulate and gave it to Azel.

"Fill it out, I'll send you the papers you need. In theory, if all the documents are in order, you'll get your visa. I'll arrange to send the consulate an employment contract for you. Be careful, and don't talk about this to anyone—I'm superstitious!"

Azel knew the visa application routine by heart, having already gone through it at least three times, but he had the feeling that this time he would get lucky.

He tackled the job as if he were back in grade school, writing slowly and keeping the form clean by resting his hand on a blotter he'd found in an old notebook. The questions were simple but specific. His father's family name, his date of birth. He wrote "Deceased," and in that case had to provide a death certificate. Then they asked him for his mother's family name. He'd forgotten it. He asked Kenza, who couldn't remember it either.

"But why ever do they need my family name?" asked Lalla Zohra in astonishment. "You're the one emigrating, not me, at least for the moment. . . ."

"Bureaucratic red tape. You have to answer all these questions even if they're idiotic. So, what's your full name?"

"Lalla Zohra Touzani."

Date of birth: 1936, supposedly. Azel remembered his grandfather, who had often told him the story of the Spanish Civil War. He had been one of the Riffian soldiers forcibly conscripted by Franco.

Ocupación actual: Azel did not know what to put down. Out of work? Student? Tourist? Zero . . . *Nombre, dirección y número de teléfono de la empresa para la que trabaja.* But he wasn't working. . . . *Finalidad del viaje:* to visit a Spanish friend. *Fecha de llegada* and *Fecha de salida:* he really didn't know anything about his dates of departure and return.

When everything was ready except the papers Miguel was to send him from Spain, Azel put the application in a manila folder and wrapped that in one of his mother's scarves.

"Here, Ma, this is my fate, it's in your hands. Take this bundle and say one of those prayers of yours over it."

"You want me to bless it?"

"No, Ma, I want you to wish me good luck, but do it with your words, your prayers that go straight to heaven. Without your blessings, I'm lost, I'm nothing, you know that. Your prayers have to be strong: some prayers don't even get past the ceiling!"

"Yes, my son, my little boy, light of my life."

8

Dear Country

For the first time in his life, Azel was taking a plane—and leaving Morocco. His mother and sister had come with him to the airport, weeping bitterly and embarrassing an already keyed-up and excited Azel, but when he realized that they weren't the only ones wailing, he felt less conspicuous. Lalla Zohra had packed a bag of food—honey cakes, crêpes, and black olives—that Azel was refusing to take with him in spite of his mother's entreaties. He was ashamed. The police and customs officials were minding their manners. The plane hadn't arrived yet, which made Azel even more nervous. He decided to reread the letter he'd written to his country the day he'd received his entry visa and residence permit for Spain. He went to the cafeteria, ordered a coffee, got out his notebook, and began to read. He was smiling, but wary of being interrupted. Now and then he stopped reading to sip his coffee and observe the other travelers. At one point, when a bee came buzzing around the table, he caught himself following it with his eyes. Then there was an announcement: the plane's late arrival meant that passengers would be boarding one half-hour behind schedule. Azel felt the sudden urge to slip off, to go someplace completely different to read his letter aloud, a letter that many of his friends would have wanted to write:

Dear country (yes, it must be "Dear country," since the king says "My dear people"),

Today is a great day for me: I finally have the opportunity and good fortune to go away, to leave you, to breathe the air of a new country, to escape the harassment and humiliations of your police. I set out, my heart light, eyes fixed on the horizon, gazing into the future, unsure of what I will do—all I know is that I'm ready to change, ready to live free, to be useful, to attempt things that will transform me into a man standing on his own two feet, no longer afraid, no longer dependent on his sister for cigarette money, a man finished with odd jobs, who'll never need to show his diploma to prove he's useless, a man who won't ever again have to deal with that corrupt drug-dealing bastard Al Afia, or be the flunky of that senile old fart El Haj, who feels up girls without bedding them. I'm off, my dear country, I'm crossing the border, heading for other places, armed with a work contract: I will finally earn my living. My land has not been kind to me, or to many of the young people of my generation. We'd believed that our studies would open doors for us, that Morocco would finally abandon its society of privilege and arbitrary misfortune, but the whole world let us down, so we've had to scramble to make do and do everything possible to get out. Some of us have knocked on the right door, ready to accept anything, while others have had to struggle. . . .

But, my dear country,

I am not leaving you forever. You are simply lending me to the Spanish people, our neighbors, our friends. We know them well. For a long time they were as poor as we were, and then one day, Franco died: democracy arrived, followed by freedom and prosperity. I learned about all this sitting outside cafés: that's where the rest of us Moroccans have chosen to study relentlessly the coasts of Spain and recite in chorus the history of that lovely country. We wound up hearing voices, convinced that by staring at those shores, we'd conjure up a mermaid or an angel who would have pity on us, come take us by the hand to help us across the straits. Madness was slowly stalking us. That's how little Rachid ended up in the psychiatric hospital in Beni Makada. No one knew what afflicted him; he could only say one word, over and over: "Spania." He wouldn't eat, hoping to become so light that he could fly away on the wings of the angel!

O my country, my thwarted will, my frustrated desire, my chief regret! You keep with you my mother, my sister, and a few friends; you are my sunshine and my sadness: I entrust them to you because I will return, and I wish to find them in good health, especially my little family. Free us, however, from those thugs who feed off your blood because they enjoy protection where they should meet with justice and prison; rid us of those brutes who know the law only to twist it. Nothing stops them. Money, as my mother says, sprinkles sugar on bitter things.

I'm not a very moral guy, not absolutely honest, and I'm far from being perfect, I'm just a bread crumb at that feast where the guests are always the same ones, where the poor person will always be out of place and his poverty a crime, a sin. "Hey, the money's there," I used to hear Al Afia say. "All you got to do is take it. Want to stop being poor? Just set your mind to it!"

And I was tempted to act like everyone else. But my mother's hand, and the hand of my father, whom I hardly knew, set me back on the right path. I thank them for not having chosen the easy way.

I must stop here, however; I'm tired. I am imagining myself on the plane. I'm not frightened, I'm excited—curious, dear country, to see you

from above, and I hope the pilot will have the bright idea to fly over Tangier
just for me so that I can say au revoir, so that I can guess who's in that distant
shack, who's suffering within those crumbling walls, who lives in that slum,
and how long they'll be able to keep bearing this wretched poverty.

A short, well-dressed old man was waiting for Azel in the airport
in Spain with a sign bearing his name in block letters, and he
spoke right up.

"I'm called Chico, it's a nickname, I work for Señor Miguel.
I'm short but I don't give a damn about that."

Azel wasn't sure what to say, so he collected his suitcase and
followed him. Chico didn't open his mouth during the entire
ride. Carmen, Miguel's elderly housekeeper, showed Azel to the
living room and asked him to please wait for Miguel to return.
Something was bothering her; it was written all over her face. She
knew Miguel too well not to know what was coming, for she'd
seen him fall in love many times, and it always ended badly.
Miguel was too trusting and let others take such outrageous advantage of him that it even seemed he might be doing that on
purpose, to punish himself through some obscure sense of guilt.

Dead on his feet, Azel was still dazzled by his new environ-
ment. He marveled at the number of paintings on the wall. Waiting in the living room, he hardly dared light a cigarette. Everything
was so neat. Not a speck of dust. Silver bibelots, a small army of
rare and precious objects, gleamed in a display cabinet.

Carmen brought Azel some coffee. His mind was reeling. Exactly what was expected of him? His first thoughts were of his
mother, and of Kenza, too. They would be proud of him some

day. Perhaps he might even be able to send Kenza some money and bring her to Spain. Right now, though, he had to face the present. Miguel. And the difficult moments that would inevitably arrive, sooner or later. . . . Miguel was not doing all this through pure altruism. And yet he was a sensitive, intelligent man: surely he must have divined how much Azel loved women. . . .

Miguel hurried into the living room, as dapper as ever, but rather distant, quite soberly dressed, and wearing a black fedora.

"Did you have a good trip?" Without waiting for a reply, he added briskly, "We must see about your papers right away. We'll go tomorrow to the police station with your passport to fill out a ton of paperwork. Then we'll see my lawyer to draw up the final contract for your employment here. For the moment, you'll stay in the maid's room on the top floor. It's very irritating, but we absolutely must go through all this strictly by the book."

Azel hesitated a moment before asking him exactly what his job would be.

"Oh come on, don't play the idiot, you've understood perfectly well. . . ."

"No, Monsieur Miguel, I assure you. . . ."

"Enough of this pretense! Let's deal with these documents now; we'll see about the rest later."

That evening Azel sat alone in his little room. He wanted to go out but was afraid of Miguel's reaction. Tired and sad, he went to bed without managing to fall asleep. His head was in a whirl with images that were sometimes clear, sometimes shadowy and confused. Feeling lost, he opened the bag his mother had packed for him and stuffed himself like a kid on honey cakes, reflecting that the paradise he'd dreamed of couldn't possibly resemble a little attic room in a big villa, or this loneliness that was keeping him awake. He thought of Siham. He remembered her tears, and her body entwined with his. He wanted her. But Siham was now far away. Closing his eyes, he touched himself. Then he opened his notebook and continued writing his letter to his country.

Dear country,

Here I am, far from you, and already I miss something of you; in my loneliness, I think of you, of those I've left behind, my mother most of all. What is she doing as I write this? She must certainly be cooking dinner. And Kenza? She'll be home soon, unless this is the evening she works as a private nurse. My pals, I can just see them, they're at the café. Rachid is back, saying nothing; the others are playing cards, envying me, thinking how lucky I am. I hear them; they're speaking of me with resentment. That's crazy—I'd like to be with them, simply for one hour, and then return here. Well, no: I don't want to leave even for an hour. I want to stop thinking of you, of your air, your light. You know, from Morocco you can see Spain, but it doesn't work like that in the opposite direction. The Spanish don't see us, they don't give a damn, they've no use for our country. I'm in my little room, it smells musty in here; there's only one window and I don't dare open it. I admit that I'm disappointed—it's just that I'm impatient, exhausted, wiped out by the change of climate, and by fear, too, the fear of what's new, of not being able to cope. . . . I'll try to fall asleep thinking of you, my dear country, dearest and greatest of my anxieties.

9

Siham

While Azel was settling in at the house in Barcelona, Siham was waiting in front of the Spanish consulate to submit a request for a visa. Her file was complete. El Haj had found her a Saudi family living in Marbella that needed a practical nurse to take care of a handicapped woman. Following his instructions, she had sent them her CV and a well-written letter expressing interest in the position. El Haj had insisted that she include her ID photo, which at first made her suspect a trap, but she quickly received an answer from the invalid explaining the reasons for such a request. She preferred dealing with a Muslim woman rather than a Christian one. Siham thought about wearing a veil for the photo, which El Haj had recommended she do, but in the end she decided that was stupid. She didn't like Islamists and hypocrites. Appropriate clothing and irreproachable behavior: that's what really counted for her. El Haj, who liked her, pressed his case.

"You know, my dear Siham, the veil is sometimes a good thing. Men are less likely to bother girls who wear veils in public, and anyway, there's no good reason not to wear one! You remember Bouchra, lovely Bouchra who married a businessman much older than she was, but very rich? She used to come to my place completely veiled, I even called her the Masked Marvel! Well, when she took off her jellaba and her veil, she was another woman: she wore see-through blouses, tight pants. . . . She was superb. She wound up winning the jackpot, by the way; how long it will last I can't say, but she had the look of someone who knew how to handle herself. To top it all off, you know—I can say this to you—she was a virgin! She carefully kept her virginity for her husband."

"Is she happy? In any case, she can't be worried about money."

"Don't fool yourself, the man turned out to be a miser. She phoned me the other day, crying. She lives in a big house surrounded by maids but she's not allowed to go out. So, this veil: you're wearing it or tossing it?"

"Tossing it! You see, my grandmother, who came from the countryside, wore the haik, it's a kind of Arab cloak. It looked like a voluminous shroud, a huge piece of white cloth she wrapped around herself. No one criticized the wearing of the haik at the time, it was normal. My mother wore the jellaba without the veil, and no one ever asked us to veil ourselves, although my uncle, the one who'd emigrated to Belgium, did complain. Whenever he came visiting on vacation, in the summer, he lectured us about morality. That used to make me giggle, because his daughters smoked in secret, had boyfriends, and so on. They obeyed their father only so he'd leave them in peace to do what they wanted. I hate such hypocrisy. Keeping up appearances and being sleazy on the sly, that's the Morocco that drives me crazy."

"Don't go crazy, my dear, you'll see: even if you leave, you'll always miss your country. We become so attached to Morocco that we can't forget it completely, it really sticks to us, like an unseasoned frying pan, and we can't forget it. I traveled quite a bit in my youth, thanks to easy money and parents who never asked questions; I went far away and wherever I was, strangely enough, I missed Morocco. . . ."

"And how do you explain the fact that those who govern us do *nothing* for us?"

Siham was surrounded by young people who thought only of fleeing, leaving, working anywhere at all. Too poor to complete her studies in the humanities, she had finally found a job as a legal secretary.

Siham obtained a tourist's visa good for four months. On the day she left, her parents blessed her. Her parents' blessing was vital, but not enough, and Siham felt the need for even more protection. She made her ablutions, borrowed her mother's prayer rug, and prayed to God. She was setting out into the unknown and would be on her guard, especially against all those Arabs living in Marbella. She'd heard stories about white slavery and the mistreatment of women there.

In the port of Algeciras, it took her some time to find her way to the parking lot, where a black Mercedes was waiting for her as promised in her letter of instructions. When the driver helped her into the backseat, she felt proud to be treated like an American movie star—which didn't stop her imagination from running wild: she was being kidnapped, to be raped and abandoned in the middle of a desolate countryside! She saw herself held captive by the Saudi family, abused by the husband of the invalid woman, lying prostrate on the floor without food or water. She would scream, but no one would hear her. Attempting to cut her wrists, she would be unable to go through with it. And then Siham abruptly pulled herself together, attributing these bad thoughts to Satan. To drive such black ideas forever from her mind, she silently recited the Koranic verse of the Throne.* Useless: ever more violent scenes kept streaming through her head. Finally she decided to laugh at them. When the driver turned around, she apologized and began to watch the scenery go by.

Marbella seemed like some sort of big tourist village for millionaires, where citizens of the Gulf countries built themselves elegant homes they lived in for a few days a year. Some of those people thought nothing of crossing the straits just to go to a party. Most of the time, they took over suites in the luxury hotels of Tangier, sending out for food, alcohol, musicians, and girls. The authorities turned a blind eye. Siham had heard all this from her girlfriends, and she'd even been told that some girls had spent a whole night waiting in a room without ever being sent for, only to leave the next morning with a few dollars in their pockets. Siham did not judge them; she kept her distance and her dignity, reflecting only that everyone shared the responsibility for this increasing acceptance of prostitution.

A surprise awaited her at the villa of Monsieur Ghani, her wealthy Saudi employer. Ghita, his wife, received her immediately. Siham observed her, trying to see what her handicap might be, but Ghita seemed to move, think, and speak quite normally.

"I'm Moroccan, as you can see," said Ghita, sensing Siham's confusion. "I live here for a great deal of the year; my husband lives in Saudi Arabia, where he has his business interests and his other family. I am his second wife, and I believe I am his favorite. The problem is this: Our daughter Widad is handicapped. She's twelve years old and has trouble speaking and moving around. We need someone who will stay with her constantly, someone patient, yet firm, who will help us take care of her. We've had Spanish nurses, but they're unionized and work like civil servants—and besides, we need someone from our culture, who speaks Arabic, knows our traditions, our customs. Our little girl has trouble with everything, you understand, so there's no reason to complicate her life. I'm telling you the truth: it's hard work, tiring, but very well paid. My husband adores Widad. He'd give anything to see her happy and . . . normal."

Siham listened without showing any reaction; she hadn't been prepared for this, hadn't imagined herself working for an abnormal child. She could leave again . . . think of this trip as a short vacation, a change of scenery, a misunderstanding. Leave again . . . yes, but—for where? Morocco? Impossible: no question of going back to that cramped life and those little jobs in Tangier. Siham tried to get a grip on herself, realizing at the same time that she knew nothing about handicapped people and lacked the inner resources to take on such demanding work. But she just couldn't see herself picking up her suitcase again to take the boat back to Tangier.

Ghita was silent, waiting. After a pause, Siham asked to see the child.

"She was hospitalized the day before yesterday. A single moment of inattention was all it took: she fell and hurt herself. You would have to be constantly watchful. Are you ready to take the job?"

Siham thought of her friend Azel and reflected that there wasn't any shame in doing this.

"I accept, but you must remember that I haven't been trained for this kind of work. You can be sure that I will do my best to make things go smoothly."

Ghita gave Siham a cell phone.

"It must always be turned on. You may also use it to call your parents and friends."

Maria, the Spanish maid, arrived with a tray of drinks and sweets. Later she showed Siham to her room, which was spacious, with two beds and a bathroom. Siham understood immediately that she would be sleeping next to the child. She looked at Widad's many toys and at the photos of her on the wall, showing her from the time she was born. She was pretty, with a sad expression, but there was a kind of solemn intelligence in her eyes.

The first meeting between Siham and Widad was almost a disaster. Tired and cranky, ignoring the presence of the new nanny, the child cried and refused to let her mother hug her. Siham felt that the important thing was to avoid intervening, to wait, simply letting the tantrum run its course. Above all—no agitation, no outcry. For a long time now, as part of her effort to improve her life, Siham had been learning patience. She took a book and went to the bedroom. When Widad arrived to find

Siham sitting on her bed reading, she waved her arm to show that she wanted her to clear out.

Siham didn't budge. For the first time, someone was resisting the child. With a smile, Widad threw herself on her new nanny and tore the book from her hands. Siham realized that she had just achieved something priceless: she had won Widad's trust.

10

Siham and Azel

After Azel had spent three months in the maid's quarters, Miguel invited him to sleep in the guest room just down the hall from his own bedroom. They had settled into a comfortable routine. Azel had accompanied his benefactor several times in his travels, carrying his luggage. The rest of the time, he took care of the art gallery, answered the phone, ran small errands. He wore nice clothes, some of which had belonged to Miguel, and that's how Azel discovered the luxury of cashmere jackets and sweaters, tailored shirts, and English shoes. He lived among Miguel's things as if he were inside another skin. For the first time in his life, he felt good, and made an effort to take care of himself. Miguel signed him up for classes in exercise and yoga, and Azel was as enthusiastic about the workouts as he was bored by the yoga sessions, which he dropped without telling Miguel. Siham often phoned Azel, whom she wanted to come visit her in Marbella, since she could not leave her young charge. When Azel finally decided to go see her, he lied to Miguel, claiming that he had a sick uncle in Málaga. It was the only way to obtain permission to get away for a while. Miguel merely said, "I hope you're not going off to meet one of those women who are always fluttering around you!"

"But what women, Monsieur Miguel?"

"Don't you ever lie to me!"

"I swear to you, I'm not lying."

"Liars always swear they're not lying!"

As for Siham, she had wangled a free half-day from Ghita.

"He's my fiancé, he works in Barcelona, a really nice guy, cultivated, educated, everything. We're from the same city, the same neighborhood."

Ghita replied that Siham's private life was her own business, as long as it did not upset her relationship with Widad.

"Don't worry, Madame, there won't be any trouble."

The reunion was brief, but intense: they were wild with desire for each another. After lovemaking, a bottle of wine, and a few cigarettes, Azel made his confession.

"I've become Miguel's lover."

After a long silence, Siham, who felt like crying, asked him if it gave him pleasure.

"I don't know. When I make love to him, I think really hard about a woman—you, for example. There: now you know everything. I'm naked in your eyes. And if one day I get married, it will be to you, because we understand each other, we talk to each other, and then, I've always felt comfortable with you."

"You know, to tell the truth, I kind of suspected. Don't tell me any more about it. The important thing is that we should both be able to see each other, to breathe, regain some strength, and do our work well."

Azel was ashamed. He asked Siham about Widad.

"I'm glad to be taking care of the girl: it's work that stimulates me, does me good. It's a tough job, full of surprises, and violent, but I've discovered that facing up to these difficulties encourages me. Her parents give me a free hand. I'm building something positive for this innocent child who suffers so much. She was born like that, it's no one's fault. Even though I sometimes wind up doubting the existence of God . . . You know, it's as if these children were sent to earth to spread humility and honesty among people. At the moment, not only am I earning my living and supporting my family, but I'm on a good path. Whenever I think back to El Haj's parties, I get depressed. Here, at least I'm useful. Back home, I might have lost my way like so many other girls and become part of one of those networks—yes, it's true—but I met you and fell in love with you. It didn't last long, but at first I was out of my mind, you were all I could think of: you were considerate, attentive, not in love, of course, but you were around a lot . . . and here you are now with a mustache!"

"Uh, Miguel's the one who asked me to grow it, he said it would look good."

"Well, if it's for your job . . ."

"You're so wonderful! I'd really like to see things as clearly as you do. But I've never fallen in love in my life: it's an infirmity, something I was taught—that love was something for women. Men, well, they're supposed to be strong, unshakable, you know, all those clichés. Now I feel guilty: I work for this man during the day, and at night I have to pleasure him. I don't know how long I can hold out. I need to see you more often—I'm so afraid of ending up doubting my own sexuality."

"Don't get upset—sexuality's not the only thing in life. To me, you're Azel first of all, the man I loved and still do. Whatever you do to earn your living, I'd rather not think about it."

After holding each other in a long embrace, they parted.

That evening, Azel set out to explore the bars of Málaga. He met some compatriots, many of them undocumented, and bought them a few drinks. One of them even offered him some hashish, "pure Riffian." Azel smoked a little, politely refused the advances of an African whore, was approached by a Tunisian who tried to sell him a cell phone or a gold watch, and felt as though he were back in Tangier, in the labyrinth of the Petit Socco. He heard children torturing a sick cat, smelled the nauseating sewer odors of the kasbah, watched youths in suits and ties singing languorously on Moroccan television, glimpsed a former guide—now blind—drinking his café au lait, saw a beggar woman dragging two young children around with her, and above all, thought he'd spotted Al Afia with his long, bushy beard, sitting in his big white jellaba at a table at the Café Central next to Mohammed-Larbi. Azel felt as if he'd been caught in a trap. Unknown men had slipped a hood over his head and tossed him into a truck bound for Morocco. He was struggling, shouting, but no one heard him. Azel was hallucinating. The alcohol and hashish must have been taking their toll on him; he had to leave that neighborhood infested with Moroccans, and right away. He took a taxi back to the hotel. In his room, he felt like continuing the letter to his country, but was much too wasted to write.

The next day, before going to the train station, he could finally reopen his notebook.

Am I a racist? Can you be a racist against your own side? Why do Moroccans exasperate me so much? They don't like themselves, yet they show their vulnerability by flying into rages at the slightest criticism of their country. Why do I prefer to avoid them? Am I not actually avoiding myself? Fleeing from myself? I'm on the run. Hardly a glorious achievement. The Moroccans I met yesterday remind me too much of what I might have become. They spew hot air, buzzing around like bees in an empty honey jar. They've got almost no imagination. They put up with everything while scrambling for a way out with their little schemes, pathetic stuff, grubbing for next to nothing. And for that they need to re-create the joutya, *the village souk, to be among themselves again even when they can't stand one another, pretending at least to be back home, to feel safe.*

I'm ashamed. I don't feel proud of myself. O dear country, if you could see what I've become! I keep trying to find excuses, ways to justify myself. When Miguel touches me I close my eyes, I leave, abandoning my body to him: I go off for a stroll, I pretend, I fake it, and then I awaken, get up, and can't face myself in the mirror. I'm so humiliated.

Oh, if my mother were to see me. . . . I can hardly bear thinking about it. How can I tell her that her son is just an attaye, *a faggot, a man*

who crawls on his belly, a cheap whore, a traitor to his identity, to his sex?
In any case, she's no fool, and has surely understood everything on her own.
Her son is virile, all right—he makes loves to a woman, to a man. . . . One
can't talk about such things.

And let's be honest. Miguel is an admirable man, refined, attentive. He
can certainly see that I'm uncomfortable with him in bed. The other day, he
was absolutely furious when he found some condoms in my jacket pocket.
He was shouting. "You'd better not be going with other men! I'd almost
prefer—I said 'almost'—that you screw some cow with huge tits rather
than a man, which I will not put up with. You hear me? You Moroccans,
you like big breasts, you're still wallowing in nostalgia for your mama's
bosom."

That was my chance to admit to him that I've been seeing Siham.
Siham, with her tiny breasts!

That evening, Miguel shut himself up in his room. Me, I fell asleep in
the living room, in front of the television, clutching the remote in my hand.

II

Mohammed-Larbi

Mohammed-Larbi was a quiet young man. Off in his corner, all alone, he was putting together his plans to leave the country at last and realize his dream. Twenty years ago his maternal uncle, Sadek, had gone to Belgium and found work, and he had promised to bring his nephew there one day. Sadek was now a leader of the Muslim community in the northern neighborhoods of Brussels, familiar with all possible and imaginable networks for leaving Morocco, thanks to his contacts throughout most of the Moroccan émigré diaspora. When he left Morocco, Sadek had been twenty years old, remarkably industrious, and determined to succeed, but he hadn't been a particularly observant Muslim. Nowadays he saw the children of immigrants "going bad" time and again, their parents helpless, overwhelmed, and above all clinging desperately to a culture reduced in general to major religious occasions like Ramadan and Aïd el-Kebir,* although it was becoming increasingly difficult to cut sheep's throats in a bathtub or backyard. Neighbors and animal protection agencies had protested, and the state had been obliged to intervene. Sheep now came from the slaughterhouses ready to go into the oven or be

TAHAR BEN JELLOUN

cut into pieces, which deprived the feast of some of its original meaning and spirit, but the faithful would have to adjust to this as best they could. Sadek could read and write, and one day he had drawn up a list of the typical cultural objects in his daily life: prayer rug, prayer beads, polished black stone for ablutions, Andalusian music, Arab and Berber pop songs, jellaba for going to pray, couscous after prayers on Friday, satellite dish to receive Moroccan television, honey pastries, brass teapot, mint tea, low table, incense, rose water, red tarboosh,* yellow babouches, clock with a picture of Mecca on the face. . . .

And then, abruptly, he'd stopped.

"Language!" he exclaimed aloud. "What tongue do we speak with our children? Oh—our Arab dialect is so poetic at home and so foreign here. . . . We speak a bad Arabic stuffed with bad French!"

Concluding that Islam was the culture he and his fellow immigrants needed, he began the long, arduous process of convincing the municipal authorities to build a mosque. Thanks to Sadek, after three years the faithful were offered a modest but convenient site for worship in the heart of the Muslim community. That was in the early 1990s, at the very moment when the Algerians had gone to war against themselves.

As for Mohammed-Larbi, he obtained his visa with the utmost discretion. Azel had been friends with him for a time, and at one point, realizing that he hadn't seen him for a while, he wondered if he'd disappeared, or simply changed neighborhoods and friends. No, Mohammed-Larbi had not disappeared: instead of going out at night, he was working in a bakery. A nondescript

86

man, neither short nor tall, with the usual dark eyes and complexion, he'd simply been forgotten. Azel did remember that he spoke rapidly and that when he drank, he soon became tipsy and began ranting, insulting religion, jumbling together things sacred and profane. Azel recalled in particular an evening when Mohammed-Larbi took on the entire planet, cursing God and the prophets, spitting at passersby with whom he tried to pick fights. He was strong, and his companions had struggled to restrain him. Nobody knew why he had these fits of anger, but a keen observer would easily have seen that he was psychologically unstable.

Then Mohammed-Larbi changed his appearance and attitude overnight: he began going daily to the mosque instead of the café, and he no longer spoke to his pals in the neighborhood. When Kenza ran into him in their street one day, she went up to give him a friendly kiss, the way she used to when they'd played together. He pushed her firmly away.

"If you want me to shake hands, wrap yours in a Kleenex, and I'd also prefer that you not speak to me in the future—it's a question of respect."

He obtained a visa and his friends never saw him again.

As soon as Mohammed-Larbi arrived in Belgium, his uncle Sadek took him in hand, inviting him to join a small group he'd organized that met every evening to read the Koran and listen to an Egyptian speaker, a self-styled *alem,* or religious sage. There was something lugubrious about these meetings. Already indoctrinated by his uncle, Mohammed-Larbi would never speak, but he listened and heeded the advice of the *alem,* who addressed a different topic every time, for example, the relations between the sexes: how to maintain the absolute superiority of men over women, how to defeat Western propaganda seeking to destroy masculine power, how to perform one's conjugal duties without slipping into vice, and so on.

The *alem* did not mince words.

"Never forget that women's wiles are terrible: God Himself has told us so and put us on our guard. Know that Evil springs from the heart and body of woman, but that Good also knows how to take form there: think of our mothers. . . . Above all, pay attention to the future of your daughters, here, on Christian soil. A few days ago, did not the police of this country summon a friend of mine, a virtuous man, to find out why he had beaten his disobedient eldest daughter? She had wanted to go out for the evening wearing makeup and ready for who knows what! God forbid! Do you realize that here they punish a family man for protecting his daughter's virtue? The West is diseased, and we don't want it to infect our children. Have you heard about those laws allowing men to marry among themselves and even to adopt children? This society is losing its mind! That is why you must be extra vigilant with your children, especially your daughters, so that they do not stray onto the paths of vice. Just look at the walls of Brussels: they call that advertising! Half-naked girls showing their bottoms to sing the praises of some car or other! Men made up like women, posing to sell perfume! We have nothing in common with all this depravity, this abandonment of values, of the family, of respect for the elderly. We—we are here because such is our destiny: God has wished this, and we are in the hands of God, who is watching us and testing us. Shall we offer this impious society our children? Shall we stand by without saying anything, doing anything? No, my brothers. We are Muslims, responsible and united, we belong to the same house, the same nation, the *Umma Islamiya*! No one can leave this great house. We are born Muslim and Muslim we shall return to the Creator."

The *alem*, naturally, was simply repeating what other immigrants were saying in the cafés. There was nothing original about his talks at all, and Mohammed-Larbi had probably already heard this speech even in Tangier, especially during the summer when immigrant families would return on holiday. Perhaps, on the other hand, he remembered only those arrogant vacationing teenagers, uneducated, violent children neither wholly European nor truly Moroccan, who drove around in fancy cars. This last detail was particularly galling. Where did the money come from? Some people claimed the cars were one of the perks of smuggling kif, while others said they were rented, just for show. It was all rather shady and did not present a pretty picture of immigration.

Mohammed-Larbi knew the Koran because he had learned it by heart as a child, and although he hadn't understood what he was memorizing, he still remembered the verses. In Brussels, where his uncle had found him a job in an appliance parts store, he returned for the first time to a serious reading of the Holy Book. The *alem* had given him a copy, saying that he would explain certain chapters to him when he had read the entire book. Meanwhile, Mohammed-Larbi had learned that the *alem* had two wives, who lived under the same roof. One day, after Friday prayers, the *alem* invited him home to share the traditional couscous dinner. As he was taking off his shoes, Mohammed-Larbi glimpsed the face of a pretty girl watching him from behind a curtain. The father had not noticed anything, and went on preaching as if he were still in the mosque. Later, as he was preparing to leave, Mohammed-Larbi felt something in his right shoe; pulling out a crumpled note, he quickly stuffed it into his pocket. As soon as the *alem's* back was turned, Mohammed-Larbi hurriedly smoothed out the paper and read: *Call me at this number between five and six o'clock in the afternoon—Nadia, the girl behind the curtain.*

Although quite intrigued, Mohammed-Larbi hesitated awhile before calling. It was a cell phone number. After considering various hypothetical scenarios, he called from a pay phone. Nadia answered and went straight to the point, speaking quite rapidly.

"I'm being punished, confined at home by my father because he saw me talking with a boy outside my lycée—I'm not allowed to go out and I think he's told the principal that I've dropped out of school. Can you help me, save me? Don't tell anyone, but find an excuse to come back to the house to ask for me in marriage, take me away with you—I don't want to get married, but if it's my only chance to get out of here I'll take it. I'm seventeen and a half, I can't breathe in this house anymore: my father has gone crazy, all my sisters have already been married off to men they didn't want, and I suspect my father is arranging the same for me! If you like, we could escape together. I have to hang up, this is my big brother's phone and he'll be coming back from the mosque, where he went with my father. Do you have a number where I can call you?"

"No, I'm speaking from a pay phone."

"Call me Thursday at noon."

It so happened that later the same week, the *alem* gave Mohammed-Larbi a cell phone in preparation for the young man's coming trip to Egypt, where he would be studying religion. His uncle had told him it was an excellent opportunity.

"You have the *alem*'s trust: do not disappoint him. There will be ten or twelve of you leaving for Cairo, where our brothers in faith will take care of you. It's beautiful, Cairo, you'll see, and the brothers are fine people, good Muslims at war against corruption and immorality."

The first call Mohammed-Larbi made was to Nadia. The *alem* answered, and recognized the number. He did not become angry, said nothing, simply shut himself up in his room and made some phone calls using coded language. On that day, Mohammed-Larbi's fate was sealed. From Egypt he was sent on to a training camp in Pakistan and was never seen again.

12

Malika

Little Malika was Azel's neighbor. She had knocked on his door one day to ask him to show her his diplomas. Wondering at this curious request, he invited her inside and offered her a glass of lemonade. Hanging framed on the living-room wall were his two certificates for completed studies in the fields of law and international relations.

"There," said Azel. "Five years of courses in Rabat. Five years of hope and then, no luck. My mother's pride and her chief anxiety. But you—I hope you'll finish high school, at least, and that you'll go to university so you can get a good job. What do you want to do later on?"

"Leave."

"Leave? But that's not a profession!"

"Once I leave, I'll have a profession."

"Leave for where?"

"Anywhere, across the water, for example."

"Spain?"

"Yes. Spain, França—I already live there in my dreams."

"And you like it?"

"Depends on the night."

"Meaning?"

"Actually, it depends on the clouds: for me they're the carpets I travel on at night; sometimes I fall off and then I wake up with a little bump on my forehead."

"You're some dreamer!"

"More than that. I've got ideas, plans, anyway you'll see, I'll get there."

Azel gave her an apple and took her home, touched and astonished by the fierce determination of this spirited girl.

And girls like her, he saw them every day. He watched them go by in little bands, swathed in their headscarves, silent, courageous, ready to brave the chill of the shrimp factory.

Malika's dream had the perfume of childhood. She'd had to fight to convince her parents to let her go to the Ibn Batouta Secondary School in Tangier. She walked to school there, often arriving late; there was a bus she could have taken, but she hadn't enough money for the fare. She walked quickly, head down, and along the way she thought of so many things that she sometimes got lost. Her feet always carried her to the boulevard Pasteur, which ended at the Terrasse des Paresseux with its famous view of the harbor and, on clear days, the Spanish coast. Malika would stop to watch the boats coming and going; she loved to see the white ships and observed them for a long time, slowly forgetting where she was. Then suddenly she would ask a passerby what time it was and dash off to school.

Malika never managed to get good grades in class. There

wasn't a proper place in her house to study or do homework. Sometimes she went outside to learn her lessons beneath a streetlight. Whenever he found her there, her father would hustle her roughly into the house. He was a peasant from the Fahs region who had come to the city after the drought of 1986. Working in construction, he earned very little money, and he saw absolutely no reason why his daughter should attend school. As far as he was concerned, girls stayed at home, and Malika would be better off working for someone as a maid while waiting for her family to find her a husband.

When she turned fourteen, Malika's father decided that she'd learned enough. He pulled her out of school, telling her that it was useless in any case.

"Look at Azz El Arab, the son of Lalla Zohra, our neighbor: he studied for a long time, and his mother made sacrifices so that he could finish up. He has diplomas, important ones, and you know, they don't help him at all, you saw them in his living room, just like I did. It doesn't matter that he looks everywhere, he can't find a thing. So—you, and a girl besides! And don't you dare cross me!"

Like her girlfriend Achoucha, the neighbor lady Hafsa, her cousin Fatima, and hundreds of girls in her neighborhood, Malika went off to shell shrimp in the Dutch factory down in the free zone of the port. Every day refrigerated trucks brought in tons of cooked shrimp, caught in Thailand and shipped through the Netherlands, where they were treated with preservatives. In the factory, small hands with slender fingers shelled them day and night, after which the shrimp traveled to yet another destination to be canned before debuting at last on the European market. In Tangier, the girls were paid a pittance. Even with the best will in the world, only a very few were able to process more than ten pounds. Malika, in any case, had never managed it, and went home in the evening with around fifty dirhams at best, which she handed directly to her mother. She complained constantly of the cold. And her fingers had become almost permanently numb.

In the factory, she sorely missed her days at school and her little forays of escape to the Terrasse des Paresseux to look at the sea. At work she never raised her head. She moved like an automaton, without wasting any time. Walking home, she no longer took an interest in anything, although when she occasionally went by her school, she thought about what she might have made of herself. But her dream of leaving, of working and earning money, had become a cruel joke: her back hurt, and her fingers, all pink and battered, now resembled the shrimp she shelled all day.

Malika quickly realized that she could not last long in that factory. Their fingers eaten by eczema, girls were constantly leaving after six months, some of them stricken with pneumonia.

Seeing Malika weak and ill, her eldest sister, Zineb, took her into her own home to care for her. Malika had not given up her dream, but dared not speak of it to her sister, preferring to treasure it in her heart. One day, she was sure, she would finally take the boat to Algeciras or Tarifa, disembark in Spain, and find a job there. She would be a saleswoman for El Corte Inglés, for example—she'd heard a lot about that chain of department stores—or a hairdresser, or (but she hardly dared even imagine it) maybe a model: that way she'd wear lovely clothes of every color, and be photographed, and be beautiful. First she would wait until she was eighteen to get a passport. But perhaps, like others, she wouldn't wait that long. She would cross the straits in some old tub or the back of a shrimp truck. . . .

Zineb's husband was a fisherman, a kind and upright man. Bearded in the Muslim fashion, he never missed any of the five daily prayers. He was appalled at how the factory had exploited Malika, and had welcomed her into his home. For hygienic reasons, Malika had worn a headscarf when cleaning shrimp at work; now she wore it in her sister's house to please her pious brother-in-law. She didn't want to cause any problems, and besides, he was treating her as if she were his own daughter. Malika helped her sister, taking care of the children, and all the while she cherished her secret dream. She soon noticed that the fisherman didn't care much for the Spanish, whom he accused of being prejudiced against *los moros*,* and of pillaging the Moroccan coasts by fishing with illegal nets. He had never been to Spain but had heard about it from his brother, who worked in El Ejido, in the province of Andalusia.

All of fourteen years old, Malika wasn't going anywhere at the moment, in any case, but she did discover a ladder leading to a sky that was always blue. She would ascend it silently, without arousing her brother-in-law's suspicions, to escape for a few moments to a little terrace where she could be alone and close her eyes. She would take off her scarf to let the wind caress her hair, allowing herself to be carried effortlessly away, as far as possible, without a word or a cry. She was happy, hovering over a sea of limpid blue.

Shelling more and more shrimp had turned her fingers completely transparent. Malika was afraid of losing them, afraid they would fall off like autumn leaves. She could bend them, but they hurt. When she went sailing with the wind, all her pain vanished. Often, in the air, she would encounter other children, each wrapped in a white cloth. They were going away somewhere, looking a little lost, but at peace. She had once been told that when children die, they become angels who go straight to paradise. Malika had just discovered that the way to paradise went past her terrace.

Climbing back down to her tiny room that first day, she felt a pang of doubt: the angels weren't going to Spain, but heading in the opposite direction, toward the interior of Morocco.

She promised herself that next time she would verify the precise route the angels were taking.

She spent that entire night coughing, shaking from the cold. It wasn't the first time she had fallen ill. All the "shrimp girls" went through this. Her frail body and delicate health were hard pressed, and to resist, to forget, she thought of the ladder and the pure blue of the sky. That night, she saw herself in turn enveloped in a white cloth and floating on water. Frightened, she awoke in tears. Her sister held her in her arms and gave her an aspirin.

13

Soumaya

Azel resolved to go to the brothel at least once a week. This was an important decision for him. He slept with Miguel, but found his own pleasure with women. Given that Siham was hardly ever free, Azel felt he absolutely had to keep up his virility with the North African Arab girls he met at the Café Casbah, a bistro that smelled of cigarettes and cheap wine. Frequented mainly by Moroccans, it was a place where girls in trouble could find refuge. The owner, a former shepherd from Nador, was called El Caudillo because he looked like Franco. He had married a Spanish woman and never again set foot in Morocco. He claimed not to miss his homeland; his childhood had been a hard and unhappy one, and he'd spent his entire youth in small-time smuggling between the Rif and the Atlas mountains. Anyway, he concluded, he'd had no luck with "made-in-Morocco happiness."

Whenever he was asked to describe his country, he would launch into some general observations sprinkled with a few home truths: in Morocco, you have to do as everyone else does: cut the throat of the sheep with your own hands on Aïd el-Kebir; marry a virgin; spend hours in a café backbiting people (or at best comparing the prices of the latest German automobiles); talk about TV programs; drink no alcohol from three days before Ramadan to three days after it; spit on the ground; try to push in front of other people; announce your opinion about everything; say "yes" when you think "no"; remember to punctuate your sentences with *makayene mouchkil* ("no problem"); and come home after having a few beers with friends to park yourself at the dinner table and stuff yourself like a pig. To round out the day, this pig will wait in bed for his wife to finish cleaning up so that he can give her a poke, but if she lingers a bit in the kitchen, he'll wind up asleep and snoring.

Azel liked El Caudillo, especially since the man never asked him any questions about his life, his past, or where he came from. It was at El Caudillo's place that Azel met Soumaya, a girl from Oujda who had come to Spain with a husband who'd decamped and left her destitute—a story she told at the drop of a hat but which everyone suspected was somewhat embroidered in certain respects. The truth was less romantic. A Kuwaiti lover had promised her the sun and the stars, marriage and the good life. They had left together for Spain, where they had taken a room in a hotel. One evening, however, without telling Soumaya, the Kuwaiti had paid the hotel bill for another month, left her a tidy sum of money, and taken off to rejoin his little family in Kuwait. Of course she soon found herself completely broke. Instead of returning to Morocco, she let herself drift into debauchery and the easy life. That was how she'd landed in the Casbah one evening when she'd had no idea where to go anymore. El Caudillo's wife had taken her in, offering her a job in the kitchen.

The first time Azel saw her, he knew she would become his mistress. Her way of looking at men was a real plea for love. Since she'd begun working for El Caudillo, she hadn't been doing too badly. The Moroccan dishes she prepared were quite popular. She lived in a small room on the top floor of an old apartment building not too far from the Café Casbah. From time to time, though, she cried over her fate. She missed her country so much, but before she could go home, she had to earn a little money. Whenever she called her family, she would tell them about Salim, her Kuwaiti husband off on a business trip, and say she'd soon be coming to visit them.

One evening when she was homesick, Azel took her in his arms and consoled her, singing a popular ditty that brought tears of laughter to her eyes. Shyly, she confided in him.

"I would never have believed that one day I would be slaving in a bistro kitchen. If my parents ever saw me, they would lose their minds. My father is an important official in the administrative district of Tangier, and my mother teaches Arabic in a private school. They spoiled their daughter—that's where I get my curves. . . . Men have no objection to a full figure. Salim, he just adored me, he would kneel at my feet and say, 'Your wish is my command!' He loved me, but he had his responsibilities, and men from that part of the world are not free, I'd been warned about that. They come to Morocco, buy themselves a good time, then take off again after making a heap of promises. Even so, I do have a friend, Wafa, who managed to marry a Saudi. She lives over there; I don't know if she's happy, but she certainly doesn't work in the kitchen of a Spanish bar. She hasn't ever been back to Morocco either, and her parents haven't been able to get a visa to visit her. Maybe she's dead, or just kept captive in one of those palaces where the doors are closely guarded. . . ."

"How kindhearted you are!" exclaimed Azel. "What I mean is, you're so full of goodness!"

"And I'm good in bed, too! You know, it's so rare to be able to speak freely with a Moroccan. With you, though, I feel at ease. Tell me, why is it so frowned on to love men? People often reproach me for showing that I love them. But I'm someone who can't hide her feelings—when I see a man I like, I let him know it. What's wrong with that?"

Making love in a small bed required the skills of an acrobat. Soumaya and Azel ended up falling onto the floor, laughing at the complicated positions they had to take. They liked each other and said so. Soumaya wore a strong perfume to cover the kitchen smells that clung to her no matter how many showers she took, but eau de toilette, perfume—nothing helped. Azel didn't have the heart to tell her.

14

Azel

"The next time you go see your whore, let me know; I'll buy you a bottle of perfume to give her from me."

Miguel wasn't angry, simply put off by the all-too-obvious signs that his lover had been straying.

Without replying, Azel hung his head, then shut himself up in the bathroom. He knew he'd be sleeping in his own room that night. Actually, it didn't bother him to be alone again. He understood that one day he would be leaving Miguel, although that was still in the future. And there was another consideration: his mother and sister had been nagging him lately, phoning him several times a week. When his mother called, she would speak to him in a murmuring voice filled with tenderness and longing.

"How are you, my beloved son? You have everything you need, I hope? Are you eating well enough, at least? Tell me what you do all day. You think of me now and then? I wish so much that I could see you again! I never go to sleep without sending you all my blessings. God hears me, you know! Have you done what I asked you to do the last time, for Kenza? Have you spoken

to him, to the Christian? He's so kind, so generous, he won't refuse to do that favor I asked of you, right? So, well, here's Kenza
and I give you a big hug, my darling boy."

Kenza got straight to the point.

"Did you ask him?"

"Not yet."

"Look, I need to know! What are you waiting for?"

"It's not that easy, you see. . . ."

"But what is it with you? You're waiting until he doesn't love
you anymore to ask him for this favor? Waiting for him to meet
someone else, someone handsomer, smarter, more clever than
you are?"

"I'll call you soon, I promise."

Azel was at a complete loss over this problem. Before approaching Miguel with his request, he wanted to wait at least until the
anniversary of their first meeting. Azel suggested to him that
they throw a small party at the house just for friends, and Miguel
liked the idea. A party to forget gloomy times, see a few people
again, have faith that love is stronger than everything else: after
all, why not?

Miguel, for his part, wasn't fooled. He knew for a fact that
Azel was not in love with him, that he was mostly taking advantage of the situation. Of course, it wasn't that simple, and there
were often real moments of affection between them, times when
they felt close to each other, but Azel never let himself go. He was
always watching himself, afraid of his impulses, and couldn't

manage to be spontaneous when they made love. When he was with women, there were pretty speeches along with the sex. With Miguel, Azel closed his eyes and said nothing.

Miguel had never considered the differences in their ages and cultures to be a problem. He saw Azel as a lost young man, destined to wind up among the dregs of Tangier in spite of his diplomas and intelligence. The boy was appealing and aggravating in equal measures, an incoherent collection of opposites with a distinct penchant for laziness, a readiness to coast along. Miguel often felt like shaking him, making him wake up and take more interest in what was happening to him. Miguel would have liked to see his lover change, take charge of things, the way he himself had done at Azel's age, but he tried not to make comparisons. Life was even harder now, a constant battle; nothing was ever acquired or settled for good, whether you were a sexual outsider or the son of Catholic petty-bourgeois supporters of Franco.

Azel took care of things at the gallery in an uneven fashion. He astonished his employer with his sharp business sense and skill with people, charming clients, playing on his Oriental allure while at the same time relying on the Western efficiency he'd picked up from watching Miguel. Now and again, however, he would go off the rails, disappearing without warning for a few days only to return dirty, unshaven, and sad, not even deigning to explain himself to Miguel, who complained bitterly but helplessly. Miguel was growing convinced that Azel had fallen into the clutches of some drug dealer or pimp—but on that score, he was completely mistaken. When Azel went off on his own he was simply running to Soumaya, with whom he was discovering erotic delights he'd never had the time to explore with Siham. Soumaya was shameless, observed no taboos, and gave herself without hiding any of her passion for what she called "vice." She had a special way of languorously drawing her tongue all along Azel's body, always lingering on his buttocks and between his legs. Whenever he asked her where she'd learned all these things that brought him so much pleasure, she told him it was intuition: freedom guided solely by desire!

One day, after Azel had returned from one of his brief stays with Soumaya, Miguel tried to put an end to his wanderings once and for all.

"You smell of women! In this house, you hear me, no one is allowed to smell of females. And while I think of it: do not shave, and absolutely do not touch your mustache. Tomorrow we're going to have some fun!"

Azel took a shower and awaited instructions. Miguel had invited some thirty people for a disguise party with the theme of "The Orient: Think Pink!"

Miguel was dressed as a vizier of the *Arabian Nights*, while most of his friends wore Moroccan jellabas or Turkish jabadors* and sarouals in every shade of pink. Shut up in the maid's room, Azel didn't know what to expect; he could hear the noise of the party but sat still, waiting. Then Carmen brought him a caftan, a wig that was almost red, a belt embroidered with gold, babouches, and a veil. Nothing but women's clothes! Azel realized immediately what Miguel had in mind.

"You get dressed, and you come downstairs only when I've rung for you," Carmen told him.

"At your command, you old bag!"

Pretending not to have heard, Carmen disappeared. And then Azel abruptly saw, in his mind's eye, his friend Noureddine, who had drowned in the straits. Terrified, Azel rushed to his mirror but saw only his own face, so tired and drawn it was almost a mask.

Rising to the challenge, Azel decided not only to play his employer's game but to astonish him as well. He made himself up like a bride, took care to dress properly in the women's clothing, adjusted his wig, and sat down again to wait. The little bell finally rang around midnight. Azel left the room and went slowly down the four flights of stairs. When he pushed open the door to the living room, everyone fell silent, gazing at him in admiration. Then the men began to compliment him.

"But what a lovely statue!"

"And such a perfect *mélange*—half woman, half man! Isn't Miguel just spoiling us!"

"Oh—the mustache! And look at that stubble! It's simply *so* exciting!"

"The loveliest catamite of the Maghreb!"

"No, no, open your eyes, this is no pickup, and *not* some passing fancy, this is serious, I can tell you!"

Azel advanced like an actor or a dancer poised to perform his ballet.

Miguel was amazed, and agreeably so. Seizing Azel's hand, he addressed his guests.

"My friends, I'm delighted to present my latest conquest to

you: the body of an athlete sculpted in bronze, with a piquant soupçon of femininity. Quite a stud! Educated, but familiar as well with the underworld of Tangier, that city of bandits and traitors. Neither bandit nor traitor, of course, Azel is simply a most beautiful object, an object to tempt every eye. Just look at his magnificent skin! You may touch it. Get in line, but don't push, he's right here, he's not going anywhere. Run your hand along his hip, for example, and *do* restrain your impulses. He belongs to me, and I won't have any fighting over him!"

Miguel was holding Azel firmly by the hand while the guests filed past him, one after the other, pretending to caress the young man.

"Now," Miguel whispered in Azel's ear, "you're going to dance. And you'll dance like a whore. You remember the fellow at the fair in Tétouan, the one who sold lottery tickets dressed as a woman? You're that man, a bearded woman!"

Azel could not understand why Miguel was trying so hard to show him off and humiliate him; for a moment he thought Miguel might have drunk too much, or smoked some hashish.

He began to dance to some Egyptian music, moving his buttocks and thinking about his sister, so talented at Oriental dancing, but her image gradually became confused with Soumaya's. Despite the tension in the air, Azel tried hard to concentrate, telling himself over and over that he was an employee, working for a lunatic boss. Cursing life and fate, he was flooded with shame but determined not to give in to regret and despair.

Toward two in the morning, Miguel abandoned him amid all those men, some of whom were drunk while others had collapsed half asleep onto the couches, alone or with partners. A group of young musicians arrived, but instead of playing, they began to copulate here and there throughout the house. Azel headed for the door to go upstairs to his room but found the way barred by a black giant, obviously a bouncer from some nightclub. . . .

Sensing the trap Miguel had set for him, Azel tore off his wig, scrubbed his face, and went off to hide in a far corner of the kitchen, where he fell asleep like a forgotten child amid the crates of food and the empty bottles.

The next day, Azel shaved off his mustache and gathered his belongings with the firm intention of leaving that house forever. He had nowhere to go, but the bitter memory of the party welled up inside him like something sour and fetid. He could not bear to remain entangled in that situation. For the first time in weeks, he felt he had to write in his notebook, but when he opened it, no words came to him. He just drew a line across the page.

A few days later, pretending that nothing had happened, Miguel summoned him and began talking about his future plans.

"That party was a wonderful idea! Why don't we throw one in Tangier, in our house—I mean in my house on the Old Mountain."

Azel did not welcome the suggestion.

"Right! And this time I'll be disguised as a monkey, a brood mare, or a beggar—why not!"

"Really, you have no sense of humor."

"Easy to say, when the joke's not on you."

The idea of returning to Tangier wasn't entirely welcome to Azel. He did want to see his mother again, of course, to throw himself into her arms while she recited a few verses of the Koran . . . but he was afraid of confronting Kenza, who was still waiting for her answer. Afraid as well of seeing his old friends, who would certainly spot him when he showed up with the Spaniard. Azel thought of Soumaya, too, who would be unable to come with him.

"It's a good idea, Tangier. But you said 'our' house?"

"Yes, 'our' house, the way I might have said 'the' house, I mean, you know perfectly well that you're at home whether you're here or over there."

"What does that mean, 'at home'? Does it mean I can do as I like in the house, that I can do what I want with it?"

"If you want to know whether half the house belongs to you, it doesn't."

"Because it belongs to someone else?"

"Yes: to my children!"

This was the first Azel had heard of them.

"Yes, I have in fact adopted two children, orphans whom no one wanted. They call me Papa and I'm very happy about that. We see one another only over the summer holidays, because they don't live with me during the rest of the year, of course: I send them to a boarding school in Casablanca."

Azel was now completely intrigued.

"What are their names?"

"They're twins, Halim and Halima. They're lovely children and quite smart. You'll be meeting them soon. I'm thinking of having them attend the lycée in Barcelona, where they would be close to me. I miss them so much. . . ."

"They have your name?"

"Not yet. For the moment, while I'm waiting for some administrative procedures to be taken care of (and you can't imagine how complicated they are!), I look after the twins as if they were my own. They haven't any identification papers yet. This is something very close to my heart. I don't talk about it, I wait, but it's always on my mind."

After a moment's hesitation, Azel asked him why he had adopted the children.

"I belong to a Moroccan association created by some remarkable women. They take care of unwed mothers and abandoned babies, and whenever I visit them, I feel as if I've been put through a wringer. I knew that it was difficult to adopt children in Morocco; you can help them, but I don't believe you have the right to give them your name. A religious authority explained to me that Islam thinks of every eventuality, even the most unlikely ones—with an eye to avoiding, for example, the possibility that adopted children who do not know who their biological mothers and fathers are might unknowingly have sexual relations with their parents, which would amount to unintentional incest. But I was also told that there are always ways to make arrangements. To me, they are my children. On paper, however, that's not yet the case. I even intend to convert to Islam, if that would help move things along. So, Azel, now you know everything. Well, no—there's still one question: why do I absolutely insist on adopting them? I thought about their lives and my old age. My gesture is both selfish and generous. Yes, I've been thinking ahead to the time when I will need people around me. It's only human, after all; I don't want to die alone like so many little old men no one wants anymore. In your country, the elderly are never abandoned, but it's different here. Today, you are with me, a presence by my side. We even make plans together. The day will come, however, when someone else will come along, a man or a woman, and suddenly you'll go off, dropping me like an old rag. Until that time, though, make no mistake: I'm no angel!"

Azel didn't know what to say. He looked at Miguel with an admiration tinged, ever so slightly, with anxiety.

In mid-August, Miguel and Azel returned to Tangier, where vacationing émigrés jammed the boulevards and avenues with their cars, making traffic sluggish. And how they loved their horns! The police had no idea how to cope with the constantly complaining pedestrians, whom young men hired by the city were admonishing to cross the streets only at the crosswalks. Standing at intersections with loudspeakers and shouting in classical Arabic, these youths dispensed advice ignored by absolutely everyone. The city was dirty and overflowing with people, but as Miguel observed, "Here, there's life."

Azel went off to see his mother, who greeted him as if he'd just returned from Mecca. As soon as she laid eyes on him she burst into ululations, while Kenza tried frantically to calm her down. It was the return of the prodigal son. The neighbors were out on their balconies or terraces, watching as Azel arrived with two huge suitcases crammed with presents, and the only disappointment was that he'd driven up in a taxi instead of a big luxury car.

"He came by plane," shouted Lalla Zohra, "by plane, and he left the car home in Spain. . . . He returned to see his mother just before she goes away on a pilgrimage!"

Kenza made her be quiet: "Aren't you ashamed—you really think you need to tell the entire neighborhood all about your life, our family life?"

The first evening was a celebration. Azel talked and talked about himself, saying whatever popped into his head, exaggerating, lying, even though he wasn't fooling anyone. Before they went off to bed, Kenza pulled him aside.

"I can't take any more of this country. Ever since you left, it's gotten worse, there's no way out, none. Luckily Monsieur Miguel thinks of us from time to time; you're the one who sends us money, right?—but he's the one who signs the money order."

Azel hesitated for a moment; he'd known nothing about that.

"Whether it's his money or mine, it's the same thing. But it's still very hard to ask him for what you want."

"But you're the only one who can do it! I don't know him well enough to say to him, straight out like that, will you agree to a fake marriage with me?"

"I know I'm the only one, but I'm afraid we're pushing our luck, going too often to the well."

"Miguel is not a well!"

"Of course not, but we can't go too far—after all, he's a man with principles."

"Then I'll let our mother take care of it."

"No, absolutely not, she'll spoil everything! And she'd risk losing the trip to Mecca he's thinking about offering her."

It was on an evening when they were dining alone together, in a
charming little house in the nearby coastal town of Asilah, that
Azel broached the subject with Miguel.

Miguel was neither surprised nor offended. He was quite familiar with that kind of subterfuge and preferred to follow the
lead of his feelings, wherever they took him. He loved Azel and
thus could refuse him nothing. His only fear was of being betrayed, double-crossed, stabbed in the back. He could talk end-
lessly about the methods and ravages of treachery. Miguel had
read the works of Jean Genet and wondered why he loved to say
that Tangier was the city of perfidy. Miguel knew there was something in Azel's eyes that was difficult to put into words, a kind of
pseudo-smile, an implicit way of revealing an inadmissible form
of deception. But Miguel was also perfectly aware of his young
lover's weaknesses: money, women, and kif. By accepting this
marriage with Kenza, he hoped to create a stability at home that
would make Azel more manageable, more trustworthy.

"But a non-Muslim man is not allowed to wed a Muslim
woman!" he pointed out to Azel.

"Then now's the time to convert to Islam! Married, you'd
have an even greater chance of success with your adoption plan.
Two birds with one stone!"

"How does one convert?"

"You go see two *adouls*, men of religion and the law, and you pronounce the *shahada*, the profession of faith: I affirm that there is no God but Allah and that Mohammed is His prophet."

"That's it?"

"You'll also have to change your name and . . ."

"And what?"

"Get your dick circumcised!"

"No, I'm too old for that, and anyway they're not going to check up on me."

"When you go see the *adouls*, you have to make an effort to dress normally: no caftan! They'd be shocked, and might turn against you. No coral necklace, either, or too many rings. These are conventional people, there's no sense in drawing attention to yourself."

"I know Morocco as well as you do and I am aware that it's always better to be discreet. And here's a piece of advice for you: appearances can be deceiving!"

"Yes, I know: all that glitters is not gold. *Senna kadhhak we el kalb kay thanne . . .*"

"Meaning?"

"A smile on the lips and murder in the heart! I just thought that up. I like to quote proverbs now and then. When I can't remember one, well, I make one up myself."

And that is how, for love of Azel, Miguel married Kenza and changed his name to Mounir.

15

Malika

Ever since Malika had seen the pictures of floating bodies on television, she had stopped dreaming. She had counted the corpses, imagining herself as a victim of that tragedy. She would lie on her back, puff up her tummy, and float with her eyes closed. The morning mist caressed her face; chilly water rippled over her small body. She felt nothing. She was playing at death, letting herself be carried away by the waves, bumping into other bodies, then heading back out to sea. A huge wave tumbled her all the way onto the sandy shore. Seaweed wrapped her in its tangles. The water kept washing over her, rocking her as if she were setting out on a long sleep. But it was dawn, the hour for prayer; her grandmother was making her ablutions and paying no attention to her. Malika neither saw nor heard her. They were not in the same room, perhaps not even in the same country. Malika would have liked to speak to her, call her, but no sound left her throat. So she began to pray as well, but without moving, and without making her ablutions. She spoke to the sky, to the sea, to the gulls, remembering what her father had told her one day about these birds that drown if they lose the oil on their feathers. She'd tried to wash a gull with soap, and when she had let it go, the poor thing had slipped under the surface and never come up. Malika had cried; she'd thought her father had invented that story because he had so much imagination. Now, whenever she saw a seagull, she remembered the one that had died from her mistake. She had even given it a name, Zbida, which means "butter cookie."

Malika's sleep became light, hovering over depths of sadness. She no longer dreamed of crossing the straits but had not given up on changing her life. Her sister protected her, but her brother-in-law ordered her about, even though he claimed that she was like a daughter to him. Since he had a hard time making ends meet, he was often in a bad mood. Anyway, he was a fisherman, and would always have a hard time of it. And his wife selling bread at the entrance to the Grand Socco wasn't going to change that. She had teamed up with an elderly aunt who baked the bread, which she herself could go sell every day only because Malika stayed home to take care of the children.

As soon as her sister returned from the market, Malika would run outside to enjoy her daily hour of freedom, dashing through the streets to the boulevard Pasteur, down to the Terrasse des Paresseux. She would buy a packet of roasted sunflower seeds and sit down to nibble them while watching boats leave the harbor. If she was propositioned by men who took her for a prostitute, she never replied, just spat seeds at them until they went away.

She now gazed at the boats with a changed eye, watching them glide away over the calm water like giant bottles in which she was content simply to send off her dreams. She wrote them down on large sheets of paper, folded them in four, then eight, then numbered them and tucked them away in a notebook.

Dream number one is blue. There is the sea, and at the far end is an armchair suspended between heaven and earth. Malika nestles into it, and sets it swinging. Her dress is blue as well, loose-fitting and sheer. High up in her swing she can glimpse the Moroccan coast, Tangier, the cliffs, the Mountain, the harbor. In the evening, the lights do not glitter there. All is dark. So she twists the swing sideways and turns her back on Morocco.

Dream number two is white. She's in a school where everyone, teachers and students alike, is wearing white. The blackboard is white and the chalk, black. The pupils learn about the stars—their movements, their travels—and then go down to earth. There, they enter a forest where the trees have been painted with whitewash. This whiteness enchants Malika. She stops, climbs a tree, and sees in the distance the terrace of her sister's house. It's a tiny terrace where sheepskins are set out to dry. From the tree branches hang books by the hundreds, covered with jackets of every color. To learn what each book says, one need simply open it. They are magic books that do not exist in Tangier. Malika decides to go to the land where this forest of books grows.

Dream number three is a train that crosses the Straits of Gibraltar. Tarifa and Tangier are linked by a bridge as lovely as the one Malika saw in a tourism magazine. The trip takes twenty minutes. Malika is sitting in the first car, avidly observing everything about the crossing. When the train arrives on the Spanish coast, a welcoming committee greets the travelers, offering them flowers, dates, and milk. Malika loves dates. She takes three of them and eats them as fast as she can. The Spanish who greeted them propose that Malika attend the lycée there, to continue the studies she interrupted upon leaving Tangier. When she turns around, the train is gone, and the bridge as well.

Dream number four is a suitcase, an old brown suitcase. Inside it Malika has hidden the toys and objects she loves. All kinds of things: a hairbrush, a piece of mirrored glass, a pencil sharpener, three buttons of different colors, a notebook full of thoughts she jotted down quickly, a silver *khamsa** given to her by her grandmother, a yellowed piece of paper folded in four and tied up with a red thread, an eraser, a brooch, some nails, and a notebook made to look like a European passport so that when you open it, you find your photograph and all the usual information. Each of these items has a specific meaning for Malika. Secrets known only to her. She has simply written on the back of the suitcase, with a black felt-tip, the words: "This is mine."

16

Mounir

Miguel took his conversion to Islam very seriously. Of course, he had already known something about that religion, but he bought books on Muslim culture, a biography of the prophet, and a new translation of the Koran. He read and reread certain passages. Everything interested him. He was curious, and happy to plunge into a world so close to him, one he had believed, mistakenly, that he knew. He realized that Islam was only truly different from Christianity with regard to that business with Mary and Jesus. Reading the sura "Women," he paid particular attention to verses 156, 157, and 158: "They said, 'We slew the Messiah, Jesus, Son of Mary, the Messenger of God.' They did not slay him, neither did they crucify him, but were deceived by some likeness (. . .) Instead God raised him up to Him." The three monotheistic religions defended the same values. As for Islam, it recognized the other prophets and required of Muslims that they honor and celebrate them.

Miguel wished to convert through love, persuaded in fact that it is through love, because of or thanks to love, that we embark upon our most important achievements. This was obvious, one of the eternal truths. When Miguel looked back over his life, he saw it as simply a series of stages in which a loving infatuation had often been decisive. "Today Azel is leading me toward Islam!" he mused. "Ah, if my old Catholic friends could see me now! They'd say that I'm done for, that it's all over, that Azel's mother has cast a spell on me, that I've definitely been fed jackal's or hyena's brains. They would never understand how eagerly I accepted the offer from Azel's family. But none of that could change my mind: I'm going to be married, and what's more, married fair and square. This marriage, of the purest convenience, will help a person in need. My sole personal interest in the matter will be to keep close to me the loved one who gives me hope and renewed faith in life. Ah, my friends, sitting discouraged in your beautiful houses, passing your time remembering your youth—your bodies are letting you down, you drive yourselves batty thinking life is unfair, and you hang out together like old folks in a nursing home, waiting to die! Well, me, I've made my choice: I've refused to be bundled off to that home! I can still get it up, still make love, I have people around me, I'm even going to have lots of people, I'll have a family and God willing, I'll have my little twins. My friends, I will enter Islam. . . . That brings back a painful memory. . . . My great love, my first great love: Ali, the acrobat, star of the Cirque Amar, Ali who drove me wild, for whom I wanted to become a Muslim, so that he would live with me, but oh—he had an accident, abandoned everything, just disappeared, and I have never been able to find out anything about him, it's still a burning wound in my heart. I only hope things won't get complicated with the *adouls*, that they'll be open-minded about this, and that I won't flub the *shahada*—I've been practicing it since yesterday: *Ach hadou anna la ilaha illa Llah, Mohammed rassoulu Llah. Ach hadou . . .* it's simple, you just say that sentence and become a Muslim, but your heart must be in it, because God is trusting you; if it's for a joke or to cheat, that's no good, because being Muslim, it means believing sincerely in the divine oneness."

Such were Miguel's thoughts, interrupted when Azel and Kenza rang his doorbell. They and Lalla Zohra were all to meet with the *adouls* at the Mendoubia* near the rue Siaghine at three o'clock. The conversion would be first, followed by the marriage.

Miguel dressed in white and put on a jellaba.

Azel asked him to please tone it down. Miguel took off the jellaba. Miguel usually wore some foundation and outlined his eyes with kohl, but as they were about to leave, Azel asked him to remove his makeup, too.

"Your name is Mounir, you love women, and you carry yourself like a man, a real one, virile and straightforward."

Azel was taking charge, somewhat to Miguel's surprise.

At the Mendoubia, the *adouls* were waiting for them. They had been informed of how matters stood and asked not to raise any questions. They would be very well paid.

The youngest of the two, who spoke several languages, greeted Miguel warmly. The other man said nothing as he opened a large register in which he recorded the day and the hour. Next, he merely asked if Miguel had performed his ablutions, since it was advisable to say a prayer after the conversion.

"Of course," replied Miguel. "I'm quite committed to this and have performed both the simple and the formal ablutions. I always do."

In a slightly strange silence, Miguel said the *shahada,* which everyone repeated after him as if to confirm his action. Miguel was very moved. Kenza stood waiting behind the men, holding her national identification card.

Miguel, Azel, and the *adouls* rose and left to pray at the mosque down at the end of the rue Siaghine. Although Miguel had toured a few mosques in Egypt and Turkey, this was the first time he had entered one in Morocco, where non-Muslims are forbidden to visit them. Watching his friend act as though he believed in what he was doing, Azel was hard put to keep from bursting out laughing.

Back again at a small office in the Mendoubia, the younger *adoul* read the solemn declaration of the entrance of a Christian into Islam.

"In the name of God the Merciful and Compassionate, we, Mohammed Laraïchi and Ahmed El Kouny, men of law and religion, attest that Monsieur Miguel Romero López has spoken the *shahada* and thereby become a Muslim before witnesses; he has chosen the first name 'Mounir.' May God help and protect him. He hereby renounces his Catholic faith and enters the *Umma Islamiya,* which welcomes him to swell its ranks and benefit from his faith and goodwill.

"Dear Mounir, you are now our brother, welcome in the Islam of enlightenment, fraternity, dignity, and noble spirituality. We remind you of the five pillars of Islam: the profession of faith; the five daily prayers determined by the movement of the earth around the sun; the fast of Ramadan when the faithful abstain from eating, drinking, smoking, and sexual relations from sunrise to sunset for a period of twenty-nine or thirty days; the *zakat,* the charity offered to the needy in proportion to your means; and lastly the hajj, the pilgrimage to Mecca undertaken if your physical, mental, and financial capabilities permit it."

Then the *adouls* read aloud the Fatiha,* the first sura of the Koran, and prayed that Mounir's life would be a healthy and good one until the day of the Last Judgment.

They drew up a certificate to which they added their signatures and a twenty-dirham state tax stamp.

There was a pause before they began the formal marriage ceremony.

Kenza was then joined by her mother, who had been standing off to one side. While the marriage certificate was being prepared, the older *adoul* spoke to Kenza in a low voice.

"Even if he has converted to our religion, he remains a foreigner, a Christian, and even though it's none of my business, you should know that I understand what is behind all this."

"You're mistaken!" replied Kenza, so loudly that everyone heard her.

Miguel felt suddenly left out; they had spoken in Arabic, and he had not understood what was going on.

The younger *adoul* explained to Miguel why Islam forbids Muslim women to marry outside the ranks of the faithful.

"A woman is easily influenced, you understand; if she marries a Christian, she'll end up espousing his religious convictions, and then the children will follow her lead. And you must also know that the law protects women, since your future wife has the right to have certain conditions entered into the marriage certificate, such as a prohibition against repudiating her or taking a second wife."

"You know, one wife, that's more than enough, and I'd even say that no wife at all—it's not the end of the world!"

"I gather, Monsieur Mounir, that you know women well."

"Well enough to understand that married life is not always a bed of roses. In fact, that's why I waited so long to get married."

"You know what Islam has to say on the subject of marriage?"

"Absolutely: the duty of a good Muslim is fulfilled in wedlock."

"Ah! I see that you are not simply going through the motions here!"

Kenza was feeling tense. Her mother was growing impatient and muttering to herself. Off in his corner, Azel watched the ceremony while thinking of Siham. He didn't see himself asking her to marry him; he loved his freedom too much, and avoided responsibilities. He was beginning to mix Siham and Soumaya together in his imagination, which made him smile.

After making the correct replies to the *adouls*, Mounir and Kenza signed the marriage certificate, then left ahead of everyone else, holding hands.

Miguel had had a festive meal prepared at his villa. He was receiving his mother-in-law for the first time, and Lalla Zohra was impressed by the luxury and refinement of his home. She did not understand, however, why he collected all those old things—

furniture, jewelry, dark paintings, tarnished mirrors—and she even offered to take him to a merchant she knew who would sell him brand-new mirrors and solid, handsomely decorated furniture. Miguel smiled at her.

"I keep these things because they belonged to my parents and grandparents: they bring back memories!"

After the meal, Kenza and her mother went home. Lalla Zohra was crying. She had never before seen a bride return to her parents' house to sleep.

It had been a long and exhausting day for everyone. Uneasy and out of sorts, Azel disappeared, leaving Miguel alone.

17

Abdeslam

Abdeslam loved to stretch a white sheet out on the terrace of his house, and drift into a dream. He had no desire to leave his country. He was content to imagine what his life would have been like if he had emigrated. Ever since he'd lost his brother Noureddine, he had abandoned all his plans. Abdeslam had turned to religion and now prayed every day because he felt guilty for having encouraged his brother to try his chances on that damned boat. He'd even given him a good part of his savings to pay the *passeur,* Al Afia. Azel knew how that had gone, he'd witnessed the transaction.

"Listen, the boat—it's not some piece of junk, right?"

"Of course not!"

"How many people are you going to put on it?"

"The legal limit: no more, no less. Why are you so suspicious?"

"Because there've been a lot of drownings lately."

"I'm a professional, not a widow-maker. I do this to help the guys in the neighborhood. I'm not going to get rich off these paltry sums of money."

"Paltry or not," Abdeslam had replied, "it was hard for us to get this sum together. I'm handing it over to you and it's like giving away part of my flesh, it's everything I have, so you'd better make sure everything goes well and that our 'paltry sum' counts for something."

"Hey, if you keep suspecting me of stuff and threatening me, take your precious money back and fuck off."

Noureddine had calmed him down, and the deal was struck.

Abdeslam was a mason. He liked to build, to put stones in place one after the other and tell himself it was his hands that had done the work. He had the soul of a craftsman. Certain homes he had restored had even increased in value. He loved a job well done, hated getting to work late, and above all else enjoyed creating new spaces inside traditional old houses. Certain Europeans made a point of hiring him, which pleased him and made him even more demanding of himself and his workers.

Noureddine had smiled at his brother just before getting on the boat, and that image had haunted him ever since. Abdeslam had tried to form an association against those clandestine crossings and had managed to get together several families who'd lost loved ones. They met regularly at the mosque to pray together. More concretely, they had demanded that the authorities do something about this problem and had dared write to the king, begging him to put a stop to this hemorrhage. To their amazement, instead of the usual impersonal note, one of the royal councilors had sent them a lovely letter in reply. He had written with great human feeling to announce that the king would be appointing a commission to propose legislation on the problem for parliamentary debate, and that he sincerely regretted this situation that was so painful for Morocco and damaging to its image abroad.

Abdeslam was proud, because it had been his idea to write to the king. He had shut Azel up in a room so he would compose the letter. As for Azel, he hadn't believed in it for a second.

"You think the king has nothing better to do than read your letter? And even if by some miracle it reaches him, you seriously think he'll do something, he'll answer? Dream on. He's got so many people around him he can't even see out the window. They keep him from confronting reality, and all because those people, they're afraid of losing their positions, so each day they tell him, Everything's fine, Your Majesty, don't worry about a thing, Your Majesty, and Your Majesty would like to visit the neighborhoods where the clandestines leave from, Beni Makada, or Drissia, or Hay Saddam? At your orders, Your Majesty: we're arranging that now with your security detail. . . . Then they let him wait a few days while they spruce up those districts, repaint walls, clean out the undesirable elements, put a cop on every corner, and so on."

That is how Abdeslam became an antideparture militant, a dedicated opponent of the *passeurs.* He went everywhere to talk with people preparing for the crossing, to explain that they had one chance in ten of reaching Europe. He distributed copies of the royal letter in certain cafés. But what could he say when they replied to him like this?

"One chance in ten? Better than nothing! A gamble, a long shot. On the other hand, if we just sit here in this café, nothing will happen to us, absolutely nothing, and we'll still be here in ten years, drinking the same lukewarm café au lait, smoking kif, and waiting for a miracle! In other words: some work, a decent job—well paid, with respect, security, and dignity. . . ."

Abdeslam would have loved to produce miracles but he was only a mason, a man who had lost his brother and suffered day and night from that loss.

Whenever he tried to argue back, he stammered, and the men made fun of him.

"Right, here it comes, you're going to hit us with your lecture on the-country-that-needs-its-children, the-country-we-shouldn't-abandon-because-if-everyone-leaves-there-won't-be-any-country-left. Yeah, yeah, we love our country, but it's our country that doesn't love us! No one does anything to give us reasons to stay—haven't you seen how things work here? You've got money, you spread it around, grease some palms, slip it into pockets, show you can be accommodating, and *voilà!* As long as it's like that, how can you expect us to love this country?"

"But, shit, I mean, the country is *us*, it's our children, and their children!"

Azel had once intervened in the discussion at this point, when Abdeslam had been red-faced with anger, and there'd been something about the looks he'd gotten that disturbed him. The men in the café saw Azel as someone who had succeeded, but at a shameful cost. He bought a round of drinks and said his piece.

"You know, I've seen Moroccans over there who are just wretched, they're beggars, pathetic, drifting through the streets, living off chickenshit deals, it's not a pretty picture. Listen to this: I've been hearing that Europe will soon need several million immigrants—those countries will come looking for you, and you'll head off there proudly, without taking any risks at all."

"Only if we've got cute little mugs like yours!" someone called out.

Another voice chimed in: "Easy to make speeches when you don't work with your hands. . . ."

Azel rose without a word and left, soon followed by Abdeslam. That evening, Azel confided in his friend.

"They're right. I am ashamed, but I'm also sure that they're jealous. They would have done the same thing if they'd had the chance. Things are getting complicated for me at the moment; Miguel has just married Kenza, at least on paper, so she'll get a visa and be able to leave Tangier. She's going to live with us in Barcelona until she can find a job and a place to live. Even my mother's hoping to join us! Can you imagine? It's crazy! You want me to tell you something? I'm not in good shape. . . . I don't even know anymore just what I am in all this business. A *falso*, a fake through and through, always pretending, running away—I only feel comfortable when I'm with Siham, but she's busy almost all the time and doesn't even live in Barcelona!"

Abdeslam heard him out in silence. He did have one question he really wanted to ask, something hard to put into words.

"You remember, when we used to go picnicking on the Mountain, and there were never any girls along? And after we'd eaten, Kader would disappear with little Sami, that chubby guy? He'd come back and say, Your turn, and we'd go off and find Sami waiting for us, lying on his stomach. . . ."

"Why are you saying this to me?"

"Just to remind you that we had some experiences with boys! So, what I'd like to know is, how does that work with your Spanish guy? Who's on top?"

"I'm not a *zamel*, I'm a man!"

"I knew it! Well, you know, little Sami—he got married and he's got two kids, so that proves nothing is ever really certain forever. If you want to see him, he has an important job in the department of the treasury, head of a whole sector, where there's lots of money changing hands under tables. Anyway, they say he got there by sleeping around, and that he leads a double life, that his wife knows about it but keeps quiet to avoid a scandal. See, things aren't always so simple. In our country, the *zamel* is the other guy, the European tourist, never the Moroccan, and no one ever talks about it but it's not true, we're like all the other countries, except we keep quiet about those things. We're not the kind to go on TV to admit we like men!"

Azel studied his friend for a moment, then asked what he was doing with his life.

"Me, I build houses, rooms, love nests. I haven't gotten married because boys . . . I like that. No one knows it, but I can tell this to you."

"You're a homosexual!"

"No: I switch back and forth, sometimes a man, sometimes a woman. Depends on the weather!"

"Why the weather?"

"Because in the summer the girls are wild about it, whereas boys, I prefer them in the winter. You're my friend, hey—I'm trusting you, so whatever you do don't tell anyone. . . ."

18

Siham

Azel decided to return to Barcelona by train. When he stopped off in Marbella and called Siham, he found her deeply shaken: the little girl had just thrown an ashtray in her face, and the parents were off at a health spa in the south of France. Siham's wound was painful, but even worse was her dismayed realization that she really wasn't qualified to take care of a handicapped child. Siham always did her best with the girl and never complained, but seeing no progress, she felt discouraged. And so she waited impatiently for Widad to fall asleep at night, the only time when she herself could get some rest. Usually groggy with exhaustion, Siham would sit in front of the television watching anything at all. Sometimes she thought about what her life would have been like if she had stayed in Tangier. . . .

Back home, Siham would surely have become resigned to behaving like everyone else, never passing up any invitation or excuse to go out and join other girls who were in the same predicament, and by giving in to her boss (which would have allowed her—just barely—to earn a living), she would have become his mistress in hopes of one day becoming his wife. She would have fallen into every trap, run through every cliché, dreamed of every impossibility. She would have purchased fabrics imported from the Far East to make caftans she'd have worn once a year, and taken her mother to the yearly regional festival in honor of the sainted Moulay Abdeslam; gradually losing all her illusions, she would have wound up marrying a widower not too far past his prime and had problems with his children. . . . Nevertheless, when she thought about it, Siham still preferred her present situation to that of her female cousins and friends back home. She'd heard from Wafa, one of her girlfriends, a high-school student, who had just gotten pregnant. She was trapped in a complete nightmare. The guy involved had laughed and simply told her off.

"Don't give me any grief! A seventeen-year-old who sleeps with the first man who comes along is a whore, so you're on your own! Go see the woman who oversees the hammam: she'll send you to a nice doctor, you know—you turn a few tricks for a little money, and your worries are over. . . ."

He'd sounded like an actor in a play. Wafa hadn't said another word. One day she had gone to his home and asked to see his wife, to whom she'd told her story. The betrayed wife was the one who had helped her get a safe abortion.

"I'm used to it," she'd said. "This isn't the first time. My husband's a real sex fiend—he doesn't make love, he sticks his thing in the hole and pumps out his balls, he's a pathetic jerk I put up with only because we've got five children, but when they're grown, I'll throw him out!"

Azel waited in the living room for Widad to fall asleep so that Siham could finally come see him. He looked around at the décor.

There were dozens of paintings in the Orientalist style, all fake, or rather, reasonably well-made copies. What was the point of hanging a fake picture in your home? To remind you of the real one? To fill up space? To show that you're interested in the way nineteenth-century painters perceived us? Miguel had no fakes in his house, only originals.

Siham fixed dinner, Azel got out a bottle of wine, and they had a pleasant meal. She told him that she'd mentioned him to her employer, who had said that Azel could come to the house as long as she herself was not there. The only thing she had forbidden was alcohol. That evening, it wouldn't be a problem, since there was no risk of her showing up unexpectedly. They did not make love, but talked quite late into the night. Azel slept on the couch, Siham in her room.

Siham had finally signed up for a class that met once a week in a center for the disabled in Málaga. She left every Monday morning and returned at the end of the evening. One day, she invited Azel to meet her for dinner and then go to the hotel room Widad's father always reserved for her. Azel had not been in a good mood. Grumpy, ill at ease, he was smoking too much and unable to focus on anything. For the first time, he spoke about seeing a doctor, perhaps even a psychotherapist.

"I'm fed up, too: I'm not happy, I live like a leech, and things just got more complicated—Kenza will need to find some sort of job and I'll have to keep pretending, when I desperately need stability, clarity. . . ."

"What's Miguel to you?"

"He's important to me, I like him a lot; he has helped me, he's helping out my family, but people can't just live off others. Miguel, he says he loves me, that he's in love, but me—I'm not in love and there are even times when I can't stand him touching me. I can't get it up anymore, so the other day he had me swallow a little blue pill, some Viagra, do you believe that? At my age? I'm a whore, that's what I am, or at least that's how I feel."

Siham tried to make light of the situation. Caressing him, she discovered that he couldn't get an erection.

"You don't want to?"

"No, it's not a question of wanting, but I'm worried and upset, I'm not getting hard!"

"It's just temporary, it's from stress, and don't worry about me, I know you're a man and I adore it when you make love to me. Get things straightened out in your head and be honest with yourself, that's what counts."

"I have to go to a doctor."

"If we were in Tangier, I'd take you to El Haj Mbarek, he's good. Maybe you're 'blocked': some woman has it in for you, has put a spell on you!"

"Stop your nonsense, you know that stuff doesn't exist."

Later that evening, in his train compartment, Azel slept like the dead.

19

Kenza

Three months later, Kenza arrived in Barcelona like a real princess, welcomed at the airport by Miguel, who was almost invisible behind a huge bouquet of roses. Kenza's hands and feet had been decorated with henna, and she was so overwhelmed by emotion that she stumbled and almost fell.

Miguel put her in the guest room. Along with the rest of her luggage, Kenza had brought a crate of food prepared by Lalla Zohra. Embarrassed, Azel tried to smile, to say that he was pleased. Morocco was landing in Spain with *tajines* of chicken with olives and preserved lemons, quail *pastillas*, almond-flavored gazelle horn pastries, honey cakes for Ramadan, spices, dried mint, ground coriander, incense, and a file of papers to fill out labeled LALLA ZOHRA in big block letters.

Azel closed his eyes. Miguel kept him under sidelong surveillance.

"Excuse me, Miguel—I'm off to the market to buy a pound of patience."

"And just where do you go to buy that?"

"To the Jesuits!"

"Do tell. I'd never have thought of that. Don't be late getting back, whatever you do."

Kenza adjusted fairly quickly. She spoke Spanish, which helped her look for work. She wanted a job in the social services, interfacing between immigrants and the government, for example. She had decided to make her own way, determined not to be a new burden for Miguel, who had given her a few letters of recommendation and made some phone calls. By the end of the month she had been hired by the Red Cross.

When Kenza had quietly tried to help out in the kitchen, Carmen had turned her down flat to drive home her displeasure. Miguel called Kenza the "phantom wife" and took an immediate liking to her; he admired her energy, her firm intention to get ahead on her own, and her open-mindedness.

"You are the Morocco of tomorrow," he told her, watching her in action. "It's the women who will get this country moving, they're incredible, and I even admit I have a weakness for the women of your generation: I like them, and I trust them."

As for Azel, he avoided being alone with his sister and was increasingly on edge. When the manager of the gallery in Madrid fell ill, Azel was sent to fill in for him, but Miguel soon learned that his gallery was now often closed during its normal business hours. Azel was partying, then sleeping until the early afternoon. Miguel knew it was useless to talk to him; Azel was growing more and more stubborn and above all, seriously depressed. Distressed in turn, Miguel confided in an old friend, who spoke to him bluntly.

"Your friend Azel isn't made for this life. If you'd put him to work as a laborer on a construction site, I'm sure he would have been happy, because he would have been just another immigrant among thousands of his compatriots. Instead, you offer him the life of a pasha, money galore, everything at his fingertips, and to cap it all off he isn't even queer! His family has found their Santa Claus. You're going to be invaded in no time, my dear. After the son and the daughter, you'll get the mother and the grandmother, if there is one. As soon as those people find a sucker, they make themselves right at home!"

"But that's so racist!"

"No, it's experience talking. You remember Ahmed? The handsome, the sublime Ahmed? He tortured me, he robbed me, he took shameless advantage of me. It's simple: he understood that he could get whatever he wanted from me with his dick. I melted in his presence, I couldn't refuse him anything. He took off with pots of money. He was blackmailing me, threatening to spill everything to my two children, with whom I have a difficult, touchy relationship, what with their mother always encouraging them to turn against me. To avoid a scandal, I kept my trap shut. Result: he stole everything he could get his hands on. You know what he is now? An international crook, specializing in the elderly. I've heard he set himself up in Majorca because that's where the rich German queers go. He's a bitch, a high-class prostitute. If I ever run into him again, I just might kill him."

"I know, he's made a fortune with his old-folks expertise. Some day he'll trip up and run smack into a rusty blade that'll cut his guts out."

"You're saying that to make me feel better, but he's a piece of work, he even claims to be a believer, pretends to observe Ramadan. I've heard he's on the run, wanted by several police forces. Seems he caused the death of a big American lawyer by making him take a pill that's dangerous for heart cases. One of the man's sons asked the Majorcan police to investigate, he was convinced his father had been murdered. Ahmed is perfectly capable of that; one day when we were fighting about money, he threatened me by mentioning that very same pill. He's a vicious guy, I hope he pays for it some day. He's the kind to wind up with a bullet in the back of the head, dumped between two cars in a parking lot."

"Azel isn't like that. He's completely bewildered, ashamed of living off me, especially since his sister is here and she's working."

"Once you've hit sixty, my dear, seduction becomes an iffy proposition."

"Oh, isn't life grand!"

"You said it, my dear. Just grand!"

20

Moha

Moha, old Moha, Moha the madman, Moha the wise man,* came down from his tree all bright-eyed and bushy-haired and rushed to Casabarata, to a café where clandestines and *passeurs* make their deals.

With time, "Bargain House," the slum of Casabarata, had become a poor man's flea market that sold everything imaginable, from dilapidated old shoes to television sets. Made-in-China merchandise and counterfeits had gradually taken over. What interested Moha in Casabarata, however, was the men who sat drinking tea and smoking a few pipes of kif.

Moha picked up a newspaper lying on a table, asked the waiter in his deep voice for a cigarette lighter, stared at two men who had apparently smoked themselves into stupefaction, waved the newspaper in the air, and set it on fire.

I, too, am on fire. I burn like this paper that does not tell the truth, that says all is well, that the government is doing everything it can to give work to our young people, and that those who burn up the straits have succumbed to wild despair. And yes, there is good reason to have lost all hope, but life, it goes on and leaves us by the wayside (the wayside of what, go figure, I won't tell you!), that's just life, but which life—the one that crushes us, rips us to pieces? Here, gather up the ashes of the news I just burned: there's lots of it, fake news, like this young woman who writes to the column "Heart to Heart," face to face, my face your face, to ask if she should let her husband kiss her on her labia minora. Another asks if our religion allows a woman to take her husband's penis in her mouth . . . but what *is* this madness? It seems these letters don't exist, that some fellow bursting with imagination writes them and sends them to the paper, so now this left-wing paper is making a fortune—it's just crazy how much people want to know how others manage their sex lives! Okay, I haven't come here to preach: if a woman wants to give herself to her husband, let her do so and not go trumpeting it in the papers. So it seems you want to take off, leave, quit the country, move in with the Europeans, but they're not expecting you, or rather, they *are:* with dogs, German shepherds, handcuffs, a kick in the butt, and you think that there's work over there, comfort, grace and beauty, but my poor friends, there is sadness, loneliness, all shades of gray—and money as well, but not for those who come without an invitation! Right, you know what I'm talking about: how many guys left and wound up drowned? How many left and got sent back? How many dissolved into thin air and we don't even know if they still exist—their families haven't had any news of them, but me, I know where they are: they're here, in my jellaba hood, all piled on top of one another, lying low like thieves, waiting for the light in order to emerge, and that's not a life. Hey you! The fat guy with the cap pulled down over his forehead and eyebrows! You think you're so smart, you pocket the money and send them off to death but they'll gobble you up one day, they'll come find you in your bed to eat out your heart, liver, and balls, you'll see, just ask what happened to Sif, yes, the one who took the name Saber because he handled one as deftly as a revolver: the dead ripped out his throat, yes, hundreds of corpses came looking for him demanding that he settle accounts and when he drew his saber it melted in the glassy glare of the dead and with his back to the wall he was sliced to ribbons by hands as sharp as butcher knives. Leaving, yes: I, too, would like to go away, so listen, I'm going to travel in the opposite direction, I'm going to burn up the desert, I'll cross the Sahara like the wind, swiftly, invisibly, slipping among the dunes, leaving no trace, no scent—Moha will pass by there without anyone seeing him. But where are you going, Moha? I'm heading for Africa, land of our ancestors, vast Africa, where people have time to take a look at life even if life isn't generous to them, where they still take a moment to do selfless things: Africa, cursed by the heavens, Africa pillaged by Blacks wearing ties, by Whites wearing ties, by monkeys in tuxedos, even by people who are sometimes completely invisible, but Africans know this, they don't wait to be told what's going on— I'm talking about Africa because its people have walked days and nights to get here, to Tangier, after hearing that Tangier was already Europe: you can smell Europe, you see Europe and its lights, you touch Europe with your fingertips, and it smells good, it awaits you, just cross eight or nine little miles and you're even closer, or go to Ceuta and you're as good as in Europe, yes, Ceuta and Melilla are European towns, where all you have to do is clamber over a barbed wire barrier—the Guardia Civil can't keep an eye on everything, sometimes they shoot into the crowd, so dying in the frigid waters of the straits or on the asphalt of the border, take your pick, my friends, Africa is here and those guys think Europe has its border in Tangier, in the port, in the Socco Chico, here in this wretched café, and they arrive like quivering shadows, in a state of uncertainty, men drained of all substance, wandering the streets, sleeping in cemeteries, eating cats, yes, so rumor says, I believe it, some gratuitous nastiness, the Africans losing just a bit more of their souls, while we white Arabs (well, let's say brown- or olive- or cinnamon-skinned), we feel superior, stupidly superior, thinking we've found in them men whom we can finally despise, with a racism that needed to get some exercise, although we were already mistreating the poor, but when the poor are Africans with black skin, we lose all control, we feel justified in looking down on them, we act like certain European politicians, looking down on you when in fact they don't even see you. . . . Aha, here's the kingpin, the supercop who doesn't arrest the *passeurs,* you wonder why he leaves them alone, well, that's no mystery, but I'll stop here, not another word, I'll shut up, my lips are sealed, and if you hear words it's because they're coming out on their own, heading for the open sea, escaping, telling the truth—okay, give me a glass of water, little Malika needs me, she's coughing, she's sick, she caught pneumonia from shelling shrimp in the cold, we have to get her some medicines, her parents can't afford them, I'm going to take up a collection, we have to save her, she's a lovely girl who deserves to live, laugh, dance, climb to the mountaintops to talk to the stars. . . .

Leaving! Leaving! Leaving any way at all, at any cost, drowning, floating on the water, belly bloated, face eaten away by the salt, eyes gone . . . Leaving! That's all you've come up with for a solution. Look at the sea: she's beautiful in her sparkling dress, with her subtle perfumes, but the sea swallows you down and then spits you out in tiny bits. . . .

I'm off, Malika is waiting for me.

21

Azel

Carmen was not pleased. Her Miguel was losing his head. This marriage with the sister of that parasite, as she called him, simply infuriated her. She could see that her dear employer was being manipulated, exploited, that he was going along with it and refusing to listen to reason. After seeking advice from Maria, an old gypsy fortuneteller and spellbinder, Carmen came home determined to put an end to this situation. She burned incense and placed cloves in specific places around the house. According to Maria, this setup would take a little time to work; all it took was patience and prayer.

Miguel hated the smell of cloves, which reminded him of going to the dentist. He asked Kenza if she was the one using this perfume, one favored by the peasants of the Atlas Mountains. Dumbfounded, Kenza in turn searched for the source of the odor. She suspected Carmen, who'd been giving her nothing but nasty looks, but she kept her hunch to herself. As Miguel's wife and mistress of the house, Kenza had the advantage, of course, but her first concern was to defuse the situation, so she preferred to do nothing. The house was turning into a theater putting on a very bad play.

Kenza decided to go live in a room at the Red Cross and try to convince her brother to change his ways. Although she was still waiting for her residence and work permits, which would allow her at last to be completely comfortable in Spain, she knew that the real problem was Azel, whom she saw less and less frequently and over whom she had no control. It embarrassed her to speak to her brother about sex; Moroccan families simply didn't talk about such things. She knew what was going on, but how could she put that into words? Before she'd even broached the subject, Azel flew into a screaming rage one day and denied everything.

"Wait a minute, what do you take me for? I'm not a lousy whore, I'm not a beggar, and Miguel is a friend, a prophet sent by God to save a family, he's a generous man, so why are you insinuating that this generosity is corrupted by self-interest? I mean, you don't know a thing about my life, my real life, you pass judgment, you get upset, but do you even know if I'm happy, if I'm doing well, in good spirits, if I feel like blowing my brains out, disappearing, dropping off the face of the earth? Ask yourself all that and stop thinking I'm here only for unspeakable things! You're suspicious of me but you're more concerned about yourself and your reputation than you are about your own survival, and yes, I make an effort to live, to take pleasure in things, I'm neither a hero nor a monster, I'm a man tripped up by his own weaknesses, loving money, the easy life, but I see now that there's a price to pay, and I won't tell you what that is, still less how I'm paying it!

"I could have followed the usual path, found a job after my studies, respectable work, something to bring me prestige, to reassure me and make me want to go far; I might have done wonderful things, an upright man still cherishing his fantasies yet grounded in reality, useful and efficient, but no: I was broken and I'm not the only one, do you understand? There are many of us young people with blocked, rotten futures, nothing on the horizon, getting up each morning to relive the day before, existing in repetition, in the sucking return of the same damn thing, and we're supposed to keep our chins up, resist temptation, spurn a helping hand because it's attached to something else that just happens to be shameful! Going every morning to the same café, seeing the same people, hearing the same commentary on what they saw on TV the night before, hearing two educated men argue over whether the engine of this Mercedes is more reliable than the one in that BMW, whether the price of property in Tangier will go up or down, whether the summer will be muggy, whether Spain will close its borders to *los moros,* drinking the same café au lait and smoking black-market American cigarettes, feeling that time is stagnating, dragging, lazing around, the hours taking unbelievable time to get through the air, and there you are, staring into space, saying whatever comes to mind, faking an interest, feeling like sending everything to kingdom come, kicking over the table, pouring your café au lait onto the white shirt of the know-it-all who never stops talking, so you play cards, dominoes, you forget time, time that's burrowing into us like a leech, draining our energy, but we've got nowhere to use this energy that has us going around in circles, so we talk about women, those who exist and those we invent, we talk about their asses, their breasts, we let off steam, and we're not proud of ourselves, no,

I'm not proud. And on top of everything we have to behave ourselves, stay in line, keep up appearances, but my dear big sister, poverty won't let you stay in line, it roots you to the spot, pins you down on a wobbly chair and you're not allowed to stand up, to go see if the sky is more pleasant somewhere else, no, poverty is a curse and I'm not the only one it's hurting: you're its victim too, you deserve better than this fraud, this white marriage to get papers, to sweep away our hard times, our bitterness, yes, I'm not the only one, go see what's happening in Mexico, that's right, on the Mexican-American border—people sneaking across, it's a risky business, leaving their land to go try their luck in the country where money is king. . . . Everywhere people long to uproot themselves, to leave, as if there were an epidemic and they were fleeing a sickness, yes, poverty is a sickness, look at the African women who sell themselves for a trifle, the Moroccan men who smuggle like morons, and one day when they're nabbed they say the Spaniards are racist, don't like *los moros,* that's it—when you run out of arguments there's always racism, sure, we're *moros* and we're not nice, we've lost our dignity, oh, if you could see, my sister, what goes on in the slums of this city, in the backcountry of this land, you would not believe your eyes! If you saw how they treat *las espaldas mojadas,* 'wetbacks,' that's what they call us, we who've managed to wriggle through the net, and they're right, our shoulders are clearly soaking wet, we've just hauled ourselves out of the water and that salt water doesn't go away, doesn't dry, it clings to our skin and clothes: *las espaldas mojadas,* that's what we are, and before us—long before us—the Italians were called wops, the Spaniards dagos, the Jews yids or whatever, and us, that hasn't changed, we're *los moros,* the wetback Arabs, we lumber out of the sea like ghosts or monsters! And now I'm off!"

That night, Miguel called Kenza.

"I'm worried. Azel can't be found, his phone is dead; I'm afraid something's happened to him."

Kenza tried to reassure Miguel as best she could, but she knew it was useless, that her brother would not put up with the situation anymore. Kenza was truly worried; Azel was perfectly capable of entangling himself in dangerous schemes merely to prove that he was still his own man. She knew he'd been hanging out lately with some Moroccan riffraff who lived off petty trafficking. Even if he didn't like their lifestyle, he often joined them, slipping into their company as if he needed to return for a moment to the wretched life he'd left behind. Among them was a certain Abbas—no papers, no known domicile, no job—who boasted of screwing everyone: the Guardia Civil, the security forces, the immigration authorities, the informers, the undercover cops, the Moroccan consulate, Socialist and non-Socialist Spain. . . .

Kenza had been meaning to speak to Miguel about an offer from Carlos, one of his friends whom she'd met at his house; Carlos had invited her to come dance in his restaurant a few evenings every week, to earn a little money. After a pause, she brought up Carlos and his offer.

"But that's a fine idea, my dear, especially since it's a very popular restaurant, not a nightclub. Do it, I'll be in the first row, you dance *divinely* well."

22

Abbas

Abbas had an endless supply of bones to pick with Spain. Short, swarthy, with lively eyes often bloodshot from everything he was on, he had arrived in this country as a teenager, hiding in a truck full of merchandise. He had almost smothered during the trip. He was rather proud of that, actually, but above all he harbored an unhealthy grudge against Spain, which had expelled him that first time, then arrested him and turned him over to the Moroccan authorities when he was caught trying to sneak into Spain again.

"I know them, the Spanioolies: poor people who got rich and forgot they were ever poor. My father told me the Spanioolies used to come to our country like raggedy beggars, sweeping streets, cutting hair, driving our buses—they were worse off than we were, and although we had nothing, at least this was our home, but they acted as if they were above us, can you imagine! Spania, the land of patched pants, frayed collars, smelly eau de toilette, well, in Morocco they were living like kings, thought themselves our betters; my father said that when Morocco became independent they practically wet themselves, thinking we'd do them like in Algeria: in our village they were so scared they all piled into the church! It was only then that they realized we were really good people, who wouldn't massacre them. Years later, wanting to return the favor—meaning visiting them at home—I turned up at the consulate, stood on line in the sun for hours, filled out forms so nosy you'd have thought I was a wanted criminal, and guess what, after all that—*walou, nada,* no visa, no come-visit-us. So at that, I got fed up, I swore I'd get into their country without a single document, anonymous, like Superman; I wasn't going to parachute in, but I had my little brainstorm: I thought, Europe has spoiled them, showered them with dough, they've even gone democratic, and that—that's thanks to Juan Carlos, I like that king guy, I'm sure that if I appeal directly to him, I won't have any problems, he's the one who put democracy into the heads of the Spanioolies, he's clever, plus there's that P.M., Felipe, I even served him a mint tea when I was working at the Café de Paris, yes, I was the official shoeshine boy, I had my box of waxes, my blue smock, but one day there were no more leather shoes, and no more job, so I changed uniforms and became a waiter—not bad—and then I took the boat, without paying for the crossing, sidling aboard as if I were a sailor, so we got to Algeciras and they welcomed me with guns—hands up and all that jazz, unbeliev-able, I'd become important! When I said, 'Calm down, I have no weapons, no papers, not even any money to soften you up,' they handed me over to the ship's captain, a sonofabitch who locked me up and forgot me in the hold for three days and nights with one bottle of tap water, not even store-bought, the cheapskate—I was screaming, kicking and pounding on the door, famished, reduced to the condition of a hunted animal by that bastard, and when I saw him again he said, 'No, I didn't forget you, I let you stew in your own juice so you'll never ever dream of Spain again' (he couldn't have been one hundred percent Spanioolie, he must have had some Arab blood: there was definitely something of us about him, because his face wasn't white, he looked like General Oufkir,* but anyway, to be that mean he had to have been uneasy in his own skin, so perhaps he hated his face, that's why he was taking revenge, keeping me prisoner). One night, while the boat was still in port in Algeciras, a sailor set me free: 'Beat it and good luck.' So now that I'm here I'm staying put. I know them, those Spanioolies, they just can't get over the golden age the Arabs had in Andalusia, sticks in their craw: the *moros* occupied the south of our country? Impossible! *Los moros, los judíos,* Moors and Jews, everybody out, or we burn them! I don't mean that today we're reinvading, but they don't like to see us prowling around their borders again, it's a knee-jerk reaction with them: soon as they see a *moro,* they get their backs up, they see *una mala pata, una cosa negra,* they're superstitious, it's in their interest to watch out because we're inconvenient and I know what I'm talking about, the Spanioolies are distrustful but still quite naïve, you see: all those Muslims moving in, for sure they must intend to reconquer what their ancestors lost—now personally I think that's pushing it, there's nothing to reconquer, but there are some tape cassettes going around that talk about that, so I'm not convinced things won't blow up some day, since the country's moving fast, Europe's pulling it north, away from us, and although we used to think we were close, I mean that we were neighbors, only eight and a half

miles, eight and a half little miles, eight and a half miserable miles
between us, in truth there are thousands of miles between them
and us, when for them Moroccan means Muslim and they remember what the Church said about Muslims (not so hot, you've
got to admit), so—we're Muslims, poor, no papers, therefore
dangerous, and it's no good us telling them that more and more
Christians are converting to Islam: every day, their fear grows. . . .
I know them, I know what they think and I understand them,
we're a fat lot of use, you can see all those jobless guys roaming
around train and bus stations, the public squares, who've turned
the Barrio Chino into a souk and the Barrio Gótico into a filthy
medina: they have nothing to do, they wait, take on odd jobs, I'm
one of them, by the way, but me, I'm craftier, I slip through the
net and when I feel the net coming I vamoose, go sleep in the
mosque and—poof!—disappear. . . . Got to keep on your toes. I
don't fancy going home sweet home, not at all; I do little things,
I eat well, drink well, smoke a bit, and life's great, really great!
Right, Azz El Arab? Didn't you find your happiness here? You
look uptight, what's the matter? Don't like screwing the old guy?
But he loads you with dough, you should be pleased; I tried it but
wound up with a tightwad and lost my hard-on on the spot, left
him with his ass in the air, swiped his watch, a real Rolex, gold
and silver, then sold it to an Arab just passing through and lived
off that for two months, and the old tightwad didn't dare come
anywhere near my neighborhood after that—he was in politics,
afraid for his rep plus he's married with a couple kids. . . . You
know, you shouldn't get pissed off—take life as it comes, find
your niche in this country and forge ahead, forget about regrets

and remorse, be like me: I steal, traffic, nothing serious, I'm not selling drugs at the schoolyard gates, no, there, that's disgusting; what I've got is cell phones with fiddled SIM cards, the kids can call for free, not bad, hey? It works for a while, then the phone breaks down and I'm there to replace it, plus I sell cards to access all the TV channels on earth, so for a song you've got the whole world within reach, just with a cable box, no need to subscribe and pay through the nose anymore, no, thanks to pirated cards I live quite well. Mind you, the guy doing the work, it's not me, I can't find the codes on the Internet, no, it's a Pakistani, a champion pirate, who does that for me, he says it's our revenge, because we're not dumber than they are, being poor doesn't mean being stupid! I like him, he's quiet, a hard worker, and when I remember my former life, I don't have a problem with being here, even if it isn't paradise; back home people should stop going on and on about garbage like: Spain is a dreamland, an earthly paradise, easy money, girls for the taking, social security, blah blah, but I think deep down they know the truth, they watch TV, they can see how we're treated here, they know it's not heaven, but I mean, what is? Where's heaven on earth? Do you know? Well, I do: heaven is when I find myself alone in my bed smoking a joint and thinking about what would have happened to me if I'd never left home, and then I have a drink or two and let myself drift off, happy and at peace. I don't ask for too much, I sleep and have lots of dreams in living color, in Arabic and Spanish, with rainbowy fish dancing in my head to music played by the loveliest woman in the world, my mother."

———

While Abbas had been making his speech, a man sitting on a mat at the back of the tiny shop had coughed a few times. Azel asked who he was.

"It's Hamou, a guy who burned the straits partly by boat and partly by swimming. He caught pneumonia or something like that; he coughs, spits up awful stuff, he needs a doctor who won't turn him in to the police. Your friend, he must be able to arrange that, no?"

Azel did not want Miguel mixed up in this business.

"I could get some money together to buy him medicine. . . ."

"No, forget it, I think the Brothers will take care of it. They like to help out in situations like this."

Azel realized that the Brothers were Islamists. He didn't say anything, but Abbas noticed the face he made.

"Okay, I know the Brothers don't do anything for free, they'll be back to call in the favor; I didn't want to ask them for help up to now, that's why I mentioned your friend, but if it's impossible, I'm going to have to accept their offer. They've got doctors, lawyers, people of means, they're well organized—I had no idea that Muslims could be that organized."

"You're really racist!"

"You can't be racist against your own side; that's not racism, that's facing reality. I'm not educated, I make my own way, and the school of life taught me plenty, for example: if you want to get ahead, you have to put up with hearing some not too pleasant things about your own community. Now, I'll say such things to you, but with the Spanioolies, I'm more Arab than Qaddafi."

"Because you think Qaddafi is a good point of reference?"

"No, I think he hurts us, but he's one of us."

"No, he isn't. You know he's a millionaire—in dollars?"

"So? I'm a pauper in euros!"

Abbas laughed and clapped Azel on the back.

"You, you went to school!"

"Yes, but it didn't do me any good."

"Frankly, I talk big, but, well, you know sometimes I just cry all alone in my little room, yes, I sometimes sob over my life, the situation I'm in; I miss my mother terribly, I talk to her on the phone, but I can't go see her, I haven't a single document anymore, no Moroccan passport, no national identification card, no residence permit, so if I leave here, it'll be in handcuffs with someone's foot halfway up my ass. You think that's a life? I'm the all-around champ of illegal alienation: I make myself as black as night to be invisible, as gray as dawn and fog to pass unnoticed, I avoid deserted places, I'm ready to run away any second, and I've memorized all the entrances to the local churches so's I can hop in a flash into the arms of the priest—that way they can't get at me, and it's already happened once, one Christmas when they gave up the hunt and I spent the holidays with the priests. Now, they live *well*, I even said some prayers, I make the best of things, always, a real expert at fitting in! They wanted me to work with them, the idea being that I'd turn Christian, but that, never: I'm not a good Muslim, I drink, don't always do the right thing, I don't pray, but change religions for selfish reasons, no way, I've got principles, after all."

Azel bought him a drink, and told him he thought the two of them could work quite well together.

Abbas didn't take Azel seriously. He liked him, but thought of him as someone who already had it made.

Azel envied the way Abbas could talk about his life, his problems, confiding in others, which Azel didn't dare do. The cell phones in the shop were mostly contraband goods, and Azel found something attractive about this place where everything was risky and illegal. The shop belonged to a Moroccan wanted for hashish trafficking, and Abbas was running it until the other man's return. As for the police, they let things ride, hoping to pick up information that would lead them to the fugitive. To keep his head above water, Abbas had a few things going on his own and had even managed to bribe a few snitches, who protected him. Even though he really had no reason to be there, Azel still liked to hang around the shop, especially when he was depressed. When he felt low, he wouldn't take care of himself, stopped shaving, and smoked too much.

23

Nâzim

His parents had named him Nâzim in honor of the Turkish poet Nâzim Hikmet.* Tall, dark, with limpid eyes and a thick mustache, he worked as a waiter in the Restaurant Kebab, an "Oriental" establishment owned by a distant Kurdish cousin who'd come to Barcelona ten years earlier. Nâzim had left his country under uncertain circumstances for what he described as either family or political reasons, depending on his mood. He was covering his tracks.

Kenza sometimes ate at the Kebab with her girlfriends from the Red Cross, who were soon teasing her for falling under the spell of Nâzim's smile and handsome eyes, but Kenza just laughed.

Leaving the Red Cross one evening, she ran into Nâzim, who claimed to be just passing by. He invited her for coffee; she declined, since she was on her way to dance at Carlos's restaurant. Nâzim was persistent, so she promised she'd return to see him soon at the Kebab, where they could make plans to go out.

He followed her. When he saw her enter the restaurant, he became convinced that someone was waiting for her. Pushing open the door, he pretended to be looking for a friend whom he'd agreed to meet there. The waiter seated him at a small table in the back.

"While you're waiting," he said, "enjoy the show! We are featuring Estrella, the loveliest dancer in the Orient."

Twenty minutes later, Kenza appeared, wearing makeup and veils of different colors. She danced with subtlety and grace. The customers applauded, some of them tucking paper money into her belt. She, regal in her beauty, was wholly absorbed in the music and her dance, concentrating on making each part of her body move as delicately as possible. She had a matchless way of making her shoulders and hips quiver together without taking a step: standing there, she was still dancing, as if her whole body were trembling. Nâzim could hardly recognize her. The performance lasted a good quarter of an hour. She was followed by an Asian dancer, and Nâzim took advantage of the changeover to slip away.

When Kenza showed up later that evening, Miguel greeted her with open arms and a big hug. He was glad to see her and hoped especially to be able to speak to her again regarding Azel, about whom he was growing increasingly concerned.

"I'm ever so sorry, I wanted to come see you dance but I was on the phone to New York for the longest time. Well, here you are at last, and I'm truly pleased to see you. Would you like to freshen up, take a shower? After all, here you are at home!"

They ate in the living room, alone. For the first time in her life, Kenza had a glass of wine, a 1995 Rioja. Quite a good year, Miguel told her, and began to talk about his passion for fine wines, explaining to her the virtues of this gift from nature. Kenza listened eagerly, fascinated by his expertise and especially by the way in which this sophisticated man talked about something she still associated closely with sin and debauchery.

"If I've never touched wine," she told him, "it's because back home, when men drink they always overdo it and don't know how to stop, drinking until they lose their balance and their reason. In our country, we don't sip, we don't drink, we get drunk."

Actually, she didn't know what to make of that glass of Rioja. It had left a strange taste in her mouth, and she would gladly have drunk a second glass. She was feeling lighthearted, happy, and was sorry that Miguel was sitting there so worried about her brother's behavior.

Miguel suddenly remembered that he was a Muslim.

"You know, you're going to tell me I'm a bad Muslim because I drink wine, but listen: I've looked into this thoroughly, and there are contradictory interpretations on certain verses regarding wine. I think that Islam does not accept drunkenness, because the person loses human dignity and doesn't know what's going on, particularly at the prescribed moment of prayer. There, all religions are in agreement: You do not address God when you are not in control of yourself, that's obvious. I drink for pleasure, not to lose my balance, as you put it."

"Have you noticed that the same men who get drunk refuse to eat pork? They reject it, even though ham isn't dangerous to either their balance or their dignity. Strange, isn't it?"

"Ah, but if you overindulge in ham, you'll wind up with a cholesterol problem, although I doubt that's the real reason why

Muslims who drink alcohol don't eat pork. Azel even claims to be allergic to that meat. That's so hypocritical!"

After dinner, Miguel took Kenza back to her place, telling her along the way about the problems he was having with Azel and the gallery in Madrid. He'd just learned that in spite of his salary and the reimbursement of all his expenses, Azel was stealing from the till.

"Azel thinks I'm Jean Genet, you know—that French writer who used to come often to Tangier, a rebel, a great poet, a homosexual who had served time in prison for theft; he loved to be robbed by his lovers, a betrayal he found reassuring or exciting, it all depended. It's curious—even though I'm sure Azel hasn't read Genet, he must think he's pleasing me by acting like street trash."

Kenza was shocked to hear Miguel call her brother trash, although she certainly knew how badly Azel was willing to behave, doing just as he pleased and disappointing everyone. Later, she tried without success to get in touch with him. That same evening, she received a call from their mother, who was also worried. Lalla Zohra had heard on the radio that the Spanish police had arrested some Moroccans suspected of belonging to terrorist organizations. When Kenza expressed astonishment that her mother would see any possible connection between Azel and those men, Lalla Zohra quickly insisted that her son could never be involved in anything like that! Now Kenza really wanted to find out exactly what was going on, but Azel was not to be found.

It was a long, sleepless night. Ugly, distressing images swarmed relentlessly through Kenza's brain. Blood on a white shirt, shattered heads, severed hands, police everywhere, words in Arabic, in Spanish, anonymous faces moving through the night, Azel looking imploringly at an executioner, a snuffling voice reading verses of the Koran, a black cat leaping onto the bodies of abandoned children, shadows burrowing into walls, and desperate anxiety everywhere.

Sleep was impossible. She showered, dressed, and went out to walk in the streets.

Barcelona at the approach of dawn is a city that softens its sharp edges, becoming gentle, as generous as a dream in which all is well. The avenues are spotless. The houses are veiled in mist, which shrouds a few lights in the awakening city. Shaking off the robe of night, Barcelona welcomes the first passersby; kiosks set out their displays, bistros arrange their tables on the sidewalks, the aromas of coffee and toast fill the air. The city wreathes itself slowly in the first glimmers of daylight. Filled with a quiet feeling of happiness, Kenza gave no more thought to her nightmares, and suddenly, in her mind's eye, she saw Nâzim. She saw him in the crowd. She smiled, the way people do in those American films where a man and woman who've just met play out a fine romance, the kind that exists only in the movies. Kenza felt so buoyant that she was even convinced a camera had been filming her from the moment she'd stepped out her front door. A voice was telling her, "After all, you're happy in this city, you were right to take your fate into your own hands and leave Tangier, your family, that burdensome daily routine; you're beautiful, available, and lucky to have met Miguel, a gentleman, so whatever you do, don't stop now, keep going! You're at peace with yourself, you're not responsible for your brother or guilty of whatever foolish mistake he might commit. Kenza, I'm talking to you, I'm the other Kenza, the one who has always pushed you to go straight ahead, to struggle, to resist giving up, the one who made you a liberated girl, so don't listen too much to your mother, she'll swallow you. Pay attention to yourself, to your life, don't get caught in the grip of fate; look up and watch the migrating birds meeting overhead in this patch of Barcelona sky: observe how they follow the rhythm of the ballet they're performing this morning just for you, before your eyes so thirsty for light. Life is beautiful in spite of the many idiots who create and spread disaster; you are safe, out of reach. Run, live, laugh. . . ."

Kenza sat down at a café table and ordered coffee with melba toast. A moment of pleasure, a moment of lovely solitude. Then the sounds of the city began, and soon the usual hustle and bustle had claimed their morning hour. It was time to think about getting to work at the Red Cross.

That evening, she invited her girlfriends to dinner at the Kebab. She looked around for Nâzim. He wasn't there; perhaps it was his day off. In fact, he was hiding, because he'd learned that employment inspectors would be coming by. When Kenza left, she wrote him a note: "We're three women looking for you . . . and without you, the Kebab's not so hot!"

In a little while, realizing that what she'd written had been rather forward, Kenza decided to go back to tear up her note, but after one last hesitation, she resolved to let things take their course. Later, on her way to Carlos's restaurant, she heard footsteps coming up behind her: it was Nâzim, and as soon as he'd caught his breath, he apologized in impeccable lycée French for missing her at the restaurant.

"Just one drink, a little drink or some herbal tea before you go home. . . ."

He pleaded with her, but she couldn't accept, still less tell him she was going off to dance in a chic restaurant.

"Tomorrow; I'm too tired tonight. Nine o'clock at the Kebab, I promise."

While she was adjusting the costume for her dance, she felt a touch of stage fright and thought of Nâzim. Then she went on-stage, threading her way among the tables like an angel sent by the stars. The Egyptian music was perfect. She closed her eyes and followed the beat, imagining that she was at a wedding back home. The audience applauded warmly, especially at the moment when her whole body quivered delicately. She bowed, tossed her veils toward her admirers, and left the stage. She dressed quickly in the wings, autographed a piece of paper handed to her by one of the waiters, and went out into the night.

The next day she was late for her rendezvous at the Kebab. Nâzim was waiting for her with a smile.

"Listen to what Nâzim Hikmet wrote about this country," he said the moment she arrived.

Spain is a bloodstained rose blooming at our breast.
Spain, our friendship in the twilight of death,
Spain, our friendship in the light of our indomitable hope.
And the ancient olive trees, shattered, and the yellow earth and the red earth
*   pierced through and through.*

"He's talking about Spain in 1939. Nothing to do with the wonderful democracy of today. People have changed, acquired a more modern way of thinking. Only one problem remains: certain Spaniards aren't very fond of *los moros*. And on that point I'm unbeatable—here I'm often mistaken for a *moro* myself. When I explain that I'm Turkish, all they can think to say is that the Turks sure must be experts on *los moros*. One day I quoted our great poet to an Andalusian landowner I'd met on a train:

> *"I have a tree inside me,*
> *A sapling I brought back from the sun;*
> *Fish of fire, its leaves sway gently,*
> *Its fruits warble away like birds.*

"The man looked at me, laughed, and repeated, 'Its fruits warble away . . .' Then he held out his hand and said, 'You, you're no *moro!*' To him, that was a compliment."

"I can never understand this hatred of Arabs."

As Kenza listened to Nâzim, hanging on his every word, she felt her fatigue melt away. She no longer wanted to go home. The night was mild; they took a walk, holding hands. He spoke to her about the Moorish reign in Andalusia, that time when Muslims and Jews composed music and poetry together in lovely symbiosis.

24

Kenza and Nâzim

The Kebab was closed on Mondays. Kenza asked her supervisor for the day off and went to meet Nâzim at the train station café. They had decided to spend the day together in a small village a half hour from Barcelona. To get acquainted, talk without being rushed, and enjoy a kind of holiday mood. Nâzim was charming and elegant. Having arrived early, he observed the travelers; strangely enough, they all seemed alike in a curious way: they dashed about, bumped into one another, and seemed distracted. Luckily, an African family had just gotten off the train, and their colorful presence brought to the gray drabness of the station a breath of desert wind, an air of gaiety, a music that made one long to dance. While he was waiting, Nâzim went over to these happy visitors, so delighted to be there. They were from Mali, by way of Morocco, and they were not immigrants, not invaders, as the father of the family told Nâzim.

"Allow me to present myself: I am Professor Mohammed Touré, osteopath, invited here by the dean of the medical school in Barcelona to give a series of lectures. My wife is a pediatrician, and she has come to see the Red Cross organization about a program it's developing for Western Africa. Our children often accompany us in our moves. Two months ago, we were all in Princeton, it was most interesting. The only problem was that everyone spoke English, a language I understand but do not speak, whereas I studied Castilian Spanish a long time ago in school. And you, what do you do?"

As Nâzim introduced himself, he caught sight of Kenza looking around for him. Monsieur Touré gave him his card, saying, "If you ever visit Mali, call me, whether or not you need an osteopath!" The family's bright colors vanished from the main concourse of the station. And Kenza had disappeared. The crowd seemed even more dense and gray than before—at least that's how Nâzim now saw the world. Was he seeing things, or simply dismayed and disappointed? Yet he was sure he'd glimpsed Kenza only a moment earlier and hurried anxiously this way and that, no longer seeing anything. Returning to the café, he ordered some sparkling water.

Kenza appeared abruptly in a flowered dress, as if popping from a magician's box. Leaning over Nâzim, she murmured, "Let's not waste any time."

They sat face to face in the train, looking at each other, saying nothing. She thought he seemed nervous, and wondered why. Perhaps he'd been shocked by her boldness. . . . When he looked at her, she felt a strange sweetness steal over her. He had beautiful hands, large yet graceful. She studied his full lips and imagined herself biting them. She laughed. He asked her why. "Ah, my friend, if only you knew!" He couldn't guess what she'd meant and did not dare look at her shapely bosom, her laughing brown eyes, her long, thick tresses, her legs, her mouth.

Since arriving in Spain, Nâzim had gone out with only two women. The first was a compatriot who thought she had found in him a husband and a father for the child she was raising on her own. Their relationship had been brief and stormy. The second woman was Cuban, an office worker who had left her country after falling in love with a Spanish professor who'd come to lecture at the University of Havana. When her visa had expired, she'd refused to go back home and had become an illegal alien like thousands of immigrants from Morocco and Latin America. The bond between her and Nâzim had been purely sexual, and after a few months they had parted without rancor. Ever since, Nâzim had been looking for a woman more familiar with his culture. He needed to hear the Turkish language, or at least Arabic, and he wanted to thrill to the music of his country, to share thoughts and feelings. Kenza was everything he wanted. Although she looked like a Southern European, she was an Arab, unattached, beautiful, and above all a legal resident of Spain. Secretly, Nâzim hoped to take advantage of Kenza's status to straighten out his own situation. He was tired of living underground. He was careful not to mention all that, however, not wanting to seem like a selfish and crass opportunist.

At the small station in Sabadell, the police were checking identity papers, systematically stopping gypsies, black Africans, and North African Arabs. Taking her companion's arm, Kenza advanced confidently. Nâzim was frightened for a moment, but seeing how sure of herself Kenza was, he squeezed her hand tightly, as if in thanks.

They kissed on the sidewalk. Nâzim was embarrassed, Kenza not at all. She was the one who pulled him close to press her lips to his. Moved and pleased, he blushed like an adolescent. He suggested that they go have a café au lait, but she refused: what she liked was iced Viennese coffee.

Then Kenza decided to take the lead. A liberated—and determined—woman, she rose and told him, "Follow me, we're going to spend the day at the Bristol, a charming small hotel, you'll see."

It had been more than a year since she'd touched a man's skin. She undressed Nâzim and licked his body while smelling it as if it were a flower, sniffing, caressing, sucking. He let her do as she pleased, and wondered when he should reassert himself. When he did get on top of her, she pulled him toward her with all her strength, saying, "Crush me, I want to feel your whole weight on me—I don't want to lose anything of your body: I want it inside me, deeply, completely."

They made love as if famished for it. She spoke to him in the Arab dialect of Tangier, and he answered her in Turkish. The sounds of their native tongues aroused them. Going into the bathroom, Kenza sang as she danced a few steps; Nâzim had seen her extraordinary skill as a dancer, which lent an erotic note to her slightest movement, and she picked that moment to confess to him that twice a week she performed at a restaurant called L'Huile d'Olive. He would have liked to tell her that he'd already seen her dance, but preferred not to have to explain how and why.

On the trip home they barely spoke, wrapped in a fine fatigue and completely absorbed in their sense of each other.

25

Azel

The slap knocked Azel down and left him stunned. He had never imagined that one day Miguel would hit him. It even took him a moment or two to realize what was happening. When he stood up, Carmen brought him his suitcase and pointed to the door. She had warned Miguel many times about the way his protégé sometimes behaved, but until now her employer had always smiled and gestured helplessly. That was back when he was still in love.

Azel understood that this time he could not talk his way out of trouble. He had gone too far, had broken his word, and was only getting what he deserved. So he headed for the door without protest, mumbling that he would return for his suitcase. Carmen held out her hand for his house keys. Azel hesitated for an instant before fumbling through his pockets; pulling out a set of keys, he placed them on the table in the front hall. There was suddenly something pathetic about the look in his eyes, but Carmen nodded and turned on her heel as though he were already gone. Miguel had retreated to his room; he was about to go to Madrid to prepare an important exhibition of works by a great hyperrealist painter, Claudio Bravo, the artist's first show in his native Spain in fifteen years, but Miguel was waiting for Azel to be out of the house before he left on his trip. He did not like confrontations, and had left Carmen in charge of such proceedings several times before. Miguel justified his cowardice by convincing himself that a new argument with his lover wouldn't change anything. Their last fight had almost turned nasty. When thwarted, Miguel became vulgar and mean; in such moments, his Barcelona streettough side—which he detested and repressed—would abruptly reemerge. He was then capable of striking his antagonist with the first sharp object he could lay hands on. And Azel's behavior was exactly the sort to provoke him to such violence.

Azel had been growing increasingly lost, shutting himself up in an imaginary world, believing in fate and premonitory dreams, being guided by what he called "the fragrance of the perfume of death." He had become a true professional liar, an actor who knew how to turn the most hopeless situation to his advantage. He counted on his long eyelashes and his dark, laughing eyes. His mother had always told him that he was the handsomest boy in Tangier; he was finally taking her at her word, and acting accordingly.

Azel lit a cigarette. Setting out for Barcelona's main drag, Las Ramblas, he knew that he was leaving the residential neighborhood of Eixample forever. The sky was flooded with sublime light, but Azel's heart was bruised, in the grip of an alien hand. He had tears in his eyes and his mouth was dry, with a bitter taste. He told himself it was because of the cigarette, and the lousy wine he'd drunk the night before. He walked along, head down.

No desire to talk, to think. And yet he loved Passeig de Gracia, that wide avenue along which you could walk forever. This morning, however, nothing was as usual, and the people he passed looked like shadows, transparent bodies auguring some imminent misfortune. He felt as if he were running full tilt down a dangerous hill. Now and then he would stop for a moment and lean back against a tree. All of a sudden, the sounds of the city were coming to him amplified, clanging in his head with the force of a nightmare.

At the end of Las Ramblas begins the Barrio Gótico, the medieval labyrinth at the center of old Barcelona; there Azel recognized a few faces, Moroccans, small-time dealers or young layabouts who spent their days wandering the streets in search of fresh schemes or adventures. Azel didn't want to chat with them this morning; he even felt disconnected from their language, their ways, their world. He pitied them. He stepped up his pace to avoid any chance someone would approach him with something to sell or exchange for a bit of kif.

He drank some coffee without sugar, spat on the ground, and cursed the day he'd first set foot in this country. A feral cat dashed across the street. Azel envied its freedom.

Dirty, unshaven, with dark circles under his eyes, Azel rang Kenza's doorbell. She'd been sleeping soundly, to rest up after her nights on duty, and refused to let him in, asking him to come back later. He began pounding on the door. Nâzim, who'd spent the night there, got up to put a stop to that racket. When he opened the door, he caught a punch on the chin.

"What's he doing here, this kike? Unless he's one of those *khoro-tos*, those third-world guys who prey on respectable girls. . . ."

Wearing hardly anything at all, Kenza asked Nâzim to move out of the way: this business did not concern him. Then she screamed out her anger at Azel.

"He's not a kike or a *khoroto* either! This man has a first name, a family name, a country, and a job—imagine that!"

"Oh really? Then why didn't you tell me anything about him? Where's he come from?"

"His name's Nâzim, he's Turkish."

"That's just what I said, he's a *khoroto*!"

"Don't use language like that with me. I forbid you! You're such a disappointment, Azel, nothing works with you, you ruin everything."

"Fine, but I won't put up with him touching you."

"Who do you think you are, to *put up* or *not* with *anything*? I don't care what you think! Just look at yourself! You're a complete mess!"

"I don't like Turks. I don't like their language, I don't like their loukoum candy, I don't like the way they look at people."

"You're a racist!"

"So what? I have the right not to like Turks, or Greeks either. . . . Men, those who touch you, anyway—I can't bear it that you belong to them. . . ."

"Maybe you'd like to add Arabs, Jews, and Africans to the list?"

"Arabs? I could never stand them. I'm an Arab who doesn't like himself. There. At least things are clear. All right, fine, I'm out of here: you're going bad, you're turning into a whore, and you're hurting our mother."

"That's it, drag in our mother! I can think of one mother who'd be crushed if she could see what's become of her beloved son."

"It's all your fault! We could have stayed together, like the fingers of a single hand, but you, you worked up this scheme to leave the country and our family and now you're going to the dogs! A Turk fucking my sister—how do you expect me to stand that!"

Azel slammed the door and ran off. He was crying. He stopped at a bar and downed shot after shot of whiskey. Once he was drunk, he took a taxi back to Miguel's house.

He vomited on the carpet in the front hall. Carmen put his suitcase out on the sidewalk and ordered him never to come back. The shock restored a sudden lucidity to Azel, who saw the situation with clarity and precision. He knew it was the end. He realized that this was the last time he would ever cross that threshold. Then he felt something like a great relief: he was free at last to go smoke kif, drink cheap wine, hang out in the streets, and see his pals again, with whom he shared the same sense of despair. It took him a long while to walk to the Barrio, where his friend Abbas was the local big shot.

"I'm free, I'm finally free!" he shouted as soon as he spotted him. "I don't have to fuck some guy to make a decent living!"

26

Malika

Malika dreaded the night. That was when she coughed the most. Sometimes she coughed so much she almost choked, and the struggle to clear phlegm from her lungs brought tears to her eyes. She swallowed spoonfuls of honey; she loved the way it soothed her throat for a moment, but as soon as she lay down again, the cough returned like a nervous tic. Her sister's husband complained that her coughing fits woke him up. It was her sister who finally took Malika to the Hôpital Kortobi, barely a minute's walk from the house. If they'd had fifty dirhams to slip to the male nurse, they could have seen the general practitioner sooner, but as it was they had to wait all morning. The doctor was a young man who seemed overwhelmed by his work. Too many patients, not enough resources. Like everyone else, the doctor dreamed of moving downtown to find a better life. Perhaps he would work in a private clinic, or even in a hospital in Oslo, for example. Norway had a shortage of doctors and had recently recruited a few North African Arabs who weren't afraid of frigid weather. For the moment, though, the doctor had to complete his national health service in this public hospital built more than forty years earlier, right after independence. Everything in it was falling apart: walls, rooms, employees, interns, stray cats and dogs. Only the trees had grown and appeared to be in excellent health.

The doctor had barely taken one look at Malika when he exclaimed, "Another victim of those shrimp!"

It was the poor people of the city who came to this hospital, and of course it was their children who worked in the shrimp factory. Malika was sobbing with fear. The doctor promised he wouldn't hurt her, but it wasn't the examination that frightened her, it was dying—leaving without realizing her dream, leaving without ever having left the country, leaving to be buried in a hole in the cold, cold ground. Malika was afraid because she had seen in the doctor's eyes how sick she was, how upset he'd been by her condition, because in spite of his stressful work, this doctor was still a kind person at heart. He was truly angry that he could not help this child. All the same, he sent her for an X-ray, studied it, then phoned another doctor with whom he spoke in quite technical terms. Malika heard the word "pneumonia" repeatedly during the discussion.

The doctor decided to admit Malika, who was put in a room with other patients. He gave a prescription to Malika's sister, explaining to her that the drugs were powerful, but unfortunately, rather expensive. "I'll manage," she replied. She'd just realized that Malika was gravely ill. Learning in the pharmacy that the medicine would cost over a thousand dirhams, she immediately pulled off one of her gold bracelets and ran to sell it to Hassan, the jeweler on the rue Siaghine. Besides the medicine, she bought some nougat, which her little sister adored. Back in the hospital room, the male nurse, named Bargach, hinted that he might be able to take good care of Malika, so her sister gave him a hundred dirhams. He then advised her above all not to leave the bag of medicines sitting on the bedside table.

"Here they steal everything," he warned her. "It's better to bring her each day's pills and keep the rest at home. What she's taking are antibiotics imported from France, they're costly, so they're much sought after by hospital employees. Don't worry, I'll keep an eye on things, and the child will be cured—*Insha'Allah,* God willing—and bloom like a flower, because the antibiotics, they're very strong and very expensive, and the more expensive they are the better they work, that's normal, right? Aspirin, for example, doesn't cost much and, well, it cures hardly anything. I'll also give her a double serving of soup. She's okay, this little girl, I'll watch over her, you can go home without worrying; the doctor's a good man, he'll take fine care of her."

Malika didn't know how to dry her tears—it was fear welling up in her eyes and coursing down her cheeks. She looked around: everyone was suffering, in silence. When a doctor went by, heads would abruptly shoot up in a single instant and call for help.

Malika was coughing less but could not manage to fall asleep. She kept her eyes open and was convinced that death was stalking her out in the corridor or had perhaps even entered the room already to find a candidate for the great departure. Malika held her nose; the smell of death was now everywhere. Yes, she thought, death has a smell: bitter, pernicious, something between the odors of pus and mold, a summer smell smothered by the dankness of winter, a smell with a color, a kind of pale yellow turning gray, a smell that weighs on the body. Now Malika suspected that death had carried off the old woman in the neighboring bed. She wasn't breathing. No matter how closely Malika studied her chest, nothing moved anymore. She really was dead. Malika reached over to touch the old lady's forehead; it was cold, and her mouth was hanging open. Then Malika cried out. Some male nurses arrived with a stretcher, in no hurry, used to the fact that when someone cried out suddenly in the night, it was because a person had just died. Making noise and joking around as if they were carrying away some damaged merchandise, the two stretcher bearers went off to the morgue. Malika was shivering. Death had touched her with its icy breath, and she imagined that poor woman lying in the refrigerated room. "Now that she's on the other side, at least she won't feel the cold anymore. And tomorrow her family will finally be here, gathered around her in tears." How could anyone sleep, with death on the prowl? Malika still felt its presence, betrayed by that tell-tale odor. She began to drift. . . . *If only I were in France, I wouldn't be in a hospital—simply because I wouldn't be sick, because I wouldn't have been working in a freezing factory, I wouldn't have caught this lung disease, I wouldn't be enduring this nauseating stink of death that's keeping me from closing my eyes . . . which might make death think I'd stopped breathing and sweep me away as well! Death sometimes makes mistakes, awful ones, but death won't get me, not here or anywhere else. I should have left, I should have held on to Azel's hand and never let go, he's handsome and so nice, he would never have abandoned me. Oh, Azel, where are you now? Why aren't you coming to take me away across the water? I should have agreed to get into that car full of sleeping children, but I didn't want to distress my parents, they would have looked for me everywhere; my mother would have gone mad, so I refused, and yet it was easy: the man had a passport with photos of six children, he was leaving at night, and the children were sleeping, so after a glance into the backseat the customs officer would stamp the passport. I was told that story, several times. The man came from northern Italy. He would take the children to another Moroccan, who'd put them to work in the street. They'd promised me that I'd be working for a family while I continued going to school. I was tempted: learning Italian, seeing some of the world, but I could not leave my parents, I didn't even mention that plan to them, why worry them?—especially my mother, but I'm sorry now, I should have gone off on the adventure. . . . My mother told me the other day that Azz El Arab's sister has gone to Spain; even her mother, it seems, is about to go rejoin her son and daughter, all because a rich man wanted to help them. They're so lucky! If only . . .*

The drugs were beginning to have an effect; Malika was sleeping now, and dreaming. She is well again, tall and beautiful, wearing a long blue dress, walking slowly along a red carpet spread out for the occasion. Other women as nicely dressed as she is are walking beside her, then past her; when they reach the end of the carpet, they vanish as if they'd plunged over a steep cliff. Malika doesn't want to disappear, she slows down, looking for someone to hold her hand. Before she reaches the end of her path, a man clothed all in white holds out his arms to her, then takes her hand to lead her onto a podium where a very long black car is waiting. That's when she recognizes the doctor who took care of her. His expression has changed: he seems happy, at peace. The hold of an immense ocean liner is open. The limousine is parked halfway inside the opening. Malika lets herself be led along. The doctor smiles and talks to her, but as in a silent film, she can't hear what he's saying. She is now sitting in the limousine, which glides slowly into the depths of the hold, where other limousines are parked, all lined up with precision. She feels a slight sensation of motion; then, perfect calm. The ship is moving noiselessly across the sea. The doctor is gone. That's when she recognizes, sitting next to her, the dead old lady. Malika screams but no sound comes out. She tears her dress. The old woman smiles, showing her toothless mouth. Instead of eyes she has small black holes. The more she smiles, the more Malika screams. The ship leaves the port of Tangier. It disappears into the night. Now the old lady has stopped smiling. Malika has stopped screaming. It is in eternal silence that she quits the country. She has finally left. Forever.

27

Kenza

Kenza looked in the mirror and for the first time found herself beautiful. She was happy. Just for fun she hid her hair in a hideous scarf and imitated a Muslim woman in a veil. That's their freedom, she thought, and it's no one's business but theirs. Me, my freedom is to love a man who pleases me in every way and makes me happy. What she liked best about Nâzim were his pale, almost green eyes, his long, strong hands, his olive skin, and his smile. When she took a bath, childhood memories began washing over her. . . . She could hear her cries of joy the day her father gave her a bike to go to school; she'd been the only girl in the neighborhood who had one. And then she looked carefully at her body, stroking her belly, feeling the weight of her breasts. In the end she found herself quite desirable.

So it turns out that I had to leave Morocco to finally fall in love, to experience that marvelous state that makes you so light, and so present; I had to rid myself of everything that was weighing on me, holding me back, tethering me to resignation and silence—I had to get rid of all that to become a woman, a lover in the arms of a mature and attentive man, different from all the Moroccan men I've met. With him I have dared to act, and my freedom has grown stronger. When my virginity obsessed me, at twenty I decided to settle that question by giving myself to my cousin Abderrahim, who claimed he was madly in love with me. An awful memory! What a scene! I had to help him penetrate me, he was shaking so much! And when he saw some blood his thingy suddenly shriveled right back between his thighs. He was stammering and sweating. I wasn't even sure we'd actually done it. The main thing was that I no longer considered myself a virgin. Another time, I gave in to my cousin Noureddine, whom Azel had hoped would marry me. He was a vigorous man, perhaps a bit rough. He didn't make me come, but at least his penis was energetic. This was before he set out on that boat, and I can still see him, proud of himself, rinsing the cum from the sheets, talking about his trip the way our grandparents talked about their pilgrimage to Mecca. He thought of his coming departure as the solution to every problem. Obviously, I was part of his plans: marriage in Tangier, the family reunited in Brussels, kids, and everything else. I let him dream on. I had no particular desire to make my life with him; I found him handsome, agreeable, but I didn't feel in love. When I told her that, my mother said, "You mean you think I was in love with your father? Love, what you young people call love, it's a luxury, it comes with time or it never does. Your father and I, we didn't get enough time, he was carried off too soon. Listen, my daughter, don't miss out on this boy! Marry him and only then you'll make what you want out of him, I'll help you, you'll see, the woman is the one who decides everything: she makes the man believe he's in charge, when she's really the boss!"

Azel must not have known that we'd slept together. I'd had no intention of shouting it from the rooftops, but the day Noureddine died, the day his body was handed over to his family, I couldn't help myself and told Azel about the afternoon we'd spent in Agla's beach shack. I was looking at Noureddine's coffin and thinking that I'd been the last woman to have given him pleasure. I cried for a long time. Today I am a different woman, and I say that because for a while, I was afraid I would never desire another man. That death crushed me. Although my feelings had been limited to a physical attraction, death had confused my emotions and persuaded me that I'd been *in love with Noureddine. That wasn't what I wanted. For months I lived with his ghost, having strange feelings, loving a man who no longer existed, a man who was gone, dead and buried. One day I went back to the famous shack. I walked in and lay down on the bed, where the sheets hadn't been changed. I smelled them; they had a terrible odor. Death had passed by there, leaving some of its ashes behind. When I ran away from the shack, a wild dog began chasing me. A watchman saved me; afterward he kindly offered me his mare to go back up the cliff. There were groups of Africans sitting in the shade on the beach, waiting. I couldn't help thinking that some of them would soon drown in the dark of night. I imagined their childhood in a Malian or Senegalese village, and their lives: poor, but not necessarily sad. I thought of their mothers, grandmothers, and aunts preparing food; I could guess at their dreams, but I had the feeling that they were not afraid of dying. In spite of their present poverty and isolation, they were laughing and joking. Back at the house, I began crying again. I had to put an end to my plight, stop thinking about Noureddine, cease climbing the mountain of his dreams, which now lay drifting at the bottom of the Mediterranean. Seeing those Africans smile and laugh had done me good.*

So I had to . . . I had to leave my country, my family, and first become the wife of a charming person, then by sheer chance meet Nâzim—an immigrant or exile (I still don't know which) and a real man—for me to not only escape my sad story, but also experience love, true love, the one that gives you shivers, staggers you, makes you vulnerable, transparent, ready for anything. I hadn't known that state in which the body, when it is so desired and so well loved, climbs to the heights and gazes out over the city with an appetite for trying everything, for consuming and embracing everything.

In the beginning, Nâzim paid so much attention to me that I almost thought he was pretending. In bed he would caress me for a long time; he was preparing me, as he put it: he would carry me toward heaven, on his back, in his hands, his arms, he would dance, hold me close, then take me almost by surprise, entering gently and driving me wild. I'd never known anything like it. He would speak to me in his language, he made me laugh. I'd use the Arab dialect of Tangier, and he loved its high-pitched sounds. I belonged to him. I confided in my husband, and Miguel was happy for me. "You're so beautiful," he told me, "you deserve to be loved by a man like that! Oh, if you knew how much I envy you!"

Kenza stepped from her bath, slipped into a robe, and ran to the phone. It was the police, asking her to come get her brother. When she arrived at the station, she found Azel so drunk that he hardly recognized her. An officer told her that they'd found a note on him saying, "In case of emergency call my sister Kenza at 93 35 36 54." She took Azel home, put him to bed, and waited for him to sober up. Whatever you do, she told herself, don't call Miguel.

When Azel finally awakened, he took a shower, asked for some coffee, and insisted that Kenza listen to his explanations. At first she refused, because she had to go to work. Azel made her telephone to say she would be arriving an hour late. He desperately needed to talk.

28

Azel

"My sister, big sister, my friend, you must listen to me, I need you, this can't go on, I'm sinking into a hell like nothing you could ever imagine. I'm failing at everything. Last week, I went to see my friend Siham who works in Marbella. We really like each other. I've always enjoyed her company. . . . Forgive me, sister, I must speak to you about things that brothers and sisters don't talk about. The relationship between Siham and me—it was about sex more than anything else, and I needed that so as not to lose my virility, and she was getting what she wanted as well, we were partners, helping each other, and it gave us pleasure. Well, last week, *walou*! You know what that means, *walou*? Rock bottom. I was unable to be a man, forgive me, but I have to say this, it has to come out, the shame—the incredible shame, the *hchouma*! Siham was so nice, she didn't say anything except that it wasn't serious, the problem was simply fatigue, stress, the change in climate. What fatigue, what stress? And why not the dollar exchange rate and a plague of migratory locusts? I'm done for, I can't be a man anymore, I don't know what to do; yesterday I went to see the Moroccan girl who's been whoring since her Kuwaiti 'husband'

186

ditched her, I can't remember her name anymore, I just remember that she used to explode with me, screaming when she came, so, well, I saw her last night, I'd had a bit to drink to give me some confidence, I was afraid of washing out again, and when I undressed, she burst out laughing! She said, 'Where'd your friend go?' I asked her, 'What friend are you talking about?' 'Man's real best friend,' she said, 'the one who wakes up when he sees a woman, who says hello and gets all stiff to drive her insane. . . .' *Walou! Walou!* I've become a *walou*, a nothing, an absence, the memory of a man, a shadow. . . . I'm sure it's that bitch Carmen, the old woman, the one who bullies Miguel and controls his life—she never could stand me, always looked at me as if I were an intruder, a thief; she must have gone to her magicians and witches to put a spell on me, that sort of thing happens not just with us, even Europeans use stuff like that, except no one ever suspects them, people think they're rational, civilized and all that, but at bottom they're like us: as soon as sex and money are involved, they react in exactly the same way!

"I know precisely when it all started. One evening—an absolute nightmare—Miguel had some Brazilian friends over, total sex maniacs, and he asked me to make love to a gorgeous woman who was actually a guy: it was dreadful, I was disgusted, they were watching me do it while we were in the middle of the living room! At first it amused me, I was playing along, in top form, but then the she-male told me in Portuguese to piss on him, and when I didn't understand, he grabbed his dick, acting it out, so Miguel told me, 'Do what he asks, piss on him, urinate, it excites him, and you don't give a damn, no one's asking you to drink it, just to

give him a golden shower!' It was revolting. I didn't feel like piss-
ing, my penis wouldn't cooperate—I shouted and left the room.
They were crazy, those Brazilians. Why did Miguel ever invite
them? Forgive me, but it's a relief to talk to you, that's how low
I've sunk, I'm dirt, worthless, no self-respect at all. After that
episode I went to see my Moroccan pal, you remember, the guy
who always knows what to do, the neighborhood big shot; I didn't
dare tell him about this, but he could see I was miserable, so he
gave me something to drink and some smoke, I don't remember
exactly what anymore, result was, the police scraped me up off
the sidewalk at ten at night, they thought I was experiencing
some sort of malaise. In a sense they weren't wrong, but it's an
ancient malaise, very ancient, a malaise that's been going on for a
long time, a massive malaise, something that hurts, like needles
playing with my heart, my liver, and griping pains, like wanting to
vomit. The police tried to question me but I was dozing; then a
doctor gave me a shot, that woke me up a bit, but I felt awful, so
awful, I wanted to die, to throw myself under a bus. . . . That's
when they called you. And luckily, they found you, big sister!

"Can I sleep here?"

Kenza was shocked; she'd never imagined that one day her little
brother would tell her such things. She didn't know what to say,
what to do, but she could clearly see that Azel was in a bad way.
After a long pause, she stood up, went to get her purse, and told
him that she could not let him stay at her place indefinitely. He
would have to seriously consider going back to Morocco. Azel
screamed and started weeping like a child. Kenza simply had to

go to work. She asked him not to answer the phone, and above all, to get some sleep.

She called Miguel from the Red Cross office. He was in bed, laid low by bronchitis. He was the one who brought up Azel, but Kenza didn't want to upset him, since he was sick.

"He's not doing well, is he?" asked Miguel. "It had to happen, unfortunately.... You know, I feel somewhat responsible; I thought he was mature enough, knew what he was doing, when he left with me.... But his longing to leave Morocco was so strong that in the end it blinded him and corrupted everything he did. I don't want to see him anymore, he went way too far. I never admitted as much to you, but he stole some precious objects from me that he must have resold at ridiculous prices, and he behaved like the worst kind of creep. He knew that money was not a problem between us, but he wanted more, he wanted to humiliate me. One evening with friends, he was appalling, he insulted them, broke a bottle of wine, and tried to pick a fight. No, Kenza, my Kenza, my friend, my dear wife, your little brother is a lost cause, and you're right to say that he'd be better off going home, where he could find his bearings. Here, he had everything given to him too easily, he has no idea how hard I worked, how I suffered to get where I am today, but, well, when you're in love, you don't think straight, you follow your feelings, your emotions. I was in love with Azel; he never was with me, and he acted as if I didn't realize that he was pretending. Well, I'm a clever old monkey, as you know, and nobody fools me! All right, let's stop talking about him for a moment. When are you going to come fuss over your poor husband? That reminds me, I haven't told you yet, but congratulations!

Thanks to a few well-placed interventions, your case is closed, you're Spanish now, a citizen of Europe: the notice from the ministry arrived yesterday, so all you have to do is go sign and claim the document that will allow you to apply for that wine-red passport stamped with gold letters that spell 'European Union'! Afterward, we'll get a divorce whenever you like—I adore you, my lovely, you're a wonderful woman!"

Before going home, Kenza made a detour to visit Miguel. When Carmen told her at the front door that Miguel was sound asleep, Kenza bowed her head and went on her way. Then, remembering that she had promised to dance that evening at the restaurant, she hurried directly there to arrive on time. She took pleasure in letting herself go in front of her audience, turning her body into a superb metaphor for eroticism and dreams. She performed several times that evening, and took home quite a bit of money.

29

Nâzim

Nâzim was standing out in front of Kenza's apartment building. He was nervous, and worried. It was his nature always to expect the worst, which was probably why his hair had begun to turn gray when he was still young. Tonight he was determined to conquer his distress. There was no reason to let himself get upset! Kenza would be there any moment; he would take her in his arms and carry her off somewhere far away. He longed so much to be free, to have his papers in order, and have a little money. . . . Then he could take Kenza to see his native Anatolia, and show her the insolent beauty of its richly forested mountains. He thought suddenly of his family and friends, whom he hadn't seen for more than two years, people whom he missed but never mentioned, which was a vaguely magical way to keep them from his thoughts, in a limbo of waiting. He was convinced that he would see them again some day, an especially splendid day, with a heart full of light and eyes brimming with happy tears; on that truly extraordinary day, he would finally become himself again, the man he'd once been. On that day his exile would be abruptly erased from his memory.

When Kenza finally appeared at the end of the street, he ran to her and threw his arms around her. He told her how happy he was to see her, how painfully he'd missed her; he kissed her hands and recited another Turkish poem to her. Kenza, however, was in an awkward position: Azel was sleeping at her place, so she couldn't bring Nâzim home.

"Let's go to a hotel!" suggested Nâzim.

Kenza hesitated. "Why not go to your place? I don't even know where you live. Hotels are for secret lovers or prostitutes, and in Sabadell it was different, we were taking a trip."

"You know I live in a rat hole," protested Nâzim. "You deserve better than that."

Kenza asked him to wait while she went upstairs to get a few things for the following day. Nâzim paced up and down, growing impatient. Perhaps Azel had forbidden her to rejoin him. Perhaps she'd changed her mind. The light went on in the apartment. At last, after twenty long minutes, Kenza reappeared. The idea of spending another night in a hotel excited Nâzim. Along the way, he began singing in Turkish and Arabic.

You are my intoxication
I've never drunk my fill of you
I can't drink my fill of you
I don't ever want to.

Kenza laughed, wishing Nâzim could take her right away, but that just wasn't done, it's frowned on, especially coming from a woman, and an Arab woman at that. But surely he could understand— even though she'd noticed that he was almost as jealous and possessive as Moroccan men. They were now holding hands as they walked, and as they walked, she whispered in his ear, "I want you." He stopped, smiled, and backed her up against a wall, where he stood kissing her ardently. Passersby pretended not to see a thing. At the hotel Nâzim paid for the room in advance and asked for a bottle of water. There was a bottle of arrack in his overnight bag.

The room was small and ordinary, nothing special. It smelled musty. The carpet was worn, the light dreary, but their desire was blind and not to be denied. Nâzim asked Kenza to follow his lead, then blindfolded her with his black tie and began to describe their room in his own way.

"The room is small, but quite charming: the walls are covered with salmon-colored silk, and there's a leather couch in one corner next to an antique armoire; a reproduction of a pretty painting in the Orientalist style hangs next to the window; the bedspread is of fine velvet; a large Persian carpet covers the floor. Now I'm going to undress you the way one would pluck the petals from a lovely rose—don't move, whatever you do. . . . I'm taking off your jacket first, then your blouse, your skirt, your shoes, stockings. . . . Wait, wait, let me undo your bra . . . but you're not wearing any panties, not even a thong! That's wild, it's driving me insane! You're unbelievable, you guessed what I wanted . . . and how beautiful you are. . . . Our love is so strong and you're an absolute pearl, I don't know how I can possibly deserve you, be worthy of you, I'm so lucky! I can hardly keep from shouting!"

She reached out for him but he eluded her, laughing, and she called out to him. They were happy. With Kenza still blindfolded, they fell onto the bed and made love for a long time.

The lights were out, the curtains closed; they awaited the dawn in silence. Then, suddenly, the sky became white.

"Look, my beauty: this is the moment when the horses come down from the heavens to wreathe themselves in the colors of autumn and gallop around a great mountain of clouds. You see that camel bearing a wardrobe full of silk and satin dresses? He's crossing the horizon seeking the lovers who were joined together this night. Daybreak has scattered itself among the tallest trees, and you—you are as beautiful as that caress of light: you are here and I am singing so that you will never leave me again. Oh, Kenza, in the name of this lovely morning, this dream stirring up the sky, will you marry me, and be my wife?"

Kenza removed the blindfold and looked up at him.

"Do you mean that?"

"I love you. You know, where I come from, a man finds it hard to confess his love to a woman, such things are left unspoken, barely hinted at, but I feel that I am not in Anatolia but here in Spain, and we're different, no longer hemmed in by our taboos, our traditions, and I'm certain it's because we each left our own countries that we've been free to become ourselves: we love each other without fear of prying eyes or the cruel words of nosy neighbors and hypocrites. Spain is setting us free, so you and I, the Moroccan woman and the Turkish man, we will get married and forget where we came from."

"Wait, wait, don't go so fast! You never forget where you come from, you carry that with you wherever you go: you can't cut your own roots that easily. People often think they've changed their way of thinking, but it resists, and I know what I'm talking about!

194

Here, an Arab woman is called upon to change her behavior, and if she doesn't change, she is ground down, bullied, despised. Don't you see, the question is much bigger than we are. As for the two of us—I need to think, and to take care of certain problems. Let me have some time. And as you know, I'm already married. . . ."

After they parted in front of the hotel, Kenza felt herself wavering. "I'm so eager to be happy," she thought, "and to forget the past; I want to live, to do any number of things. And now I have to make up my mind." But she didn't know quite what to think about Nâzim's proposal. She knew hardly anything about this man. Whenever she asked him about his life in Turkey, he was always evasive. She had learned to be careful. Of one thing, at least, she was certain: she felt good with him in bed, where each time they were together her body discovered a new kind of pleasure. She had feelings for him too, of course, perhaps she even felt love, yet some doubt still remained. What was this man of culture and education doing in Barcelona? Why had he left his country? He'd said it was because of political problems, but Kenza was bothered by something she couldn't quite put her finger on. As she walked she thought about what she had just experienced, one of the most wonderful nights of her life. A Frenchwoman in Tangier, suspected of adultery and cast off by her Moroccan husband, had once told her that secret trysts were always the most precious nights of love, for love was strongest when it defied the force of habit. Then why get married? To avoid ending up alone?

Kenza needed to talk to her best friend, Miguel.

30

Miguel

Sitting at his desk in a white woolen burnoose, Miguel was writing letters, signing checks, putting things in order. Kenza went over and kissed him. It was so hard for her to imagine him naked at an orgy, surrounded by Brazilian queens! She had never dared speak to him about his private life.

"You've arrived at the perfect moment! I've just come across a notebook in which my father kept a kind of diary. I've learned some amazing things, I must tell you about them—or better yet, let me read you a few pages on Morocco."

June 24, 1951: I'm in Rabat, in a room in the Hôtel Balima. Our consular service has put us up in this hotel until the inquiry is finished.

There are ten of us, ten Spaniards who boarded a small boat in the port of Tarifa on the night of June 22. José the printer, fired for daring to talk about unionizing; his brother Pablo, a journalist watched by the police; Juan, a lawyer forbidden to practice his profession; Balthazar the poet, who cannot find a publisher; Ignacio, a medical student at odds with his parents; Pedro the ambulance driver, a practicing Jew who has suffered persecution;

Ramón the bookseller, attacked by pro-Franco publishers and newspapers;
García the bartender; André, a French writer living in Spain who says he
is Spanish. We are all Communists, anti-Franco militants, and we've all
been to prison. I don't remember anymore how it happened, but one day
José suggested that we leave Spain to go live and work in Morocco. The
north and extreme south of the country are occupied by Spain, the rest by
France. We were spied on, and frequently asked to show our papers in
Spain; we lived in fear of being arrested and charged with who knows what
crime. The police know how to set up things like that; we'd arrive at the
police station to find our files already bulging with misdemeanors and
things we'd never done. We had no passports, no permits to leave the
territory. We would always meet in secret but were fed up with hiding.
Before becoming a bartender, García had been a sailor, and he was the one
who found the boat. No one had done that before: leave Spain in secret for
Morocco. We could have followed the example of many comrades and gone
into exile in France, but the ten of us were drawn to this country where the
sun shines all year round. Morocco was the door to Africa and adventure.
We left on the 22nd and took turns rowing all night long in the darkness,
but we became lost. García had forgotten how to navigate on open water.
We fetched up outside Salé, a pretty little town next to Rabat. When the
French police picked us up, we told them we were a bunch of friends who'd
gone fishing and lost our way. They believed us. So did the Spanish consul.
No one had any idea that we were the first boat people in Hispano-
Moroccan history.

Before the consul realized what we were up to, we'd left the hotel and
scattered throughout the country, mainly in the north. The next day, I read
this item in Le Petit Marocain as well as in España, a daily published

in Tangier: "Ten Spanish immigrants in danger of drowning were rescued from a small boat off Salé; they vanished after receiving medical attention and are currently being sought by their families and the police."

June 26, 1951: I took the train to Tangier. At Arbaoua, the Guardia Civil were checking Moroccan passengers with particular interest, so I began a loud conversation in Spanish with Juan. The police saluted when they passed us; one of them even asked us for a cigarette. Juan let him keep the entire pack. Arriving ten hours later in Tangier, we were dazzled by the beauty of this city embraced by the sea. The peseta was the chief currency, and everyone spoke our language in this bustling international city, which was for us a place of disorienting and exhilarating freedom. We saw long, luxurious American cars, and I remember a pink Cadillac convertible driven by a very thin man, flashily dressed, beside whom sat a gorgeous European woman smoking a cigarette, just as in an advertisement. I later learned that the young man was the only son of an old Jewish family in Tangier, a very wealthy family. His name was Momy.

Within a week Juan found work in a large law firm with Spanish, French, and English employees. The Hôtel El Minzah was looking for a bookkeeper; while I worked there I met many people from the worlds of politics and literature. I remember in particular an American writer who was always drunk. Rumor had it that spies were everywhere; I never saw any, although there was one bartender who obviously worked with the police force—but which one? Each country had its own, so he must have sold information to anyone with money. I suspected that he was an informer because he began to criticize the Caudillo, trying to lead me in that direction—an obvious ploy, and when I told him I stayed away from politics, he took the hint. I spent eight most enjoyable months in that city.

I adored the "Gran Socco" with all those peasant women selling their plants, flowers, fruits, vegetables, and cow's milk cheeses, and I also loved the other Socco, "el Socco Chico," where smokers quietly savored pipes of kif, which wasn't illegal—there were even blue signs with the map of Morocco outlined by the smoke of a cigarette, above which was written "Moroccan State Tobacco and Kif Authority." Yes, at the time there was no problem with smoking kif. I also liked the Old Mountain district with its colonial villas, formal receptions, its snobbish English girls and the beautiful Spanish women who served the guests. It was at one of those parties that Juan fell in love with Stéphanie, a French girl spending her vacation with her uncle, an interior decorator who did not like women. Juan and Stéphanie were married in France and as the saying goes, they lived happily ever after. I remember an English painter and his wife; he used to draw the medina, scenes of Moroccan life. And there was a member of the British royal family who loved parties and boys and didn't care who knew it. At the time people also talked about an American writer who'd lived there for several years with an illiterate Moroccan boy, while his wife had set up house with a peasant woman. Tangier was like a circus full of those who live on the margins of society. I considered this spectacle with a critical eye and did not mix with such people.

February 13, 1952: I sailed away from there on a ship of the Paquet line, landing in Marseilles, where I was welcomed by friends in the Party who found me work at the Gare Saint-Charles. Those were difficult times. There were many Spanish refugees. One day I learned that my father had been taken to hospital, and I returned to Spain for the first time, traveling with forged papers. At home I was reunited with my wife, Mercedes, who had been working hard to raise our two children: fifteen-year-old Miguel,

the rebel, and his twin Maria, an excellent student. Life proved stronger
than my ideals; I did not become a turncoat, but I gradually distanced
myself from the Party, especially after the Soviet invasion of Hungary.
I wanted to tell the story of that clandestine crossing in June 1951.
Something historic, unique.

Miguel shut the notebook, rubbed his eyes, and looked at
Kenza.

"It's incredible! Would you ever have believed that there were
already illegal aliens in 1951, but going in the opposite direction
from today's boat people? That's crazy, no? My father never spoke
to me about this period in his life. Strange, isn't it?"

Kenza didn't know what to say. Like everyone else, she'd
thought that Moroccans had invented those dangerous journeys.

"You know, my dear, the Spaniards who occupied Morocco
were desperately poor people, without the resources of the
French. Franco drew the best elements of his army from the Rif,
then lost interest in everything that might have helped the country to develop, to really exist. He never built anything decent over
there, no dams, no roads; there was one Spanish hospital, but it
was the nuns who actually ran the place. Well, what a time that
was! That's why Moroccans have never considered the Spanish
as true colonizers. Some Spaniards, however, still feel superior
to Moroccans, *los moros,* as they call them. Enough of that: how
are you?"

Kenza wanted to talk about Nâzim's proposal. Miguel's pale
face seemed very tired, though; perhaps he was ill. She decided to
wait for a better occasion.

She was about to leave when he informed her that he'd asked his lawyer to begin divorce proceedings.

"All you have to do is repudiate me," she replied. "You say three times, in front of witnesses, 'I repudiate you'—and that's it. Then you have a letter sent to me through the *adouls*, who will inform me officially of your decision. That's how it's done in Morocco."

Knowing that a Moroccan marriage was not a contract, but an act that had no legal value outside the Muslim sphere, Miguel had registered his marriage at the city hall in Barcelona, yet Kenza had never sought to take any advantage of her position. She gave Miguel a kiss.

"You know, my Turkish friend, Nâzim . . . he wants to marry me."

"You'll have children—I'll be a father, or a grandfather!"

"I haven't gotten that far yet. I'm attracted to him, but I don't know him very well. I can't tell if he's sincere. I feel something like a presentiment. . . . Although, he is the first Turkish man I've ever met, and perhaps I'm prejudiced."

"Do you want me to make inquiries?"

"No, no, don't bother."

"Give me his name anyway, and the date when he arrived in Spain."

"He came here through clandestine channels, he's an illegal."

"How can that be? If he hasn't any papers, he won't be able to get legally married."

"No, he's suggesting that we get married and then apply to have his situation straightened out."

"As long as we haven't been properly divorced, you won't be able to remarry. As for him, if he wants to do things by the book, he has to clear up his own problems in any case. All this seems rather complicated to me."

"You're right; it's just something we were considering, we haven't decided anything."

"Are you in love?"

"Yes, Miguel."

"Don't rush into this. Wait until your own position has been completely clarified. After that, you'll do as you like. A Moroccan woman and a Turk! What a lovely mix, you'll have handsome children!"

31

Azel

Azel was familiar with the Barrio Chino, the "Chinatown" of Barcelona, so he knew it was no longer a Spanish neighborhood. Below Las Ramblas, where Indian and Pakistani shopkeepers now plied their trades, the narrow streets looked sometimes like the medina of Fès, and sometimes like the older parts of Naples. There was nothing remarkable about the area. The walls were tired. The sad people and the few African women waiting around for clients in broad daylight were the dreariest part of the neighborhood, a section of which had been taken over by the city for the construction of a film theater and library. Moroccans hung around the area, killing time; some leaned back against a wall, sunbathing, while others sniffed the air. You would have thought they were waiting for the Prophet. They tended to gather at a phone store with the odd name of *Al Intissar*, "Victory," a narrow and rather inhospitable place on the Carrer de Sant Pau, squeezed in between a tiny hairdressing salon called *Ma Sha'a Allah*, "What God Willed," and a small house of prayer, *Mezquita Tarík Bin Ziyad*.

That was where Azel found refuge. Like everyone else, he did nothing, really; he was waiting. One day, Abbas had said to him,

"Waiting, that's our new profession!" So that's where Azel was, staring motionless at the ground, his cigarette slowly burning down between his lips. He looked quite shabby, and hadn't washed for a week. When a Nigerian prostitute named Azziya suggested that he run away with her, to disappear off in India or Australia, he smiled, nodded, then asked her if she'd seen Abbas that morning. She wandered off to have a beer at the Bar Alegría.

Suddenly, a name popped into his mind: Soumaya! "If there's anyone on earth who can still save me," he thought, "it has to be her. She's the only one who can revive my soul, and help me recover my manhood. I just have to see her! Abbas must know where she is. But, in fact, where's Abbas? Is he hiding? I've been hearing talk about police raids lately; perhaps he decided to get a jump on them and has simply disappeared?"

Azel was walking in the street, following a sunbeam. He stopped in front of a Moroccan peddler offering true odds and ends: a pair of secondhand shoes, a broken black telephone, a ladle, some plastic ashtrays, three dirty neckties, a military helmet, a phone book for Seville, a map of Barcelona, a lampshade, some light bulbs (probably burned out), four coat hangers (one of them wooden), and a folded bed sheet. The two men looked at each other, smiled, then shook hands.

Azel was hoping to find Abbas in a boardinghouse in the Barrio Gótico. He walked along with his head down, thinking more and more of Soumaya, seeing her, remembering her scent; a furtive flash of heat crossed his loins: "That's it, she'll know how to fix everything, she has the power to flood my body with warmth, and her big breasts are unbeatable, she knows how to use them so well, that's exactly it, her breasts will be enough, like the first time, when she insisted that I come between them. She knows my weak spot—but is she even still in Barcelona?" She'd spoken so often to him about her intention to go home to Morocco to open a hairdressing salon. . . . Abbas would be able to tell him. . . . Abbas knew everything.

On the Carrer del Bisbe, some Moroccans were leaning against a wall, and at an angle suggesting that they were trying to keep the house from falling down. A Pakistani was selling acrylic scarves. He said nothing, simply waited for a customer to stop and wind one of the brightly colored mufflers around his neck.

The boardinghouse where Abbas lived was run by some people from Latin America. Abbas was still asleep; Azel woke him up, dragging him out of bed and off to a café on Las Ramblas.

"I'm in hiding," confided Abbas. "I was tipped off about the arrival of some Arabs from Afghanistan via Islamabad. The police are afraid of attacks—you know, from unscrupulous killers, the ones they call Afghans, fanatics without any conscience at all. So the police have thrown out a dragnet and are arresting a lot of *moros*. And what's new with you?"

"I left the Spaniard. Fucking guys—it's not my thing."

"All right! You told me that before, but then, how did you manage to get a hard-on?"

"He'd go down on me, I'd close my eyes and think about Siham or Soumaya, and I have to say he was better at it than they are."

"Oh dear, Soumaya . . ."

"Where is she? I was looking for her, I need her."

"You'd better forget about it, she has that sickness that can't be cured, poor thing; she got into drugs, one thing led to another, now you wouldn't recognize her if you saw her, all scrawny, breasts like empty bags, glassy-eyed. . . . She can't afford to get medical help, plus she's so afraid of being sent back home. Why did you want to see her?"

"No reason, just to say hello. She was always nice to me."

"I'll take you to see her tomorrow, if you want, but you'll have to leave her alone, she's so sick, poor girl. She shares a room with a Mexican woman who's down and out."

The beautiful Soumaya, so lively and luscious, had become a gray shadow, her face collapsed into wrinkles, her eyes empty, her body ravaged by the sufferings of hunger and sickness. She was sleeping . . . or perhaps in a coma. Azel's eyes filled with tears, and he had to look away. Distraught, he rushed from the room. He wanted to do something for her, to save her, if he could; Abbas told him it was too late.

Azel remembered a French doctor he knew, a friend of Miguel's in Barcelona whom he could perhaps ask for help. It was impossible to forget his name: Gabriel Lemerveilleux, "Gabriel the Marvelous." It was his real name. He was a *pied-noir*—from a family of former French colonists—from Mostaganem, Algeria. Cultured, witty, profoundly compassionate, he loved to be of service and had an acute sense of friendship but not many illusions about the human race. He worked as little as possible, giving priority to his many tumultuous love affairs with men. Intense and intelligent, Gabriel was more than just a skilled professional, for he had a true passion for helping others. People said that he "loved his neighbor"; some laughed at this, others remarked upon it with pointed irony, but everyone agreed that he had the gift of reading other people's eyes, and of always being there when he was needed. Azel had met him in Tangier at one of Miguel's parties. He found his address easily in the Barcelona phone book.

When he went to Gabriel's office, Azel had no way of knowing what he would learn there.

32

Gabriel

Gabriel was certainly the person who knew Miguel the best. Even though they rarely saw each other, they kept in close touch. Gabriel knew things about his friend, but refused to talk about them. That morning, however, when he saw Azel show up at his office, he asked him to wait, not to leave under any circumstances, because he had something to tell him.

"I'm glad to see you, Azel. I had no idea where to find you. But first, what brings you here?"

After a moment's hesitation, Azel spoke of Soumaya's predicament, and Gabriel immediately reassured him. It so happened that she had come to see him a few days earlier: she was suffering from a severe hepatitis infection, nothing more. She was already taking medication that would quickly have her back on her feet.

"But I saw her myself! She's terribly sick!"

"Don't worry, she'll be fine. Thanks to a few little 'Moroccan' interventions, I managed to have her admitted to a clinic run by the Red Cross. She must rest, and above all, she must live a cleaner life, poor dear—she's been abandoned, and has let herself go very badly. I even told her that before anything else, she would be wise to take a bath. To look at her, you'd have thought she was at death's door."

After a pause, Gabriel added, "You hurt Miguel a lot, you know."

"Oh, let's not be dramatic: I helped myself to a few of his knickknacks because I had a debt to pay, that's all. Miguel was very generous to my family, but I've lost everything, I'm ruined. I'm the one to be pitied, not him."

"Well then, at least listen to what I'm going to tell you. Miguel is not the man you think he is. He is a self-made man, but in a way, he took the same path as you. The family he was born into was quite poor. His father had to go abroad to Morocco and then France, where he worked in the port of Marseilles. His mother was a concierge in a residential neighborhood, and to survive, she was forced to surrender her children to the child welfare author- ities. At your age, Miguel was in much more desperate straits than you are today. He left Spain as soon as he could, to save his own skin. To do that, like you, he had to follow a man, a rich and powerful English lord, a stern and complicated person. Because Miguel was so handsome, this lord took him under his protection and set him up in one of his homes after his return to London. Miguel was his lover, his devoted slave, his servant, his valet, and the lord even required him to sleep now and then with his sister, an old hag no one wanted. Unlike you, Miguel had already had sexual relations with men in Spain; he liked that and had no problem with it, even though society viewed such matters harshly at the time. Miguel submitted to his master and satisfied him, knowing that one day he would be rewarded for his service. So, being sly and intelligent, he took as much advantage as possible of those few occasions when the lord would refuse him nothing. Miguel's sole objective was to escape from misery and poverty once and for all. That's why he even used the sister to obtain what the lord was most reluctant to part with: a small Picasso that Miguel absolutely adored. It took strength, let me tell you, and incredible energy to play this game to the end and above all, come out a winner. In short, when the lord died, he left his vast fortune to Miguel. The lord's sister contested the will, and even started a rumor that Miguel had poisoned her brother, but the law ruled in Miguel's favor. After that, he moved to Tangier, where he bought a magnificent house. He set his parents up in a little farm in Málaga, and put some order in his own life. He began by changing his name. He found a husband and a job for his sister. He made overtures to the Spanish royal family, and some people even say that the queen took a liking to him, which opened up some doors. Miguel loved to shine, to give large parties, spend money, and do everything for those he fell in love with. So you see, Azel, I think that with you he was reliving a part of his youth, and you deeply disappointed him."

Azel was stunned. He couldn't help thinking about what Miguel might leave him when he died. He even considered approaching him to ask for forgiveness, to get back into his good graces and slip him the famous little pill that stops the heart without leaving a trace. . . .

Now that Gabriel had reassured him, and he was less worried about Soumaya, Azel thought about his own troubles. Just as he was about to say good-bye to Gabriel, he hung his head and stammered nervously, "Listen, I can't get a hard-on anymore!"

"So? It happens to everyone, like getting a flat tire. All men go through it sooner or later, it's nothing, don't get upset about it."

"It's not physical—it's my head that's screwed up, I feel lost, my self-confidence is completely gone, I'm done for, so ashamed. . . ."

"Then call me next week, we'll talk seriously about this."

33

Flaubert

Through some strange turn of events, the paths of Azel and Flaubert crossed one cold morning on a park bench. Azel was smoking; Flaubert was not.

"Hey, you! You've got a killer way of smoking!"

"What's that mean, 'killer'?"

"You're sucking in the smoke full strength to keep all the tars in your lungs. Ev-er-y bit. You're trying to get rid of yourself. Well, that's none of my business, but like they say back home in Cameroon—more precisely, in the land of the Bangangte, in the Nde—it looks like you're afraid you'll have a dry wake."

Azel looked at him, smiled, and clapped him on the shoulder.

"You're a weird guy! Who sent you to lecture me? My mother, my sister, or my benefactor?"

"Nobody, I'm just passing through, came looking for André Marie, a cousin the family's searching hard for, over some problems with a tontine. André Marie's a tall black fellow, I think he's over six feet, left one day determined to find work in Europe, got into Morocco over the border with Mauritania, spent a few months in Tangier—where he had a tough time of it—then finally went over the water. At least, that's what he claims in the message he sent one day through a cousin who came back home."

"I see, another of those Africans so hard up they're eating all of Tangier's cats! People say they're why the rats and mice have reappeared in the harbor neighborhoods. And you, where're you from?"

"I work for a Franco-German NGO. I was in Toulouse when the family phoned me, asking me to go look for him, said I'd find him in Barcelona, in the African quarter. So I took the train and here I am hunting for André Marie. You wouldn't happen to know him? Big six-footer, hard to miss!"

"No, I don't know any Africans. Well, yes, I know Azziya, a whore from Nigeria."

"Azziya—that's no African name!"

"Right! It's the Moroccans who nicknamed her that. Where I come from, the blacks, they're often called Azzis, a rather nasty name, sometimes even Abid, which means 'slave.' But back to you: what's this business about a 'dry wake' and a 'tontine'?"

"At home, in the Bamileke country, we live with the duty to respect our word and never disgrace our family honor. The worst shame for a Bamileke, it's that people won't come to the wake, you know, the funeral. If you don't keep your word, you are no longer part of the family and the tribe. A dry wake, that's when folks show up at the funeral but don't drink, or eat, or stay very long."

"But the dead man, he couldn't care less if people come to his funeral or not."

"Not so—because with us, the dead are never dead: they change their status and become ancestors we consult when there's a problem."

"And this 'tontine,' what's that?"

"It's a system of credit. Some people get together in a small group and each person promises to pay a certain sum every month into a common fund. Then, everyone in turn has access to the complete amount on credit. The money is loaned without papers, or signatures, or anything, just a promise. If one member of the group doesn't repay the loan, the honor of the entire family is at stake, so the person's brothers and sisters will be obliged to repay the debt to cleanse the family name. I've come looking for André Marie because he took a loan to go work in France and then disappeared without reimbursing the tontine. His father isn't dead but he's sick, and he fears that because of his dishonored son, his wake will be dry. They called me to remedy the situation before the rainy season comes. I have two or three weeks to take care of the problem. Or else there will be a tragedy: he won't be able to say he's from Nde anymore."

"Nde, that's the name of your village?"

"It's more than a village, it's like a county, and it means 'Nobility, Dignity, Elegance.'"

Azel thought he was joking.

"With all those traditional values where you come from," he asked, "why do you need to leave? I always felt terrible seeing Africans drifting along the streets of Tangier like lost shadows. They're gentle, not bad or aggressive people; they beg, clean cemeteries, do demeaning work for lousy pay. Some of them stand along the roads, especially around the city of Ceuta, and call out to drivers, gesturing to show they're hungry. It's really sad to see. What forces them out onto the roads?"

"We leave, but it's always to come back. We live our lives in terms of our families, for which we each feel responsible. Let me tell you about Apollinaire—not the French poet, but my cousin, who now works in the transportation of goods. A few years ago, his father died suddenly without having repaid a loan his family owed to a tontine. His wake was more than dry: no one came to honor the dead man, it was a deserted wake, arid and miserable. So Apollinaire decided to emigrate to France to make the money his father had not had time to earn. Apollinaire managed to sneak into France and worked selling used cars. In barely five years he'd saved up a goodly sum. He came home to Douala and arranged everything for his father's funeral in their village. Obviously, he had repaid the debt."

"But hadn't his father been dead for five years already?"

"Yes, of course, but the family had to be cleansed of shame, even five years late. That's the story of Apollinaire. Today he's rich, influential, healthy, has several wives, and he manages his business at home. His mother is convinced that he owes this fortune to his respect for a promise given."

"So, I gather that you like things back in your country?"

"We've got economic problems, most of all, and troubles with government and corruption, among others, because we haven't yet hopped off the lap of Madame-la-France, who treats us like retarded children. And the worst thing in all this, you know, it's that we go along with it!"

"So it's because of Madame-la-France that you left your country?"

"No, I'm one of the lucky ones, able to come and go as my work dictates. And above all, I need my mountains the way you need your cigarettes."

"You cling to your homeland on account of some mountains?"

"It's much more than that, it's the land of my ancestors, and they are essential to us: without them, I am not alive."

Azel looked up at the sky and dreamed of Africa. He wondered why Moroccans did not feel African and knew nothing about their own continent.

"You know," said Flaubert, "strangers and foreigners are welcome among us. If you feel like it, you could sell rugs up north in my country, in Maroua, or Garoua; the Aladji would buy them from you. They love Moroccan carpets, especially prayer rugs. So think about it, if you feel like forgetting your troubles: leave Europe without going back to Morocco—Cameroon will welcome you! These aren't idle words, don't forget: we are the land of promises given but above all, kept. Here, let me give you my family's phone number in the Nde. You can call whenever you like."

"You certainly do trust me! Knowing nothing about me, you're already inviting me to visit!"

"It's better to start from the premise that man is good, you know; if he turns out to be bad, he's the one he hurts. A question of wisdom."

"Do you think I could consult a marabout?"*

"Of course, but everything depends on what it is you expect from him."

"To be cured."

"But of what?"

"Of everything. Of myself, my life, my failures, my fears, my weaknesses, my inadequacies. I want to be at peace, that's it, at peace with myself."

Before he left, Flaubert held out his card.

"By the way, what's your name?"

"Azz El Arab."

"That's a writer's name?"

"No such luck!"

34

Kenza

The paperwork on the divorce was moving along. Miguel had warned Kenza that he would be away for a few months. Shortly before his departure, he sent her a package containing a gorgeous antique necklace and a considerable sum of money, along with a note: "My dear, I'm going far away, I'm rather worn out by everything that's happening to me, so I'm looking for just the right distance between my hopes and this complicated life. It isn't easy. I need some air, and most of all, to tend a garden of forgetfulness. Be happy, make me some children with this Turk, and I'll raise them to keep sadness from spoiling my old age."

That last advice was tempting, but Kenza still had her doubts about Nâzim. Whenever she spoke of the future, he became elusive. She was loving; he was hesitant, unable to express his feelings, whether from modesty or calculation, she couldn't tell. They had been seeing each other for more than a year now and were still as perfectly compatible in bed. Kenza wanted to move forward, make plans, and start a family as soon as her divorce from Miguel came through. She loved this country, sent money regu-

larly to her mother, still performed at L'Huile d'Olive, and occasionally agreed to appear at weddings, where Oriental dancing
was fashionable. She was saving money, and had decided not to
worry about Azel. Each to his own life and fate, she kept reflecting, as if to convince herself that he was not her responsibility.

And then Nâzim vanished overnight. Kenza looked for him
everywhere, expecting the worst. She'd heard that the Spanish
Department of the Interior had summoned a hundred illegal
aliens from Mali and Senegal; lured by the promise of receiving
proper documents, they'd all turned up at the police station at
the appointed time. The police had been so nice to them that a
few illegals had even started dancing in front of the station. Then
they had been served hot drinks and little cheese rolls; no pork
rolls, though, and they had appreciated that cultural courtesy. After their meal, the authorities had escorted them to a large hall,
then apparently forgotten about them for the next hour or so,
long enough for the sleeping pills dissolved in the drinks to take
effect. The Africans all fell deeply asleep. Well-trained officers
slipped handcuffs on them and bused them to a military airport
where a plane awaited them. A few of the prisoners opened a
drowsy eye, but could not manage to speak; their vision was
blurred, and they couldn't understand what was happening. On
the plane, other officers gagged them and used an especially
strong tape to bind them to their seats. The plane took off. A few
hours later, the passengers awoke to find they had landed at the
airport in Bamako, where the same officers released them from
their bonds. Inside the plane, blows suddenly began raining down
as seats went flying. The crew had shut themselves up in the

cockpit; the pilot disapproved, of course, but preferred to ignore the whole thing. Going along with it, but not exactly consenting. Orders. There you are—he'd had his orders, although no one had gone into detail about the operation. . . .

Meanwhile, the Malian authorities were in a spot, and wondered why the plane couldn't have landed in Dakar. The revenants—as the Department of the Interior called them—were therefore released into the wild. The Senegalese took off, some for Dakar, others for northern Morocco. They wanted to return to Spain. They had nothing to lose.

It was the Spanish press that broke the story, denouncing the inhumane methods of Aznar's government. The prime minister responded with his usual cynicism: "There was a problem, there's no more problem, so where's the problem?"

This sordid scandal tormented Kenza. Perhaps another charter had been arranged for Turkey? She reassured herself with the thought that there weren't enough Turks in Spain to fill a plane. She went by the restaurant, where one of the waiters told her they hadn't seen Nâzim for a week and gave her an address where she might find him. Kenza took a taxi to what proved to be a dark little street between the Barrio Chino and the Barrio Gótico. The entryway was dirty. A tipsy Latino was begging; she gave him a coin and asked him if he knew a Turk, tall, dark-complexioned, with a thick black mustache.

"Ah, *el moro,* top floor in the back, the red door."

She knocked on the door and called Nâzim's name several times. Inside, she could hear only the voice of a child. She knocked louder.

"Nâzim, it's Kenza, open up, it's important."

The child was crying. Kenza could hear a woman trying to comfort him, and thought she must have been sent to the wrong address. Nâzim couldn't live in this derelict building. Unless he was married and lived there with his family. . . . Kenza felt guilty immediately for thinking that—and yet, anything was possible: Miguel had told her that, time and again. Now her doubts about Nâzim burrowed deep inside her, taking up all the space, gnawing at her, playing tricks on her and making her suffer. There was only one thing to do: find her man and put the question to him straight out.

The next day, toward the end of the afternoon, Nâzim reappeared, seeming tired and preoccupied. He explained to Kenza that he'd had to leave for Galicia for a well-paying job, which he hadn't wanted to tell her about, because it had meant taking some risks. After a moment of silence between them, he took Kenza by the shoulder and spoke softly to her.

"You know, Kenza, my life is complicated, I have debts I must repay to a very bad man. I can't go into details, and anyway I haven't even the right to talk about it, I'm asking you just to trust me."

They had gone to a café. He put his arms around her. Kenza felt like crying, while her intuition kept telling her, Watch out, watch out. Nâzim got up to go to the bathroom. Then Kenza noticed that he'd dropped his wallet. She picked it up, placed it on the table, and stared at it. An insane idea came to her: If you open this wallet, you'll discover something important. It was like a sign from fate. Still, she didn't dare touch the wallet, but Nâzim was taking a long time. . . . She reached out slowly toward the wallet and flipped it open with one finger. A photo. Showing Nâzim hugging a young brunette with long hair, flanked by two children. A family photo. The classic photo that fathers carry in their wallets. She couldn't hold back the tears trickling down her cheeks. Nâzim finally reappeared, smiling, ready to spend a wonderful day with his beloved. Kenza had regained control of herself. She rose without a word, left the café, hailed a taxi, and vanished, leaving Nâzim alone on the sidewalk.

35

Nâzim

The secret had almost corrupted his mind and body. He had kept it locked away, as if in a box firmly shut upon memories that wanted only to return to life, scraps of a previous existence kept prisoner for a few months, perhaps a few years. He had steeled himself not to revisit them, not to recall them. He knew that memories exist only when they are brought back to the present. Sometimes he did circle around them, breathing their perfumes, intoxicating himself with loneliness, taking a good look as if to convince himself that there was no point in going back and forth between his past and present lives. Now there were no more precautions to take. He carried the foul disgrace inside him and thought he could get rid of the dirty, stinking, shameful thing by shoving it down into the realm of inadmissible crimes. He had lied through omission. He'd kept quiet, that's all. Kenza had never asked him specific questions about his past. What would he have said if she had asked him if he'd been married in Turkey? He would have mumbled a few words, then changed the subject. Me, married? Of course not! Naturally, I could have married my

neighbor, but she'd been promised to her cousin. And as the great
Nâzim Hikmet said:

> *I tore the gazelle from the hunter's hands, but fainting still, it could not be revived*
> *I plucked the orange from its branch, but it could not be peeled*
> *I slipped in among the stars, pell-mell, but they could not all be counted. . . .*

It was now two years and three months since he'd seen his wife
and two sons. He sent them money, called them from time to
time from a phone booth, telling them anything at all, saying that
he was working in a private university whose name he never mentioned, that he lived in Madrid but also taught mathematics in
Toledo. He invented, made mistakes, became confused, apologized, then curtly hung up the phone. He knew that he could
count on his wife, who worked for a firm of architects; she was
quite capable of taking care of the children, and she would wait
for him. He had left Turkey because of massive gambling debts,
when he'd found himself suddenly brutally pressed by one of his
creditors, a wealthy and perverted man.

"I know that you have nothing, not a thing," the man had said.
"You could never pay me all that you owe me. Killing you, that
wouldn't bring me back my money. You can't imagine how much
money I have, but you see, I love Evil, I love to see my fellow man
suffer, I can't explain to you what happens inside me, but I get off
on seeing someone, especially someone nice, like you, slaving away
and suffering the worst humiliations in life. Your punishment—is
exile. I'm throwing you out of the country. Sending you to hell,
not prison, that would be too simple, no, I condemn you to exile.

224

I take you from your wife and children, on whom I will keep my eye. For three years, do not set foot in Turkey. My men are everywhere, they're ruthless, and delight in cutting their fellow men into very small pieces; that's how it is, and you owe me three million, so I sentence you to three years' nonexistence in Turkey. Got that? And do *not* make me cry: when I cry, I turn mean. You're lucky, you know, your punishment isn't cruel enough, so consider yourself fortunate to have wound up with a creditor of my stamp. Wait, don't leave yet, you haven't heard where I'm sending you. Someplace where Turks don't usually go. Hey, Spain, for example: it's a lovely country, Spain, very hospitable. You'll make discoveries there, might even like the place. Don't apply for a visa, you'll never get one. Just set out, walking, day and night, and think of me if you get tired—I'll be getting off. You have forty-eight hours to disappear. Listen, take this phone number: the guy's name is Omar, his friends call him Taras Bulba; he's not a poet, but he likes to butt-fuck men like you, so give him your ass and he'll help you get out of the country. It's up to you; Omar's a sicko, soon as he spots some buttocks, he whips out his dick to try having a go at them—a strange fellow, loyal, he's never betrayed me, has no feelings or emotions. Unless you'd rather tackle everything on your own. . . . Don't think you can mention our contract to anyone, or ask for political asylum, for example; I know Europeans are bleeding hearts, soon as they see someone looking a little lost, they slip him political asylum—not in your interest to try for that, I've got your family in the palm of my hand. Mind you, you don't have to go to Spain, you could try Germany, but that would be too easy, with all the Turks they've got. Germany, that wouldn't be exile. Exile's an icy-cold place. But don't forget, even there, I've got my spies."

Nâzim knew he was dealing with a twisted man. He had no choice but to leave, flee, get out of Turkey and into Spain as fast as possible, staying three years, exactly as ordered. His creditor must have had his henchmen there; Nâzim took all his threats seriously and already saw himself, as in films about the Mafia, pursued by killers, with his wife and children in danger. His debts were enormous. How had he come to this? A kind of mindlessness, a madness, a curse. Gambling for him had been like drinking for alcoholics, a true plunge into hell. His wife, though, had never known a thing. He would never, ever, have told her about it. He simply used to disappear now and then, saying he had meetings at the university or that he'd run into some childhood friends and would be getting home late that night. His exile in Spain was a punishment, of course, but he also saw it as a chance to free himself from gambling. Before leaving, he explained to his wife that the university was sending him to Europe for a few months; he didn't go into details. He kissed his children as they slept, packed a bag, and vanished, blinking back tears.

That's how he'd wound up in Spain after a short stopover in France and a few troubles along the way.

36

Azel

What is an undocumented alien? A foreigner in an irregular situation. A clandestine who has burned all proofs of his identity to make it impossible to return him to his native land. But also, sometimes, a foreigner who has entered a country legally but no longer has a work permit, a residence permit, or any reason to remain in that country.

Azel was in that last category. To renew his residence permit, which had expired a few months earlier, he had to have a work contract with an employer and a home address attested to by a water, electricity, or telephone bill. And he could not provide any such documentation. He knew he had tumbled into illegality, the marginal zone patrolled by traffickers and other recruiters always ready to hire you for unsavory jobs. He knew this and wasn't worried about it. A fatalist, he felt that his destiny was to follow this path, not resist it. And so he had broken with everyone, even Kenza. He lived heedlessly, as if he wished to atone for some serious offense he had once committed. He now had no one to talk to, to confide in. His life had lost all meaning. He spent most of his time with Abbas, who slipped him counterfeit watches to sell, or sometimes a few matchboxes crammed with hashish sticks. Now and then, when a woman would brush past Azel, he felt he had recovered his former sexual prowess and would dash off to a café to masturbate in the men's room. One day, Azel sold a fake Cartier watch to a passerby, who thanked him in Arabic. A moment later, the man returned and asked him if he had time for a coffee. He didn't know this city, he explained, he was just passing through. Could Azel give him the address of a mosque in this neighborhood, where he could go for the evening prayer? He wanted to pray, he'd be so unhappy if he couldn't.

Azel didn't know of any mosque in the area.

"So," the man asked him, "you don't pray?"

In reply, Azel made a face that meant prayer was not his thing.

"It's a great pity, my brother, not to speak to God, even just once a day. Did you know that you can gather the five daily prayers together in the evening and say them in peace that way?"

Then Azel understood that this man was in fact a recruiter using the same approach and friendly patter as the one who'd tried to rope him into an Islamist movement in Tangier. Azel let him talk, listening to him without imagining the guy in grotesque situations the way he had with the first recruiter. That time, he'd still had the energy to defend himself against this kind of seductive political come-on. Now he was tired, and hoped in some confused way to take advantage somehow of whatever propositions this man would surely offer him.

"You understand, brother, that here, we are in the land of our ancestors, those whom Isabella the Catholic expelled after burning men of faith, our Muslim ancestors, at the stake. She ordered the destruction of places of prayer, she forced those unable to flee to convert to Catholicism, she outlawed the writing of Arabic and the wearing of traditional garments. That was in the past, five hundred years ago, but the burning wound is still here, in our hearts, in the heart of every Muslim, every Arab. Islam has been driven from this country. It is our duty to bring it back, to make it respected. We've had enough of humiliation, of our unworthiness in the eyes of the Christian West. Consider how our Palestinian brothers are treated, how America supports the policies of Israel, and how our countries treat their own citizens. We must do something, react, spread, listen to the voice of Islam and other Muslims. Tell me, you've studied, haven't you, you're not illiterate like most of your brothers?"

"Yes, I'm a graduate of the law school in Rabat."

"I could tell right away. I knew I was dealing with a cultivated man of good sense. I would like to invite you to join us for the evening prayer. Not today, of course, but if some other time you happen to feel like meeting some compatriots who are neither drug dealers nor the dregs of society, come see what we're building, what we're preparing for our country's future."

Azel realized that the man was lying to him, and asked, "Are you Moroccan?"

"As much as you are."

"Then why do you have the Near Eastern accent? You sound like one of those men from the Gulf states who lecture us on TV."

"It's just because I went to the Wahhabi university in Jidda."

"Wahhabi . . . you're Wahhabi?"

"Come to see us, then I'll explain to you the doctrine of our guide Abd al-Wahhab,* who lived in the eighteenth century."

"I know, you don't need to draw me a picture, it's the hidden woman, veiled from head to toe, it's Sharia instead of the law and civil rights. You cut off the thief's hand, you stone the adulterous woman . . ."

"All those things, they're just preconceived ideas. I'll make an appointment with you for next week, same time, same café. Here's my card with my cell phone number. You can reach me whenever you like, except during prayers, of course. And I forgot to tell you that by some magnificent coincidence, my name just happens to be Abd al-Wahhab!"

Azel was not surprised. He studied the card, reading and rereading what was on it: *Ahmad Abd al-Wahhab; Import/Export; Barcelona–Madrid–Tangier; Tel. 34 606 892 05.*

That evening, Azel managed to unload his entire stock of watches from Abbas. He was about to leave the café when a scuffle broke out between two immigrants. Responding with exceptional speed, the police arrested everyone.

"Identity check!" shouted an officer. "Papers, passport, work permit, residence permit, unemployment card, I want to see every card, and those who don't have any, step to the right, while those who think theirs are all in order, step to the left! All Spaniards, beat it! This concerns only *moros.*"

Azel hesitated, then moved to the left. He had his passport with him, but all his other documents were out of date. He noticed that the police let two North African Arabs go without even demanding their papers. Informers. Perhaps the very ones who'd alerted the police.

Azel was taken to the police station, where he thought about calling Miguel, but didn't dare get him involved. Azel's fate had to pass through that café and his arrest. He was sure of that. There was only one thing he didn't want: to be sent back to Morocco. The shame, the *hchouma,* and the *hegra,* the humiliation—no, never, anything but that, even prison but not the boot up the backside, hard enough to land him in a few seconds on the heights of the Old Mountain of Tangier. He had left. Left to return only like a prince, not like garbage tossed out by the Spanish. The police found Azel's two matchboxes full of hashish. Now he was in worse trouble.

"So: this man whose papers are not in order—is also selling hashish!"

He spent the night at the station, lying sleepless on a bench next to a Latino bum who stank. Azel thought about his mother. He called to her; she didn't hear him. He knew she couldn't hear him. He saw her sitting on the terrace of their house, looking at the sea, thinking of the day when she would rejoin her children. She'd had enough troubles in her life to want to end her days in a happy country with her two successful children at her side. Everyone has a dream. . . . Azel's was broken beyond repair. For the moment, he had to find a way out, something that would convince the police of his good faith. Hard to plead innocent with fifty grams of hashish in your pockets. So he had to put his cards on the table. In the morning he asked to speak to someone in authority, an officer with whom he could negotiate.

"Negotiate! Negotiate! This is a police station, not a court of
law! You're a lousy drug dealer hawking fake watches and you
want to *negotiate*? Just who do you think you are?"

The officer finally arrived. He spoke Arabic.

"*Assalam Alikum! Issmi Khaïmé, atakallamu larabiya wa aʾrifu al Maghreb.
Madha turid ya Azz El Arab?* Bonjour, my name is Jaime, I speak Arabic,
I know your part of the world, the Maghreb. What do you want,
Azz El Arab?"

"*Mina al mumkin an ou inoukum.* I could be useful to you."

Jaime abandoned the Arabic and began speaking in French
and Spanish.

"Useful? You want to turn informer?"

"Well, more precisely, I could supply you with information
about certain Islamist groups."

Jaime left to make a phone call, returning with another officer, evidently higher in rank than he was.

"You think you can be a police informer just like that? It takes
time: building trust, showing results, being tested. . . ."

After an hour, during which Azel felt the atmosphere change,
a third officer joined them.

"How can you prove that we can trust you?"

Azel got out Abd al-Wahhab's card and handed it to him.

"This man tried to get me to join a movement, a kind of group
to defend Muslim interests in Spain. He talks constantly about
revenge, about Isabella the Catholic, Andalusia, the return of Islam to Christian and infidel lands. I'll be meeting him again next
week. Give me a chance."

That's how Azel became a snitch for the Spanish police. He saved his skin but sold his soul. Perhaps in a good cause. Actually, he didn't give a damn whether he was on the right side or not. Despair had hardened his heart. The next day, he felt rather sick, with pins and needles all over his body. Tiny insects were running up and down his limbs, gnawing at him, and he felt paralyzed. He wasn't suffering terribly, but he did see his right foot detach itself and get carried off by a thick column of black ants, after which praying mantises tore off his other foot. He would have liked them to carry all of him away like that and bring him a completely new body; maybe he would recover his virility, and experience once more the pleasures of his former life. Azel's face felt like a stone mask. When he tried to stand up to go look in the mirror, he couldn't budge. Something was holding him back, a powerful exterior force that clamped him to the earth. Entirely enveloped in a transparent blue veil, a lovely Moroccan woman was now holding the mirror out to him. Smiling, dancing, she invited him to join her. Remaining absolutely still, Azel watched her; this was the first time he had ever felt such a change in his awareness of the world. He thought of Kafka and The Metamorphosis, which he'd never read, but he remembered a wonderful lecture his philosophy professor had given on the subject.

I'm going to transform myself, become someone else—that would be a good thing, after all: I'm changing from one person to another; I add a bit of treachery, a touch of denunciation, even if it's for the right cause, and which cause is it, anyway? I mean, really, it's disgusting to be a spy for the cops.

He needed a little time to get used to his new duties. His mind was almost down to its last scruples. Gone, no forwarding.

Gone for good. Gone to die. He was planning to visit the city cemetery. *If I die, bury me here, in this land I dreamed about so much. I wouldn't like to be interred in the earth of the Marshan Cemetery, I know it much too well: the dead folks are our neighbors, and we know all their visitors. Dying, what does it matter. . . .*

One morning, when he got up, he felt the need to do something positive. He went to the post office to send a telegraphic money order to his mother. Then he phoned her to announce that he had a new job, that Miguel had gone to America for a long time, that he himself was doing well and would soon visit her in Tangier.

When his mother began to speak, her tone was melodramatic.

"You see, my son, I don't know how much more time God will grant me in this life, so you know what obsesses me: to see you married, to see your children playing in my house and making noise, lots of noise. . . . I would not like to die without experiencing such wonderful moments. You know, your cousin, lovely Sabah, she's waiting for you, she just refused a rich and quite promising suitor; Sabah thinks about you, her mother confirmed that to me yesterday. Come, take a wife and give me grandchildren. May God grant me life and your presence at my deathbed."

Azel said nothing beyond the conventional phrase: "May God grant you health and may your blessing protect me."

Protected . . . he didn't feel protected at all. How had he managed to get himself mixed up in so many conflicts? He saw himself at an intersection, unable to cross; in the rush of cars coming from all directions, he felt like a headless puppet. After everything he'd lived through that past month, how could he possibly find himself? How could he find peace? There was someone inside him driving him to sabotage his own life.

Possessed. That's what his mother would have said about him.

They've cast a spell on you. They've hunted you. The evil eye, hatred, jealousy. There, my son, is the explanation for everything that is happening to you. You cannot imagine what malice springs up in people, in life, whenever anyone stands out from the crowd; they try to hurt you: you're handsome, intelligent, successful (you managed to leave, in any case, and make a fine career for yourself in Spain), so you unleash ferocious hatred, dreadful envy—oh, we're all persecuted by the evil eye, and I know, you young people today, you don't believe in it, you think logic is everything, that nothing happens beyond what you see, but you must learn to see what doesn't show itself, because even our prophet Lord Mohammed recognized the existence of the evil eye. Jealousy can wreak havoc, just look at what befell that poor Hanane: she's beautiful, educated, from a good family, and was going to marry an engineer, from an important clan, so everything was ready, even the invitations were printed, and you know what happened to her? No, she didn't die: worse! She was abandoned by her fiancé, who preferred to marry her aunt! So the evil eye, I know it well. My son, don't forget to read the Koran: God will protect you. Know that from where I am, far from you, I never stop blessing you, you and your sister.

37

Kenza

Alerted by the emergency service of the Red Cross, Miguel emerged from his voluntary seclusion to sit at the bedside of his wife, who had tried to commit suicide. Kenza was frighteningly pale, with dull, empty eyes. An unhappy love affair. A cruel disappointment. She had suddenly lost all desire to live. When she did not answer Miguel's questions, he felt that her silence was the result of some specific trauma, that something dreadful must have happened. Miguel searched her handbag and pulled out a book of poems, *Human Landscapes*, by Nâzim Hikmet. He looked at the photograph Kenza had used as a bookmark. It showed her next to a tall man, darkly handsome, with a mustache. They were standing in front of a restaurant called the Kebab. Miguel wondered if Kenza might recover her power of speech if she could see the man in the picture again, and with the doctor's encouragement, he began to search for him. It took Miguel some time to find the Kebab, a modest hole-in-the-wall squeezed between a dry cleaner's and a cell phone store. The chairs were dirty and the tables were covered in plastic. An old man was nodding behind the counter, but when he saw Miguel arrive in his beautiful coat, he jumped as if the king in person had just walked in. Miguel narrowed his eyes; there was a poster on the back wall with the picture of some actor or singer, and when Miguel looked more closely, he thought he recognized the man beside Kenza in the photograph.

The old man smiled at Miguel.

"Ah, you too are an admirer of our national star! All the women are crazy about him. He's a magnificent singer."

"Where does he live?"

"He's the kind who has palaces wherever he goes. Everyone is a fan, whatever the government: left, right, military, civilian, Muslim, secular—he's always loved and applauded."

"He doesn't live in Spain?"

"No, he came last year for a television special. Thanks to Touria, our prettiest waitress, we had the honor of receiving him here. He even sang without any music because there were some thirty compatriots in the room who kept clamoring for a song."

"Who is he?"

"His name's Ibrahim Tatlises,* which means 'sweet voice'! He's from Urfa, southeastern Turkey, not far from the Syrian border. He's a lady-killer. Wherever he sings, husbands hide their wives. Touria cries at the very sound of his voice."

Miguel showed the man the photo.

"Do you know this woman?"

"Her, no, but the man, yes, he worked here for a few months. He kept mostly to himself. I don't know where he's gone. He never gave me any cause for complaint. Did he do something wrong? Wait a minute, it's true, he does look like Ibrahim, but of course it's not the same man!"

Miguel stammered a few words of thanks and promptly left that dark and dreary place. Suddenly he realized that Kenza had fallen in love with love. She wanted a man in her life, and had thought she'd found him in Nâzim.

How had that quiet girl, apparently so levelheaded, who'd worked to put herself through nursing school and done so well there—how had she convinced herself that this man she hardly knew was eager to start a family with her? Once again, Miguel felt somewhat responsible for this mistake, and especially for the present crisis. He reflected that he should have kept a better eye on her, paid attention to what she was doing, introduced her to people and even men who might have made her happy. This mysterious and seductive Nâzim had clearly hoped to obtain papers, perhaps even to become a Spanish citizen through Kenza, who had never considered—or rather, had refused to consider—that possibility. She had defiantly decided that he would be her husband and the father of her children. The lovers had spoken about it only once, though, and Nâzim had been difficult to pin down. Kenza had talked about it with her mother, however, who'd been pressing her for a long time to find a husband. Lalla Zohra believed in the affair with Nâzim and was sure Kenza had found the right man. In reality, her daughter had done nothing but concoct a fantasy that fulfilled her every desire: to get married, be like everyone else, have children right away, and above all, go home at last with her head held high to make her mother happy.

Nâzim had come along, and Kenza had chosen him to play the main role in her story. Nâzim had never had any inkling of what was actually going on. Now, Kenza's world had collapsed. The blow had been devastating.

She had to be saved, brought back to reality, persuaded to accept therapy. She had to forget that man and perhaps even consider returning to Morocco in the end. Miguel now realized that there was something terrifying about the loneliness of immigration, a kind of descent into a void, a tunnel of shadows that warped reality. Kenza had let herself be caught in the maze, and Azel, well, he had gone desperately wrong. Exile revealed the true dimensions of calamity. Miguel remembered how much the long psychoanalysis he had undergone had helped him with this aspect of his life, perhaps even saving that same life. But Kenza was no more inclined at present than Azel to lie down on a couch and talk about the secrets of the soul. . . . A question of culture and tradition, and money, too. In any case, they both thought that only crazy people went to psychiatrists.

And now Miguel understood how urgent it was to send Kenza and Azel home to Morocco, since their return was certainly the only thing that would help them find their footing again and begin to heal. Miguel contacted Juan, the consular official who had helped him with the initial paperwork involving Azel. Now he wanted him to have Azel arrested and expelled to Morocco. With Kenza, Miguel would take the time necessary to convince her to remake her life in her native country. After a few inquiries, Juan informed Miguel that his protégé had changed protectors: he was at present working in Madrid as an informer for the antiterrorist police, so Miguel no longer needed to worry about him. Despite the fact that his feelings for Azel had changed, Miguel had a hard time dealing with such a shock. So their relationship had really been a failure all down the line. . . . Miguel had to face facts: no one can change the course of fate.

38

Azel

Azel could have found another way out of his predicament, but homesickness had wounded him deeply. He saw things clearly, and was ashamed.

I'm ashamed of failing at everything, ashamed of clasping a hand held out to me in a bed where silken sheets gleamed as enticingly as sin; I wanted to convince myself that my manhood was strong enough to satisfy both men and women: what pretension, what folly, and how sorry I am that I followed Miguel, that kind and generous man, of whom I never managed to be worthy. . . . At first I told myself it was just an experience like any other, I even remembered doing a few things with Mehdi, my cousin who so enjoyed having his buttocks stroked, but with time I discovered that I couldn't tell lies for very long, and I lied, masturbating in the dark before reaming Miguel, doing things without pleasure or joy, sometimes laughing at myself, especially when I was on top of him; I'd hit him in the back, he liked that, so I'd take advantage, wanting money, which he'd give me, and then I saw myself as a whore, a private gigolo. I had everything I wanted and afterward I'd feel bad, guilty, dishonest, a leech, so I'd provoke him to make him mad, make him let go of me—I'd try to exasperate him, and I did, and then the old woman Carmen would butt in with her nasty mouth! She spared me nothing, she saw what was going on—she used to scream, especially when he wasn't there, calling me **moro hijo de la calle,** *dirty Moor-boy from the gut-*

ter, and one day when she called me hijo de puta, a whoreson, my blood boiled in an instant and I gave her a bitch-slap she won't forget anytime soon. . . . Attacking my mother, that—she had no right! My poor mother who made such sacrifices for her children, taking risks by smuggling, and to call her a whore—I could have strangled that Carmen, so then I knew it was time to go, which I did in a mean way: I stole, I ripped the silk sheets, pissed on Miguel's handmade shoes, broke a crystal vase, went on a rampage; I wanted to bring a real whore, crude, drenched in cheap scent and plastered with makeup, and fuck her in Miguel's bed, but I couldn't do it. I left with my head hanging because the old woman had the last word and I couldn't speak my whole mind to Miguel, when I wanted to shout and denounce all those flush Europeans who come shopping in the poor neighborhoods of Tangier, Marrakech, Essaouira; I can remember the plight of the shrimps—the shrimps, they're the still-fresh little adolescents whom Europeans pay with a sandwich, that's right, not only do they fuck them or get fucked but they don't even pay the shrimps fairly. I was struggling like a dement, trying to earn a living and above all take good care of my mother who'd had such trouble raising us in dignity—how many times did she go off to cook for rich people celebrating a wedding or anniversary, when she'd leave early in the morning and drag herself home late at night, with a little money and some food, the leftovers from the party, pieces of meat and a little sauce in plastic bags? Then she'd heat it all up and tell us, "Eat, it's your mother's cooking, eat your fill, take what you can while we wait for better days," and to me she'd add, "You, when you grow up you'll be a doctor or an engineer, you'll take me traveling, first to Mecca, then Cairo—I so long to see the land of Farid al-Atrash* and Oum Kalsoum, you'll buy me jewelry and lengths of silk, I'll live a new life, a queen's life, a little queen without a crown or king but you'll be my prince, you'll always be my prince, so work hard in school, bring me home good grades, be a good son, you'll have my blessing forever. . . ." Given what I've done, it's hard to say that I've made her dreams come true, and the whoring clings to me—all my pals at the Café Hafa know that I left with the Christian from pure self-interest, that I've always chased women, that I'm not, as they say, who people think I am, that I was ready to do anything to get out of Morocco, and besides there were some who envied me, who'd have loved to meet someone who'd pack them up in the luggage; some were looking for women but hey, they were ready to go off with guys, everyone knows, it's common talk in cafés, our reputation is widespread and it's not a pretty one—there are even hotel concierges or fellows out on terraces, they alert their buddies when they spot a pigeon, usually a woman of a certain age, preferably rich, alone or with a woman friend, often a widow or divorcée, or sometimes, but rarely, still young, free, available for True Love, dreaming of the Orient, harems, and pretty little clichés. Everything's divine at first, all wonderful, the sex works just fine, plans are made, the woman's dazzled by the pleasure the guy gives her, she's ready for anything, can't imagine leaving Morocco now without her little Moroccan, so off she goes and pulls every possible string to bring him to her native Holland or her American town, and it's only much later she discovers she's been had; then it's disappointment, hatred, depression, and rejection of anything even remotely resembling an Arab. . . . None of that means anything anymore. . . . I can't get an erection, I'm punished, I punished myself, convinced myself I no longer deserved to have sex—that's it, a self-mutilation that's making me suffer atrociously; I sit crying off in a corner, not even wiping away my tears, weeping over my country, over everything it was unable or didn't know how to give us, weeping over all those young people wandering the streets looking for a helping hand, over my family who will be so disappointed and so in need of comfort, but me—who will comfort me? Who will embrace me and put me back on the road to life? I struggle to breathe, I'm choking, but no one cares; I watch others pass me by and I envy them, I imagine them living, laughing heartily, planning for the future, breathing deeply, setting stones one upon the other, building a house, being as strong as stone, feeling desire and bringing it to climax, while I'm here, and I try to be useful, to be somebody else, a real man instead of a liar, a thief, or a fake, but how will I manage that? I need help: maybe a sleep cure would be good for me, but I haven't the right to go away, to

*put my head in the sand, I just need to finally forget that time when I left Morocco—
if I could only stop thinking about that. . . . There: that memory does not reflect anything I did, I can look all I want, I'm not finding a thing, forgotten, erased, that
moment when I left and was writing to my country. . . .*

Azel's dearest wish was to wipe out all memory of his departure from Morocco, and to return home like a hero. Was he not
personally helping to combat the terrorism that was threatening
Europe? Now he dreamed of appearing on television, introduced
as the good Muslim responsible for thwarting a dangerous plot.
All this had pushed Azel's sexual problems to the sidelines; he no
longer fretted over his penis, looked at women, or had erotic
dreams. He had become another man: courageous, subtle, and
strong. He moved with clear agility and ease between the antiterrorist police and the radical Islamist movements dedicated to
sending the West up in flames. He knew, however, that this equi-
librium could not last forever. From one day to the next he feared
some fresh collapse provoked by his chaotic life in Madrid. As a
front, the police had found him a part-time job in the legal department of a large bank; no one was supposed to know what he
did with the rest of his time. At long last, Azel felt useful and
respected. He dressed elegantly, drank abstemiously, but could
not manage to give up kif, which he often abused to the point of
making himself ill. Only a mixture of aspirin, paracetamol, and
codeine could relieve his violent headaches.

When several days passed without any sign of life from Azel,
his police contact became annoyed and decided to visit him. The
concierge claimed to have seen Azel the previous day with two
men, *"Moros,"* she added. The policeman rang and rang Azel's bell,

but no one came to the door. He called for reinforcements to break it down.

Azel was on the floor, his throat cut, his head in a pool of blood. The Brothers had slaughtered him like a lamb sacrificed for Aïd el-Kebir.

39

Kenza

Waiting. Kenza had spent her life waiting. She had explored all the mysteries of boredom, because to wait is to dive into a sea of ennui. It's like growing old, in other words—watching the future shut down, fade away, lose all promise. If she could have at least known what she was waiting for. . . . Although Kenza had always managed to get through her life without too much fuss, her mother never stopped saying things like:

"Tell me, how do others manage to do so well, finding a husband of good family, with fine financial prospects, a handsome, respectable man? Look at you: you are beautiful in every way, your studies enable you to work in a clinic, you're from an honest and upright family—not rich, but not poor, either, so, tell me, what are you waiting for to meet a man? I'm waiting for you— every day I pray God that you meet someone, I pray and ask God to consider my condition, my age, and my hopes. . . ."

Kenza had had enough of such admonitions. She was simply unlucky. She lacked the savoir-faire of her married girlfriends who preferred not to notice that their husbands were merrily cheating on them. At least they had a home.

Before leaving Morocco, Kenza had even dared take part one day in a program about marriage on Radio Tangier. The moderator had gathered together four unmarried women between twenty-five and thirty-five years old, whom she introduced with the remark that after the age of twenty-five, it was time to get seriously worried. Kenza had just turned thirty and had lost her virginity years before. She wanted to defend the idea that a woman could be single and happy, free and honest, loved and respected. She was waiting not for a husband, but for love. She had an exalted idea of love, of the relationship between the sexes, especially in a beautiful country like her own, and although she knew that she was cherishing some illusions, she persisted in her ambition: to find love—true love, real and sincere, overwhelming love, and for once, just once, to experience those sublime moments described so tellingly in the films and novels she had adored. She remembered in particular *The Alexandria Quartet*, which her philosophy professor had given her; *Gone with the Wind* and *The Lady of the Camellias* had deeply moved her as well. It was through such works that she had formed a precise idea of what would make her deliriously happy. And it was also how she had realized that she would not find such a love in Morocco, not because Moroccan men were incapable of such emotion, but because daily life and public opinion would always stifle true love in the end.

She had learned much about Morocco in the hammam, the ideal place for sociologists, psychoanalysts, historians, novelists, and even poets. For it is there, as they bathe, that women talk. It is the greatest divan in the world, a collective space, like taxis, where everyone has the right to speak up, to confide, to complain.

It is there that women have for centuries been shedding tears and sharing those truths that the outside world wishes to neither see nor hear. It was in this haven that Khadija the seamstress had dared tell how she had caught her husband abusing the little apprentice who worked in her home, a sweet and talented girl of thirteen. The husband was sneaking into her bed and entering her from behind to avoid taking her virginity, and to punish him for this crime, Khadija had deprived him of insulin for an entire day, which had almost driven him insane. It was in the hammam as well that Kenja had heard the story of Saadia, possessed by the jinns* that lived in her old house: as soon as she lighted a lamp, an invisible hand would snuff it out. Now Saadia was familiar with every marabout in the country and spoke of nothing but what the jinns had commanded her to do. It was also in the hammam that Kenza had learned of the miraculous recipe to restore full potency to a man; at least three women had attested to the marvelous change in their husbands after they'd taken this potion. And it was in the hammam that Kenza had heard that pregnant African women were choosing to make the dangerous clandestine crossing in hopes that the police would take pity on them if they were arrested, and let them give birth on Spanish soil.

She had "learned" Morocco in the hammam the way one learns a language both foreign and familiar. Silences, for example, could be translated. Back home, women who kept silent did so not because they had nothing to say, but because few people were capable of listening to and understanding what they did have to say. Now Kenza paid attention to women who kept their own counsel. The raw language used by women among themselves had been a shocking revelation to her: they spoke openly about genitals and accompanied their words with obscene gestures, showing no modesty, as if they were all sharing at last in the power of complete freedom. If they could have lived their whole lives in the hammam, they would have done so. It would have become the land of women, where they would summon men, to consume them as they pleased, returning them afterward to their humdrum lives laced, of necessity, with cowardice and compromises great and small, a social routine where appearances are naturally intended to mask everything else. Imagine an immense hammam as the City of Women, with veils of vapor in the semi-darkness, so conducive to speaking freely and in confidence, and secret networks of cellars, taverns, trap doors, antechambers where sexuality would at last be free, unfettered by modesty or moral judgment. Women would gather there to reorganize the relationships of society, or at least those between men and women. That would be a nice little revolution! "Wife, where are you going?" the husband would shout. "I'm off to the hammam to bathe, pluck my eyebrows, and perfume myself just for you, so that tonight I may be yours, to do with as you please!" The husbands would complain, "Oh, the hammam again!"—and have no idea how much they'd be missing; yes, you poor husbands, everything escapes you, but you'll never have a clue, never learn what goes on there, where women are so fond of gathering among themselves for a few hours undisturbed by husbands or children. "A curse on this place from which men are banished!" husbands would cry. "We men, when we go to the hammam, we don't dawdle and linger there, we wash, all done, then it's off to work."

And that's how Kenza went to school in the hammam of Marshan. Which hadn't prevented her from spending the rest of her time waiting, waiting, and waiting some more. Then the angel Gabriel arrived: Miguel, the friend in need, bringing with him both order and disorder. Without meaning to, he would seriously damage the life of her family, but no one would ever reproach him for that. Unlike her brother, Kenza was grateful to Miguel. She did not hold him responsible for her self-destructive fantasies. She'd felt this burning wound inside her for a long time, well before the advent of Miguel: the wound of waiting, ennui, and a future whose mirror had shattered.

Kenza had dozed off peacefully. Light music was playing on the radio. As if in a dream she heard: "The king is dead; long live the king!" Then a cry, followed by applause, and then: "Hassan II is now at rest; may his son be ever blessed!" Images began tumbling through her mind: men and women clothed in white immersing themselves in a river, then going to pray in a vast prairie bathed in light. No one was weeping. Children were running in all directions yelling, "Long live the king!"

But it was not a dream. Rising, she felt an unfamiliar sense of profound well-being, and even felt like shouting "Long live the king!" Going to look in the bathroom mirror, she saw a radiant face there. It was hers. She was happy, and did not even try to discover the reason for this sudden joy. She ran cold water over her head but decided not to dry her hair; she liked feeling the water drip gently down her chest and shoulders. She was alone, and needed no one else. Later that evening, she watched a rebroadcast of the king's funeral, followed by scenes of allegiance being pledged to a young man, who was deeply moved by his duty to carry on the centuries-old traditions of his dynasty.

It was then that Kenza felt the hour had come for her to go home at last to Morocco.

40

Returning

For several days now a few of them have already been on the move, guided by an irresistible longing to head far away, to put out to sea. They walk along, crossing cities, chilly wastelands, forests, fields. They walk day and night, driven by a force of such unsuspected strength that they feel no fatigue, not even the need to eat and drink. Borne along by winds bound for home, they advance without questions, without wondering what is happening to them. They believe that destiny is there, in that march, drawing them back to their roots, to their native land, a destiny that has appeared to them as a kind of command, an indisputable order, a time outside time, the ascent to a mountaintop, a wonderful promise, a shining dream, pressing on, heading over the horizon. They take to the road, heads high, with a warm breath at their backs: the wind of freedom. Sensing that this is the moment, this is the hour. This is their season, a season for no one but them, for all those who have suffered, who have not found their place in life. Without a single regret, they've left everything behind and have already forgotten why they ever left home. They head for the port, where a familiar inner voice tells them to embark on a boat christened *Toutía,* a modest craft aboard which the captain has planted a flowering tree with a sweet perfume, an orange or a lemon tree.

The captain is a man from another era, a kind of dandy with sideburns and a well-trimmed beard. His body is frail, and he is assisted by a graceful young woman with gray, almond-shaped eyes, a dark complexion, and long brown hair that blows in the wind. Some people claim she's a countess; others that she's a fashion model from Brazil; still others believe she is the captain's wife, for does he not gaze at her with loving eyes? She is there to welcome the new passengers with open arms. Tattoos emblazon her forehead and chin. She places her right hand on the shoulder of the captain, who calls her Toutia the Sublime. And when the captain gives the signal, she sings an Andalusian Arab song in a clear, true voice; the song is suffused with wrenching nostalgia, and her voice breaks with emotion. Toutia closes her eyes and sings with all her heart. Everyone, on the dock as well as the ship, stops to listen to her in silence.

They arrive in scattered little groups. There is pride in their eyes: what they have just accomplished was not simply a duty, but a necessity. Some of them have succumbed to fatigue; it's nothing, only a touch of rheumatism. In the heat of midsummer, it is the cold of exile, a pernicious chill, that attacks you: you stand up only to find your right leg giving way, that's how it is, who knows why; the doctor told me it was age but he was lying to me; the mind is fine but the body can no longer keep up. How dare he say that to me, when I've been wandering these roads for so long?—

but I can see he's not familiar with this illness that quietly torments us . . . well, good for him, after all; I feel fine at the moment, I don't know who I am, but I feel fine, in spite of the doctor's opinion. I've lost my name, I'm told my face is gone—it's amazing how mean people can be—and my rheumatic pains have disappeared as well. This boat seems both familiar and strange to me: perhaps it isn't a boat, only a model, some trompe-l'oeil, a simple image projected out onto the water; this is the first time I've ever boarded a boat without knowing its destination, which is a beautiful thing, actually. . . . I'll sail across the waves until the day the last day dawns, until the moment when the Master of the Soul will come to reclaim his due, and as for me, I'm ready, been ready for a long time now, ever since my mother taught me that the great good-bye is nothing and that the only things to fear are sickness and the wickedness of men. A wing will dip down and gather you up to bear you away to other skies, that's what death is, my son, a dream in which suffering no longer exists.

Miguel walks with a cane. He is still smartly dressed, but his face has an unhealthy tinge and is marked by illness; he advances silently, alone. He, too, is answering the call. Who alerted him? Who told him about this expedition? Miguel put all his affairs in order before leaving his house. No one is aware of what he has meticulously prepared. Everything has been laid out in a letter left to Carmen and Gabriel.

In a few days, a few weeks, perhaps, I'll be going away. No tears, please, over my condition; I must admit that I've been happy, and have experienced some difficult moments as well as extraordinary joys, and today I have no regrets, I leave at peace, with a light heart, asking only one thing of you: that no one should know about the disease that consumes me and will carry me off. I'm counting on your sense of responsibility, your love, and your friendship to ensure that my sendoff will be as beautiful and elegant as my life. Discretion, restraint, dignity, and generosity: that is my wish. I hate noise and bother. On the day when I feel my end coming, I will enter a hospital with "bronchitis" and die in my bed there. You will then be informed, and will come get me even if it's the middle of the night. Under absolutely no circumstances will you leave me in the morgue, not that I'm afraid of the cold, but it's a dirty, unsavory place, and you will take me home immediately, to my old house, and there you will ask my neighbor Lahcen, a religious man and the soul of honesty, to come prepare my body. Next, you will buy flowers, all the flowers you can find in the market of Fès; place them everywhere, burn sandalwood, and whatever you do—do not call a priest: remember that I have become a Muslim. Lastly, invite all my friends, and offer them food and drink.

I have already bought the grave, which is at the Cemetery of the Moujahidin, one hundred tombs to the left as you enter: the site lies beneath a tree on a rise overlooking the city, with a view of the Mountain, the sea, and old Tangier. I like Muslim cemeteries; they're so much less depressing than the well-organized graveyards of other religions. Muslim cemeteries are simple, humble, and open; life shines on them with a magnificent light. I am not a deeply devout man, you know that, but I respect religions. When I have been laid to rest (I wish no coffin, only a shroud), you will say prayers you have chosen because you love them, and perhaps some poems or Sufi* songs. After that, it will be time for us to say adieu.

As to my estate, my lawyer, Maître García, will keep you informed. One more thing: I ask Gabriel to supervise the studies of Halim and Halima, my children. He knows what I expect of him and has only to carry out my wishes. Regarding Kenza, let him make sure that she receives her rightful inheritance.

Miguel boards the boat unaided, greets the captain, kisses Toutia's hand, and goes off to rest in a chaise longue in the shade of the tree. There he hears a voice murmur to him, *You are in a world where spent passions are marked by a great love that still glitters in the darkness beside the flowers you so cherished, flowers bearing a life overflowing with memories.*

Kenza arrives alone. She is radiant, dressed all in white, her hair hanging loose, and she speaks to no one, but she seems happy and at ease. Time has done its work; spring has left a little of its pollen-dust behind. Kenza's life has been shaken, and some memories have fallen free like fruit from a tree. Some good ones, some bad. She has not had the strength to sort through them. There will be time enough to bring order to all that. She is no longer anxious and feels relieved, as light as on the day of her first period, when she ran through the streets as if flying like a swallow. This morning she had that same feeling. It was so good: changing bodies, putting some distance between herself and the world with its misfortunes, moving beyond that great sorrow and not choking with shame in her sleep. Kenza calmly boards the ship; a sailor shows her to a pleasant cabin. This cabin has a view of the sea, he tells her, and the dolphins that escort us—they're intelligent, they talk among themselves and we understand them. They'll come greet you, but don't worry if sharks sometimes drive them away and swim along with us for a while. Rest now; look, here's a thermos of tea, and some cookies. Kenza falls swiftly and serenely asleep, pleased to be going home again. Bending over her, Toutia gently strokes her cold face. Then she kisses her forehead and tucks the covers in around her shoulders.

Soumaya, the beauty, the woman who believed everything men told her, who gave herself to them freely, Soumaya, lost and found again, comes aboard, covered from head to toe. No one dares speak to her. She wears the white haik of the peasant women of the Rif, hiding her body from which the last few years have stripped all charms. She is her own victim, and answering the call, she, too, has joined the ship. Soumaya has not become a Muslim sister; if she remains veiled it's to conceal her face: her right cheek is scarred, and she is missing a few teeth. When asked she says she had an accident. "Yes, an awful crash on the road between Toledo and Madrid, he was driving like a madman, he'd been drinking, an oncoming truck plowed right into us and that's all I remember; later when I came to, I looked in the mirror and screamed. Disfigured. . . . The insurance company paid me some money and the doctor said, 'Go, go back home, there's a boat waiting for you in Tarifa, you'll see, you won't be the only one going aboard: it's a magic ship, and on it life will seem beautiful to you, the sun will always shine for you, so go, my weary beauty.' I set out enveloped in my grandmother's haik; it was to be her shroud, but when she died in Mecca I inherited it: Egyptian cotton, very soft, very strong, and no one has noticed me, I can disappear into this shroud, it was perfect for crossing the country without being bothered or questioned by the police, so I blessed my grandmother for having the good sense to die in Mecca. They told me she died smothered in the crush of the crowd, in the place where they stone the devil;* it seems that often happens, people lose control, trampling the weak and elderly . . . but they also say that dying over there sends you straight to paradise! Me, I don't want to die, I'm still young, I want to start a family, have children and tell them stories. . . ."

When Flaubert arrives dripping with perspiration, no one pays any attention to him. He's been running, convinced he was going to miss the boat. Tall, slender, his eyes shining, he can't stand still, and talks loudly. "The day I found out the return boat was waiting in Tarifa, I dropped everything and hit the road. Took a good week to get here. I had to run, lost a few pounds, but I feel fine. So, where are we going? Why doesn't anyone answer?" He looks for a familiar face. Everyone is off in a private world. There's nothing for him to do but follow their example. Flaubert has an idea, though: "What if this ship were just a fiction, a novel cast upon the waters, a book in the form of a bottle tossed into the sea by all those weeping mothers so sick of waiting? If I'm right, now I finally understand why my parents named me Flaubert. So, all I have to do is enter the novel. But how does one become a fictional character? What's the way to slip between the pages and settle comfortably into the most beautiful chapter in a story of love and war? *Madame Bovary*—there's no more room for me, it's full up, and anyway there's no black guy in that story. . . . Where can I find a hideout, a cushy spot? There's always *Gone with the Wind*, but who'd want to be in that? If I could only find it, this novel where I could be a character, I wouldn't need to work any-more: the novelist would take charge of me, give me a role, fit me into the story, make me live, love, yell, and die in the end because he wouldn't know how else to wind up the story. But I don't want to die, not even as a paper character; I don't want to burn or get pulped, that happens a lot, when books that haven't found their readers get sent to a paper factory or shredded into papier-mâché to make cardboard boxes. Can you imagine! My character, multi-plied in thousands of copies only to be thrown into a grinding machine that squishes my head over here, my balls over there, now it's the feet, in short—it takes a mere few minutes to subdi-vide me into millions of tiny paper scraps: I wind up as confetti! Or writing paper or a movie poster or even toilet tissue. No, for-get it, better I should look for an epic novel that's still in the works, and sneak in among the main characters—as a museum guard, for example—and watch the amorous goings-on between the heroine and her lover, a diplomat hounded by his wife who's two-timing him with the head of the diplomatic corps. . . . What if I asked that English woman who wrote the book everyone's reading now, it's about a magical character—that guy, no ques-tion, his book won't end up in the shredder! That novel would suit me; problem is, it's already written, so how could there be a new version for me to appear in? Shouldn't I start by reading it? Someone on this boat must have it, millions of copies were sold, so I'm sure the rats have one in their nests for the hard times of winter, definitely—rats stock up on summer novels for those long cold nights. The only difference from us is, rats don't read, they nibble the paper to get all those vitamins in the ink. That's what my cousin Émilzola, a librarian in Douala, told me one day. Now that I think about it, becoming a character in a novel is the best thing that could happen to me. My cousins and so forth in Nde won't believe me, they'll think the horrors of exile have driven me round the bend. I can just see them chuckling. 'Flaubert? Ho yes! He escaped! Right out of this world! Found fictional work in a work of fiction! He prances around in books, sleeps in pages perfumed women open daintily to read. You get it? All day he sleeps in the purse of some fabulous woman, follows her everywhere, even when she's taking a bath: she reads him, he ogles her, licking his lips, while here we are still wondering what to do about this inheritance, since there's still the matter of the tontine. . . . What a guy, that Flaubert—he found a way to avoid dealing with reality, yes, *real* reality, the kind that sticks to us like glue, and hurts. Him, he's an old fox, got it made, sitting pretty on a library shelf waiting for some hand to reach for him, open him, flip through him, then put him right back because there's no sex, nothing erotic in the novel, just politics that won't interest hardly anybody, leastways that's what we heard . . . .'"

And now it's Flaubert's turn to find himself a small space, next to the lemon tree where, lulled by its subtle scent, he falls asleep like a child. The lemon blossoms take only a few moments to waft him on their perfume all the way to the terraces of Fès, to the old city where women spread the aromatic flowers of citrus and jasmine trees out to dry on big white sheets, after which the blooms are steamed to extract the essential oils that make the finest perfumes.

The captain is sitting in a large wicker armchair. He's smoking his pipe and reading an old newspaper reporting on the landing in Normandy. Wielding a fan from Seville, Toutia is cooling him and keeping the flies away. Now and then, with a sort of silver holy-water brush, she sprinkles him with rose water. He looks up from his paper only to keep track of the new arrivals. The ship will sail as soon as its twenty-five passengers are aboard; three are still missing. A big fellow turns up suddenly, claiming to be one S. Panza. After consulting with Toutia, the captain asks him about his master, Don Quixote. "He's coming, he's coming, Captain; he was detained by the border police because his papers weren't in order. Actually, he hasn't any papers at all! Plus, customs confiscated that sword of his he's so fond of, so, you see, things are a bit complicated . . . but don't worry, I'm sure he'll finagle his way out of all that."

The captain is astonished. "So your master travels as if this were the sixteenth century, sans passport, sans laissez-passer? But, where does he think he is? And you—how did you manage to get through?"

"I told them I would go let you know that my master had been delayed."

Flaubert, who always keeps one eye open, wakes up when he hears Panza's footsteps.

"Flaubert, at your service!"

"Please, don't get up," Panza apologizes. "Just tell me what documents you used to come aboard."

"Documents? My name is Flaubert, and that's enough. No

need of papers here. We are the guests of destiny. So what use would documents be? Go, go fetch your master: tell him that Flaubert awaits him, standing firm with a vigilant eye, his wits about him, head squarely upon his shoulders, and above all—ready to go adventuring upon the high seas!"

Without a word, the captain continues to smoke his pipe and check the horizon every so often with his ancient binoculars. Flaubert asks Toutia to lend him her fan. She doesn't reply. When Don Quixote appears—or at least he claims that's his name—the captain rises to stand at attention.

"Welcome, Monseigneur! We were waiting just for you in order to set sail. Your wish is my command."

"My thanks, dear sir! And yet, I do believe we lack one person more, or rather, I would say, a personage. This ship was conceived especially for this mission, with room for five and twenty passengers precisely; she will not leave without every last one."

Consulting his lists, the captain agrees.

"Then let us await any last-minute arrivals."

A few hours later, just as the sun slips gently to the horizon, the passengers see two men in military garb appear, carrying between them a large crate that looks for all the world like a coffin. They set it down on the dock, then leave without once looking back. Soon, a man—or rather, a tree—comes forward and walks around the crate. A face is visible inside a hole cut into the bark, and two flexible arms stick out of the trunk. When the tree-man (or the tree inhabited by a man) prepares to board the ship, two officers of the Guardia Civil rush forward to stop him.

"Halt, there! Where do you think you are? A zoo? A circus? Your papers!"

The tree rustles, shaking from its branches leaves that are still green: identity cards from several countries, cards of every color, passports, administrative documents, and a few pages of a book written in some unknown language. Suddenly, from these pages burst thousands of syllables that fly at the officers' eyes and blind them. The letters then gather together in a banner that says: *Freedom Is Our Job.* Ignoring the officers, the tree boards the ship and goes to stand beside Don Quixote, whom the captain questions in a low voice regarding the identity of this personage.

"Which one? The one in the tree or the one in the coffin?"

"The one in the tree. My men will bring the coffin on board. We are to deliver it to the authorities upon our arrival, but since I have no conception of time, or space either, for that matter, I can't make any guarantees. So tell me, who is hiding inside that getup?"

"He calls himself Moha, but with him you're never sure of anything. He's the immigrant without a name! This man is who I was, who your father was, who your son will be, and also, very long ago, the man who was the Prophet Mohammed, for we are all called upon to leave our homes, we all hear the siren call of the open sea, the appeal of the deep, the voices from afar that live within us, and we all feel the need to leave our native land, because our country is often not rich enough, or loving enough, or generous enough to keep us at home. So let us leave, let's sail the seas as long as even the tiniest light still flickers in the soul of a single human being anywhere at all, be it a good soul or some lost soul possessed by evil: we will follow this ultimate flame, however wavering, however faint, for from it will perhaps spring the beauty of this world, the beauty that will bring the world's pain and sorrow to an end."

Tangier–Paris
September 2004–November 2005

Notes

3 Tangier is the main link between Europe and Africa, and the legendary Café Hafa perches on a rocky promontory with an unbeatable view of the Straits of Gibraltar. With its original décor seemingly unchanged since 1921, the café has fallen on harder times, but its terraces—later re-colonized in the Stoned Seventies by rock stars—were long frequented by le beau monde and writers such as Jane and Paul Bowles, Tennessee Williams, William Burroughs (who called Tangier "Interzone"), Jack Kerouac, Allen Ginsberg, and Truman Capote, some of whom helped make Tangier a well-known gay resort, which it remains—to a lesser degree—today.

The two most prestigious districts in Tangier are La Marshan, a historic residential neighborhood west of the kasbah, and La Montagne, "The Mountain," a district of grand villas and gardens favored by artists.

7 A jellaba is a loose-fitting hooded robe worn by both men and women in North Africa; in the Near East, a caftan is a

full-length women's tunic with long sleeves and a sash at the waist, and is decorated with embroidery.

8 The Rif is a mainly mountainous region along the northeast coast of Morocco. Populated by Berbers and Arabs, the terrain of the Rif Mountains is often inhospitable, and Riffians are considered a tough, hardened people. The major cities of the Rif include Tangier, Al-Hoceima, Chefchaouen, Nador, Tétouan, Ceuta, and Melilla. Portugal invaded Ceuta in 1415, Spain invaded Melilla in 1490, and although Morocco lays claim to both cities, they remain to this day the only two European territories in mainland Africa.

10 One of the five pillars of Islam—they are all listed on pages 122–123 of this translation—is the hajj, the pilgrimage to Mecca every good Muslim should make at least once in this life, after which he or she is entitled to use the honorific title *hajji* or *hajja*.

31 Once banned in the West, Sir Richard Burton's 1886 translation of *The Perfumed Garden* by Sheik Nefzaoui has been called the Arabic Kama Sutra. The chapter titles for this Islamic sex manual reveal a focus on—among other things— both admirable and contemptible behavior by men and women; matters that either favor or impede coition; various causes of enjoyment, sterility, or impotence; the "Sundry Names" given to the sexual parts of men and women; and

"Prescriptions for Increasing the Dimensions of Small Members and for Making Them Splendid."

37 Lined with cafés and bazaars, the lively rue Siaghine is the main street of the medina (the "old city"). At its northeastern end lies the Petit Socco, the heart of the medina; *socco* is Spanish for *souk*, the traditional Middle Eastern marketplace or shopping quarter, and the "little souk" occupies the site of the city's ancient Roman forum. Heading southwest, the rue Siaghine links the medina to the Ville Nouvelle (the "new city") through the main market of Tangier, the Grand Socco, famous for the colorful ambiance provided by peasant women in picturesque native dress selling their fresh produce from the fields and farms of the Rif.

59 Lighter than the jellaba, the gandoura is an ample, almost sleeveless robe that sometimes serves as an undergarment in East Africa; babouches are Turkish slippers.

75 This is sura 2, verse 255, the Ayat al-Kursî, the celebrated Verse of the Throne:

Allah! There is no god but Him, the Living, the Eternal. Neither slumber nor sleep overtakes Him. To Him belongs all that is in the Heavens and the earth. Who can intercede with him except by His permission? He knows what is before them and what lies behind them, and they can grasp only that part of His knowledge which He will. His Throne embraces the Heavens and the earth, and it tires Him not to uphold them both. He is the All-high, the All-glorious.

85 The hajj takes place from the eighth day to the twelfth day of the twelfth month of the Muslim lunar calendar, and the end of the pilgrimage is the three-day worldwide celebration of Aïd el-Kebir, "the great festival," also known as Aïd el-Adha, "the festival of sacrifice," during which an animal is slaughtered to commemorate Abraham's willingness to sacrifice his eldest son at God's command.

86 The tarboosh is a red cloth or felt cap, a kind of fez, usually sporting a blue silk tassel and sometimes worn as the inner part of a turban.

96 Islamic invaders began occupying and settling large areas of southern Spain in the early eighth century, and modern travelers in Andalusia still marvel at the surviving wonders of their civilization. By the fourteenth century, however, the *reconquista*—the wars of reconquest waged by the Catholic monarchy—had reclaimed almost all of Muslim Spain from *los moros*—the Moors. In 1492, the year Columbus planted the flag of Isabella of Castile and Ferdinand II of Aragon in the New World, his patrons drove Mohammed XI, the last sultan of Granada, from his besieged city, ending Moorish rule in Spain. As he fled to Morocco, the sultan bade fare-

well to Granada at a spot now known as the Moor's Last Sigh.

105 A jabador is an embroidered vest once favored by the Arab aristocrats of Andalusia; saroual are baggy, calf-length pants fastened at the knees and worn under the jellaba.

118 The *khamsa* (from the Arabic word for "five") is a symbol or design depicting an inverted hand. Called the Hand of Fatima by Muslims and the Hand of Miriam by Jews, this ancient talisman is often placed at the front door of a dwelling to ward off the evil eye.

121 Near the Grand Socco rises the brilliantly colored minaret of the Sidi Bou Abid Mosque, set off by the luxurious Mendoubia gardens with their eight-hundred-year-old trees and the former palace and offices of the Mendoub, the sultan's representative during the international administration of Tangier, which lasted from the Treaty of Algeciras in 1906 to Moroccan independence in 1956.

123 The first sura of the Koran is the Fatiha, "the Opening":

> In the Name of God, the Merciful, the Compassionate.
> Praise be to God, Lord of the Universe,
> The Merciful, the Compassionate,
> Sovereign of the Day of Judgment!

You alone we worship, and to You alone we turn for help.
Guide us to the straight path,
The path of those whom You have favored,
Not of those who have incurred Your wrath,
Nor of those who have gone astray.

140 In Tahar Ben Jelloun's 1978 novel, *Moha the Mad, Moha the Wise*,
Moha is a holy fool, a voice from the crowd who speaks like
a traditional North African Arab storyteller: he recounts
the country, its mistakes, hopes, and dreams. Moha is the
voice of exclusion. Here is a sampling of texts that illuminate Moha's role in *Leaving Tangier*.

Moha took the path of the tree. To love the tree. [. . .] It's a
dwelling for silence, a little palace where death bites its own
tail. My special place for absence. [. . .] The forest! But the
forest is gone. There is neither forest nor desert, only a plain
planted with zinc and broken mirrors. Ever since it grew
rich, the city has spewed out poor men who wash up on the
outskirts of life. They are my children. [. . .] If you meet my
children, don't run away. Let them rob you just a little. It's in
a worthy cause. Then laugh along with them. [. . .] You will
thus deserve my blessing and perhaps a piece of the tree, a
bit of paradise. [. . .] I bear within me a rage of the utmost
purity ever since the French wounded our land almost a
century and a half ago. [. . .] Me, I'm a hundred and forty
years old. I've seen everything, known everything. I'm only
passing through. [. . .] Why does death sail away with us to

the horizon? [. . .] Even when they lock me up, I press on.
[. . .] Anyway, I'm not dead. How can one die when one has
never existed? I have no name. I am hypothetical. I'm from
nowhere. From a hill. A plain. The vague horizon and the
mint of time. That's what they've decided! Moha has never
existed! What a lovely mirage for their pale desert. It's true,
I have no identity papers . . . and how could I have any? No,
I'm not talking about corruption, but I don't intend to fill in
any blanks; I cannot write anything on the dotted lines. . . .
Neither date nor place of birth. I have three hundred and
fifty-two names, one name for each moon. My date is written in the sky. Go read in the labyrinth. . . .

152 General Mohammed Oufkir, Morocco's much-feared chief
of police, tried to seize power in 1972 by having King Hassan II's plane shot down. After the coup failed, Oufkir was
liquidated and his wife and six children—one of whom was
only three years old—were imprisoned under appalling conditions. In 1987 several of the children escaped and managed to contact French journalists before being rearrested.
The family was finally freed in 1991.

158 Nâzim Hikmet (1902–1963) remains Turkey's most famous
and revered poet at home and abroad, acclaimed for the
modern stylistic innovations he brought to Turkish literature as well as for the lyrical power of the novels, plays, and
poetry through which he mounted an impassioned crusade
against injustice and oppression in Turkey and throughout

the world. Persecuted for decades by the Republic of Turkey for his Marxist-Leninist convictions, he spent nearly two-thirds of his adult life in prison or in exile, finally dying of a heart attack in Moscow after long years of separation from his beloved country and family.

While imprisoned, Hikmet wrote a massive work intended to be his masterpiece: *Human Landscapes,* an extraordinary depiction of his homeland and the turmoil of the twentieth century, and although the Turkish government cruelly suppressed his poetry for nearly half his career, this collection of poems is today considered to be one of the greatest patriotic literary treasures of the Turkish people.

216 A marabout is a Muslim hermit, holy man, or the leader of a sect, especially among the Berbers and Moors in Northern Africa.

230 Mohammed ibn Abd al-Wahhab (1703–1792) was the founder of Wahhabism, a branch of Sunni Islam that seeks to restore the supposed theological purity of the Muslim faith during the first three generations of Islam, a purity grounded solely upon the Koran and the Hadith (a kind of appendix to the Koran containing traditions related to Mohammed). Ibn al-Wahhab reintroduced Sharia—Islamic law—to what is now Saudi Arabia, where Wahhabism has become the dominant theology. Heeding their teacher's call for jihad against "polytheistic" Islam, modern-day Wah-

habis violently oppose what they call perversion, superstition, and heresy in the Muslim faith.

237 A Turkish singer of Kurdish and Arab descent, Ibrahim Tatlises (1952–) is one of Turkey's most prolific recording artists. He has his own television show, has appeared in numerous movies, and has recently enjoyed increasing international success.

242 Farid al-Atrash (1915–1974) was one of the idols of twentieth-century Arab popular music. A Syrian composer, singer, and musician, he specialized in romantic love songs and composed the songs and instrumental music for more than thirty Egyptian musical films in which he starred.

More than thirty years after the death of Oum Kalsoum (1904–1975), the "Star of the East," there is still no one to rival the phenomenal impact and artistry of this Egyptian singer. She began singing at an early age, and through her artistic dedication and the canny management of her career, she turned her truly extraordinary voice into one of the wonders of the Arab world. She sang of the joys and sorrows of love and loss in bravura performances that might last for as long as six hours. During these performances two or three songs would become the means through which, improvising in response to her public's ecstatic energy, she would create an intense bond with her audience, who repaid her tremendous outpouring of emotion with their undying love.

248 In the West, a jinn is usually thought of as a "genie in a bottle," but in pre-Islamic Arabian mythology and in Islamic
culture, the Jinn are a race of supernatural creatures, lower
than angels, capable of assuming human or animal form and
influencing mankind for good or evil. The Koran says that
the Jinn were created by Allah, "from the fire of a scorching
wind," from "fire free of smoke"; one connotation of the
word *jinn* is invisibility, and jinns are invisible to humans unless they choose to be seen by them. The Jinn live in their
own societies like humans (they eat, marry, and while they
may live for hundreds of years, they do die), but, like angels,
they have no substance: whole communities can live comfortably on the head of a pin or cozily in a vast desert waste.
In the sura devoted to them, "El-Jinn," a company of jinns
listens to the Koran and pledges allegiance to Allah, but
some dark jinns, called Ifrit, will work black magic upon
people when summoned by a magician or human evildoer.

255 Sufism is a wide-ranging tradition of Islamic mysticism
practiced by many different Sufi orders, all dedicated,
through differing practices and beliefs, to the individual experience of divine love through religious ecstasy: by seeking
truth and self-knowledge, the human heart strives to heal
itself and turn only toward God. Sufism is perhaps most familiar in the West in the person of Jalal ad-Din Mohammed
Rumi, the great thirteenth-century Persian Muslim poet,
jurist, and theologian, whose poetry speaks of the universal
longing to reunite with the lost beloved. After his death,

Rumi's followers founded the Mevlevi Order, long known for worshipping through dance and music as the Whirling Dervishes.

258 An estimated two million people now converge on Mecca from around the world to perform the rituals of the hajj, which have become closely scripted to safely shepherd massive crowds through these rites. Each pilgrim must circle the Kaaba counterclockwise seven times; "kiss" (point at) the Black Stone; run between the hills of Safa and Marwah; drink from the Zamzam well; stand vigil on the plains of Mount Arafat; gather pebbles at Muzdalifah; and throw them at walls ("the devil") in Mina. Manuals go into minute detail about every aspect of the hajj, noting even the prescribed size of the pebbles for the "stoning of the devil" (1–1½ cm). This lapidation reenacts Abraham's pilgrimage to Mecca, during which the devil appeared to him at three different heaps of stones; each time, at the Archangel Gabriel's urging, the patriarch pelted the devil with seven stones until he vanished. The defeat of the devil's attempts to stop the sacrifice of Ishmael also represents the humbling of each pilgrim's "internal despot," or selfhood, which allows the worshipper to draw closer to Allah.

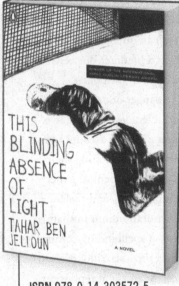

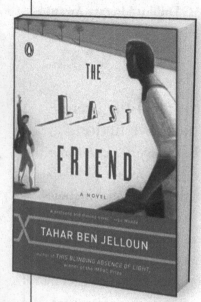